T0032511

A SECOND CHANCE
AT LIFE

What Reviewers Say About Genevieve McCluer's Work

Cold Blood

"The story is a good one, and I enjoyed it a lot. It doesn't hide what the plot is doing, though it still manages to throw in the odd surprise, and it moves at a pace fast enough to keep me wanting to read just the next bit. If you like vampires that hunt other vampires, moral quandaries, limbs going flying (and getting stuck back on again), and cute women falling for each other—grab this one."
—*Lee Hulme's Book Reviews*

"I like Genevieve McCluer's writing style. It is fast and immediate and draws me in. I loved the nod to a previous novel *Olivia*, and to some recognizable areas of the city. She makes monsters sympathetic characters and gives them entirely plausible lives alongside the other residents of Toronto. I like this world she has invented."
—*Kitty Kat's Book Blog*

Olivia

"There's a playfulness at times, but then the seriousness of the situation hits the reader square in the face. At the halfway mark it suddenly took off for me. There was one heck of a surprise, that I did not see coming at all. I enjoyed the story and would like to read more in this world."—*Kitty Kat's Book Blog*

Thor: Daughter of Asgard

"Norse mythology intrudes on a bubbly romance in this light adventure from McCluer. ...Readers will come for the gender bending mythology and stay for the light romance."—*Publishers Weekly*

My Date With a Wendigo

"*My Date with a Wendigo* is a sweet, second chance romance at its furry little heart."—*Wicked Cool Flight*

A Fae Tale

"This is an unusual tale, but a very enjoyable one. It's funny and a bit kooky, but very sweet and romantic too. Genevieve McCluer writes great humorous prose and I found myself giggling out loud a few times in the course of reading this book. Her characters are well defined and fun, and she makes her secondary characters come to life as much as the main protagonists. An enjoyable read."
—*Kitty Kat's Book Blog*

Visit us at www.boldstrokesbooks.com

By the Author

My Date With a Wendigo

Olivia

Thor: Daughter of Asgard

A Fae Tale

Cold Blood

A Second Chance at Life

A SECOND CHANCE AT LIFE

by

Genevieve McCluer

2023

A SECOND CHANCE AT LIFE

© 2023 By Genevieve McCluer. All Rights Reserved.

ISBN 13: 978-1-63679-459-4

This Trade Paperback Original Is Published By
Bold Strokes Books, Inc.
P.O. Box 249
Valley Falls, NY 12185

First Edition: July 2023

This is a work of fiction. Names, characters, places, and incidents are the product of the author's imagination or are used fictitiously. Any resemblance to actual persons, living or dead, business establishments, events, or locales is entirely coincidental.

This book, or parts thereof, may not be reproduced in any form without permission.

Credits
Editor: Barbara Ann Wright
Production Design: Susan Ramundo
Cover Design By Tammy Seidick

Acknowledgments

Thank you to Jessica, Daniel, and Alexandra for all of your support and help, and to my editor, Barbara.

CHAPTER ONE

I set my bag on the twin mattress. The walls are a far more comforting beige than the sickly off-white of my old cell, and the whole place looks like an actual house. I hear inmates moving about, but it isn't the normal clack of shoes on metal and concrete; it's tile floors and soft furnishings. They haven't simply moved me to some minimum-security prison. They've moved me to a literal cottage.

"I'll leave you to it," the officer says, and I hear her boots thud out of the cell, if I can even call it that. It's a proper bedroom. I never caught her name, though I suppose I'll have plenty of time for that. It's a life sentence, after all.

I sink onto the mattress. I need to unpack, but being back home is so overwhelming. I didn't request this transfer. I have no idea how it could've happened. I've been in Alberta for the past twenty-four years, and all of a sudden, I'm sent back to Ontario without a word.

And it means she's so tauntingly close. I could scale that barbed wire fence, and I know I'd find her within a couple hours. I could find her anywhere. And then, she'd be on the run with a fugitive. I could never do that to her.

It was so much easier in Alberta. I hold my head in my hands, forcing myself not to cry. I won't look weak my first day in a new prison. I have no idea what to expect here. I have to fend for myself.

I need to get the lay of the land, and I need to apply for work. Otherwise, I'll be stuck with far too much free time.

Jumping to my feet, I glance around the little room. It looks freshly painted and is impeccably clean. There's not the usual metal toilet that I'd want to scuff up to make it not show my lack of a reflection, and the door isn't a big metal slab with electronic locks. It's all weirdly suburban.

I unpack my meager possessions, placing my books and pens on the flimsy desk opposite my bed, and set my radio and headphones on my newly made bed.

Do I have any more ways to procrastinate?

There's a window next to my bed that's letting in enough sun that I have to avoid stepping too near it, but I can't risk covering it until later. I sold my TV when I heard about the transfer, and I'm too nervous to focus on any of my books, so it seems I can't procrastinate in my cell. None of this makes any sense, and I need answers.

I stuff my hands in my pockets and stride into the hall. My room is on the second floor, so I'd normally be walking out into the range, but it's just a normal hallway. There aren't even any sight lines for guards. The front door closes, and I realize that had to be the only guard that was in here, and she's gone. We're left to just do whatever we want? Minimum security is strange. How is everyone not constantly high?

I walk down the hall and find three women gathered in one of the bedrooms to watch something with incredibly emotional, over-the-top music on the television. There are ten bedrooms, but two don't have any possessions in them, and the other six are all full of stuff but unoccupied. This is no ordinary prison. I'd heard horror stories about Ontario's old women's prison, but I've never heard anything about this new one.

I'm back in Ontario. It hits me all over again. I can almost smell her. I take a deep breath, trying not to think about it, but tasting that lilac-like scent she always had. I could almost swear she's really here.

I could call her. Assuming she still has the same number. I haven't taken her off my list, no matter how many times I convinced myself I should.

And what would calling her do? She deserves a real life, and I can't give her that. I take one last breath, tasting that lilac, and stride down the stairs, forcing myself to look casual and the slightest bit confident. I don't want to look cocky when I have no idea who may run this place, but I can't look weak, either. Surely, even this little cottage still works like a prison. It's been years since I last had to fight anyone, and I'd rather not ruin that track record.

By the kitchen I'd passed coming in, I find the remaining four women sitting around a table with some bags of chips and a collection of *Dungeons & Dragons* books. "Hey, new girl," one of them says.

Is she talking to me? I stare at her. "Hi?" I try.

She gestures for me to come closer, and one of the women to her side giggles. Her hair is a mess of red curls, she's wearing a colorful, loose-fitting blouse, and she looks almost as young as I do. She smells like candles, the nice kind my mother always bought. I don't remember what scent they were supposed to be. "You want to join us? We were just starting a new campaign, and I have some pre-gens."

"Uh…" I stare at her and the other girls.

"I know how rough it is when you're new in prison, thought you might like—"

"I'd love to," I say. It's not even a lie, though the main point is to get her to shut up about me being new. It could raise questions, like what my crime was, if it was my first time, how long I was going to be there for, and that had all grown more awkward over the last couple decades. It'll be nice to have the distraction. I was in a long-running *Shadowrun* game in Alberta that only stopped because the GM got shanked for snitching, so while it's been a few years, I mostly know what I'm doing. "Which edition is it? I'd rather roll a character if I can, but I'll take a pre-gen if you're in a hurry."

"All we have is time," one of the other women says with a chuckle. She's older than the one who invited me and has laugh lines framing a surprisingly warm face. She also has a surprisingly strong apricot smell, though it's rather pleasant. Is this what it's like being in minimum security? People are friendly? I don't like it.

"How about you draw up your character while I tell you about the setting?" the redhead asks. "I'm Millie, by the way. Sorry, Inmate Michaels." She giggles.

I shake my head. This is strange. I can barely remember what it was like when I first came to prison, but I could swear it wasn't like this. Everyone left me alone. Though, granted, I was a famous murderer and barely able to handle being there. And I got in a few fights with the guards early on. Okay, the difference may be on me. "I'm Dinah." If they hear a guard say my last name, they'll put it together. They'll know what I did, who I am, and how strange it is for me to be here.

I watch, waiting for the recognition on their faces. The older woman smiles and reaches out her hand. "I'm Paige."

I take it, staring at it in confusion as we shake. The other two girls at the table introduce themselves as Helen and Laura, then Millie starts describing the setting, and I work on making my barbarian.

By count, we've had our first fight, our bard has probably gotten herself her first STD—or apparently, they're called STIs now—and Rachel is the farthest thing from my mind.

Until now. Well, it couldn't have lasted forever.

"Join us tomorrow?" Millie asks.

"Or later tonight if you're not too tired," Laura says.

"Definitely tomorrow. I'll see about tonight." It's nice having the distraction, and I haven't gotten to game in ages. I ran a few sessions after the old GM died, but players kept getting locked up in solitary to the point that it just wasn't worth it anymore. It might have been a gang war.

Once the guards finish making sure we're all alive—which doesn't take long in a unit with only eight people—the other women all seem to realize that they haven't eaten anything more than chips. Millie insists rather strongly that I should join them, and she makes a big show of giving me a tour of the little kitchen. It has a fridge, an oven with an actual stove instead of some meager microwave, and a cupboard with unsecured knives. "They lock those up after curfew," she explains.

I stare at them. I don't need knives, and I'm not particularly afraid of them, but I haven't seen one that wasn't made from a toothbrush in a very long while.

"Did you enjoy the game?" she asks as she starts searing some meat in a pan.

"Yeah, I've missed it."

"Oh, you didn't have anyone to play with at your assessment center?"

Right, she thinks I'm a new inmate. I should let her believe that, but if anything slips, it could come back to bite me. Lying is always a terrible idea in prison. People will assume the worst, and I've seen people sent to the ICU for far less than lying about being a famous cop killer. "No, I'm—"

"Pelletier," someone calls. I turn to find an officer peeking in through the front door. He looks oddly like an uninvited guest, nervous to be coming in unannounced. Sweat shines on his forehead like he just ran all the way here. "Your lawyer's waiting for you."

I narrow my eyes. My lawyer? I haven't had a lawyer since my trial, and that was over twenty years ago. Is this why I'm back in Ontario?

"We're just about to eat," Millie says.

How new is she? Talking back to a guard may get you some respect, but you don't do it on somebody else's behalf, and it's just as likely to make people think you talk to guards for other reasons as well. "It's fine, I wasn't hungry anyway. You can have it."

"It's your food—"

"Pelletier," the guard repeats, sounding sterner.

"You can pay me back for it with some soup." I smile at her. I'll need to find a dealer I can trade the soup to, but at least it's as good as cash in prison. I'll have to tell her why I'm here eventually, but it's hard to argue with this reprieve, especially when it may finally grant me some answers. "Coming, CO." I try to give the guard the same smile, but he only glowers at me.

He leads me through the open courtyard, the sun beating down on me. My flesh feels like it's cooking on my bones, but I ignore it. I need answers, and this is the only way to get them. I try to watch for any familiar sights, but most of the prison looks so same-y, save for the big blocky building in the center, and I was so distracted from pain and confusion when I got here that none of it means much. It's possible that it's a trap, and he's planning on murdering me, but he didn't handcuff me, and I doubt he can take me in a fair fight. I don't have to share the same fears the other girls do.

He leads me into the central building and finally opens a door halfway down one of a dozen hallways, leading into a private holding area. That would add to the murder idea if there wasn't a woman waiting in there on the other side of a small table.

She's gorgeous, blond, tall, wearing what has to be a ludicrously expensive pantsuit, and she smells odd. It's weirdly pine-scented, like there's tree sap in her blood or something. "Thank you, now let me talk to my client in private."

"She—"

"Please leave."

He grunts and closes the door, leaving me and my apparent lawyer alone. "You're not scared?" I ask.

She chuckles. "Why, do you have iron on you?"

I blink.

Her prim and proper smile grows playful. "You must be so confused. I'm sorry. I had assumed she told you something."

"I, what?" I stammer.

She laughs again and gestures to the metal chair across from her. "Sit. There's a lot to go over."

I eye her but do as I'm told. You get used to that in prison. "Who are you? You're…" It sounds crazy saying it. I've never met any other monsters. Could she really be one? It would explain why she doesn't smell human.

"If you're going to call me a fairy, you might want to know that's considered quite impolite. My wife would take offense."

"Your wife?" I stare at her, my jaw dropping.

"Yes, it's legal now."

"I know that!" I sigh. "I just hadn't expected—wait but—okay, this is all too much."

Her smile is playful as she reclines in the chair, watching me. I know nothing about fairies. Is this some weird game they do, or is this just what lawyers are like? My last one never bothered with much. "Well, you see, when a fair one and a fair one love each other, they—"

"I don't need to hear about the fairies and the bees."

She laughs, but her tone is cutting. "What did I *just* say?"

"Sorry, the fair ones and the bees?"

She rolls her eyes. "Let's try this again. I'm Dovana Gudaitiene, your attorney. I've been trying to go through cases of fiends that have ended up in the system, as it's, you know, not great for us to have that kind of exposure."

"So you're here to kill me?"

Her smile grows all the more wicked, and if there was blood in my veins, it would likely be running cold. How do you stop a fair one? Was the chair iron? I could break it off. "No. I had you transferred here and have had most of the records of your crime scrubbed from the internet. Fortunately, it was pretty small back when you were arrested, so that wasn't too big of a deal."

That's a real thing? I'd assumed scrubbing people from the internet just happened in movies. I was all over the newspaper. "Thank you? I can't afford—"

"It's pro bono. I'm more concerned with keeping the public from finding out about us. You're eligible for parole in a little under a year. I tried to have your records changed so it wouldn't be necessary, but unfortunately, some friends of the officer you killed have been keeping a close eye on your case. I had hoped I'd be able to brush this all under the rug like I did with the last few cases I've handled, but—"

"I'm a cop-killing vampire?"

She nods, the playfulness gone, her expression turning oddly sympathetic. "That kind of stuff makes the news."

"I didn't know he was a cop."

She shrugs. "That doesn't make much of a difference. They're not going to want to let you out. And more concerningly, you haven't aged a day since then, and that will make you stand out. Believe me,

I know the feeling. I became a changeling when I was twenty-one. We can still age a little, just slowly, but it gets me carded constantly." She sighs, rubbing her temple. "Could you have seriously not just run away? I know how fast vampires are."

"I didn't know at the time," I snap.

"How didn't you know? Wait…"

I nod. "We'd just been turned, Rachel and I. We were a couple of stupid homeless kids who crashed in the wrong house. When we woke up, we were starving, and we saw him. He'd come in, investigating something, maybe just us, and he was there and…" I trail off, still perfectly remembering the taste of my first and only kill. I've had blood so many times since, and it's never been as sweet. "His partner was right outside. I told Rachel to run, and I took the fall."

"Shit," she mutters. "No wonder she's so worried about you. Poor thing probably blames herself."

"She…" My mouth goes dry, and if I'd been drooling at the thought of a proper meal, I stop. Rachel is the one who sent her. After all this time, she's still worrying about me. Guilt eats at my heart. "I told her to live her life."

"She's going to try to visit tomorrow. Let her. You need some contacts in the local community if you want to make parole, and we are not having a vampire serving a life sentence. If it comes to that, you have to make a run for it. Normally, when people find out about us, someone can talk to them or kill them, as the case often is, but if we end up with an immortal prisoner, it'll be rather difficult to cover that up."

It's not anything I don't know. I've tried to convince myself to run so many times. It wouldn't be hard. But what life could I have as a criminal? I'd never be able to be with Rachel. The guilt weighs all the heavier. I've been holding out all this time for her, even after I tried to force her to move on. Why does she still care for me?

"I have a therapist who's willing to meet with you to sign off that you're not a danger to the community, and I'm trying to scrounge up some character witnesses to testify. Do you have any other friends from when you used to live in Toronto?"

I shake my head. "None that I stayed in contact with." Or who are likely still alive after that long on the streets.

"You are not making this easy for us. Can you mind control the parole board and all the witnesses?"

I hadn't even thought of that. Could I have done that to the judge? Back then, I didn't know it was a real thing, but I've had years to find out what I could do, even if I was hesitant to explore it with so many witnesses. "Maybe. I've only done it to one person at a time."

"Great." She grinds her teeth. "Don't cause any trouble here. I'll be back in a few weeks with whatever I've managed to work out, so please, be on your best behavior."

"I always am."

She smiles, but I'm quite certain she's biting back a comment about how I wouldn't be in here if that was the case. "If it comes to running, go to the Community Center. It's at the old Honeydale Mall now. You'll be able to get a new identity there."

"What's the Community Center?"

"Vaiva, you really have no idea on any of this stuff, do you? I suppose you *were* newly turned when you were arrested. It's sort of like a black market with everything a fiend could need. To my knowledge, the only one in the world is in Toronto. Well, technically Etobicoke. Other places seem to be a lot less tight-knit, but it's made Toronto sort of the fiend capital."

"So fiend is, like, the general term?"

"Yes." She sighs. "I'm sure she'll explain plenty of it for you tomorrow, provided you'll meet with her. I need to get started on setting up a better case for the parole board, and I have a trial in the morning."

I stare at her. This has all been so strange. I've never met another monster, another fiend, before. "All right. I'll try not to get into any trouble."

"See that you don't." She knocks on the cell door, and the guard opens it a few seconds later. "I'll talk to you soon, Ms. Pelletier. You take care of yourself."

The crazy fairy lawyer is escorted out, and I'm left alone in the room until the guard takes me back to my friendly little cottage a few minutes later. I knew parole was a long shot, and I've been terrified about how my non-aging may look to them, but there was nothing I could do about it.

That's all stuff I can probably handle, but I'll see Rachel tomorrow, and I have no idea how to handle that. I don't think I have the heart to turn her away again.

CHAPTER TWO

My door opens, and an officer peeks in, making sure I'm alive and where I belong. I smile at him, and he doesn't acknowledge me, instead moving on to finish count. It's not much nicer of an awakening than the lights coming on and the doors clicking open. I glance at the window to make sure the plate and blanket are properly keeping out the light before I get up. I had the entire night to try to think of what I was going to do—any way out of seeing Rachel—any way to convince the panel that I deserve parole, and I came up with a grand total of nothing. I slept some, but I don't really need it anymore.

I walk out into the hallway and blink as if I'm still sleepy, forcing a yawn. I'm too stressed. I need to take my mind off it. Where's a good DM when you need one? I head downstairs, my mind still whirring. Am I really going to see her today? How can I let myself? She deserves so much better.

My fists ache from how hard I'm clenching them. I look like I'm ready for a fight. That's not a good way to look in prison if you don't want to end up with someone's brains all over your knuckles. I take a deep breath, forcing myself to relax, and shake out my arms.

A couple women are in the kitchen, and I smell eggs, though it's far less appetizing than the women, so warm and close, with blood thundering in their veins. Great, that's not a good sign. I haven't eaten in far too long, and my housemates are growing nearly mouthwatering.

"Morning," one of them mutters.

"Good morning," I try.

"You're the new girl." It's not a question so much as a statement of fact.

"So I keep being told."

She nods and turns back to the eggs.

If I stick around here, I'm liable to eat them. I head back toward my room. I need to figure out a way to source food. It was easier when there were more of us, but eight people isn't a lot to reliably feed on without leaving any signs.

Millie's door is ajar. Are we friends yet? Can I go knock on her door and see if she's awake? I have so much on my mind, and I need to distract myself, but I'm also scared I'll eat her, and I'm never quite sure how to act with these sorts of things. I'd say it's because prison rules can be rather arbitrary, but I've been in prison longer than outside of it, so at a certain point, it starts seeming more like it's a me problem.

I head over and gently knock on the door, but that makes it slide open a crack farther, letting me see in, and showing Millie tapping away on what I have been assured is a phone. I let out a surprised squeak and back away, not wanting to let her know that I saw. I can't be playing around with contraband, and she can't think that I'd squeal on her. Though it could be worth it to find out how she got it in. It could make my time here a lot more tolerable.

She bolts up in bed and hurries to the door, shoving it open and meeting my gaze. I haven't made it that far away. Maybe I was too surprised, or maybe I didn't want to use superspeed in case there are witnesses. Surely, there's a camera in here, isn't there? "Dinah." Relief shows on her face, still tinged with fear.

"I didn't see anything," I say firmly.

"Did you need to use it?" she asks. "I'm sure you're going crazy not having internet. Or maybe there's some guy you want to talk to?" She winks at me. Who winks at people?

I've heard about the kinds of things you can do online. You can see everything a person is doing and learn everything about them. I've been tempted before to ask someone so I could find out what was going on in Rachel's life, but I didn't want to have to ask how it worked, and I knew it would only make it that much harder not to talk to her.

But now I don't have a choice. I *have* to talk to her. Should I google her or whatever it's called? "I don't..." I trail off. I have no idea where to begin. Clearly, I can't pass as my age. I could control her and tell her to teach me, but that'd feel so violating when I'm trying to be a friend to her. I'm already lying by omission.

"I've never used a smartphone before," I finally say.

Her eyes widen, and she tilts her head.

"Forget it. You can, um...do whatever it was you were doing. I'll—"

"Come in." She gestures into her room. "It's Sunday. I don't have work until tomorrow, and *D&D* isn't until this afternoon. There's plenty of time to show you."

I can probably make her forget everything if it comes to it. I follow her inside and take a seat on the plush chair next to her bed. She seems to have everything. There's a TV on her desk with some sort of system hooked up to it, a wide assortment of snack foods, and a cell phone under her pillow.

"Oh, help yourself to whatever you want." She points at the pile of food. "I ate your dinner, so I kind of owe you."

Why couldn't there be a pack of blood? I grab a bag of Fun Dip and face her, trying to figure out what to say. "Thank you."

"You've really never used a phone?"

"I've used a phone. I've even used a cell phone. Just the kind that had buttons, and if you hit the internet one, it would give you a loading screen and never do anything." She doesn't need to know that I only used one of those in prison.

She stares, seeming to study me. There's not much to learn from appearances, unless she's going to put together that the pale, oddly young girl isn't human. "How old are you? I assumed you were younger than me. I've only been here for about a year."

"How old are you?" I'm avoiding the question, aren't I?

She chuckles. "I'm twenty-two."

Right. Should I lie? Should I say, me too? Could she google that too? Would it tell her who I am? Mrs. Gudaitiene said that she scrubbed any record of me from the internet, but what does that really mean? Would I come up blank, or just the newspaper stories are gone, or what? I didn't even know what googling was to start with. "I was in prison in Alberta for a while. I was just transferred yesterday."

"Oh." She chuckles. "I'm sorry, I just assumed—"

"It's okay. I'm not against being the new girl. I've just been in prison long enough that I don't know a lot of stuff from the outside world." I should've bought a phone when I had the chance, but I didn't want to try to figure it out or have that temptation. Or end up in solitary again. I'd starve.

She shrugs. "All right, let me show you how to use this." She pats the bed, so I give in and sit next to her while she taps away on the screen. I would think that should smear it, and it wouldn't read anything after a little while, but it seems to work despite it somehow. "Was there anyone you wanted to look up? I'm assuming you don't have Instagram?"

I shake my head, staring at the screen, feeling the words rise up in my throat while I try to force them back down. I shouldn't. I don't need to know. Even if I'm going to talk to her tonight, I don't need to know more than that. "Could you look up Rachel Evans?"

Her eyes widen again, and she slides back. "Is she, like…"

I didn't think I'd be that obvious. I must've sounded too wistful or romantic. "You don't have to—"

"No, I was just surprised. I was expecting some boyfriend on the outside, not, well…" She barks out an awkward chuckle. "I'm sorry. Rachel Evans, you said?" She types it into something and holds the phone out to me. "This her?"

I stare at it. I'd know Rachel anywhere, no matter how much she changed, and the white girl with pink hair is decidedly not her. I shake my head. "No."

She exits out and opens something else, typing it in again. "Uh, what about this one on Facebook? I don't have an account, so you can't message or anything but—"

I snatch the phone from her. My heart starts beating only so it can stop. My mouth runs dry, and I try to ignore the smell of the delicious drink next to me. "It's her."

Her hair is in beautiful bouncy curls, and she smiles at me on the screen, and it looks so warm and genuine, just like I always knew it. Not that I ever knew her to have hair, since I always shaved it for her, but that was a minor change. It's really her. The screen blurs, and for a moment, I'm worried I damaged the phone, only for a tear to run down my cheek and fall onto the screen. "Fuck, I'm sorry."

"You've been in prison for a while, haven't you?"

I let out a shuddering breath, trying to keep from bawling. You should never show weakness like this. I can back it up, but it's still a terrible idea in prison. "I'm sorry," I say again.

"It's okay. You can scroll through there. Just move your finger along it."

It takes a few tries to stop accidentally backing out of the page, but I manage to look through the handful of pictures that she has displayed. It's really her. She's happy. She's alive. She's okay.

Fuck.

How could I ever not see her? I want to run to the visitor's room and wait there until she arrives. Though I'd probably be tackled by a guard for that.

"Thank you," I finally say as I hit the last picture. It says it's from a decade ago, and she has braids in it, but she looks just the same. I wonder how no one ever notices. It's publicly available, so you'd think someone would just look and realize she's a vampire. Do people not use Facebook?

"There's nothing to thank me for. So how long…God, girl, what is your skin care routine, and how much does it cost to have it smuggled into prison? 'Cause I'll pay it."

"Just genetics," I say. "And I bathe in the blood of virgins."

"Where do you find virgins?"

"That is the real question." I try to laugh, but it's hard when Rachel is still looking up at me.

Boots thud on the tile floor downstairs. How long have I been in here? I didn't get to shower. I thank her one more time and head back to my room as they start count. Both officers walk by each room, glancing at us without a word. When they head back past my door, I ask, "Could I get a job application form?" I have to get out of here, and that means looking good for the parole board. After seeing those pictures, I'd do anything.

The two officers look between each other. "I'll grab it before the next count," one of them says, more to the other guard than to me, and they walk off.

God, I hope I don't look like I've been crying.

I barely manage to make it through the rest of the day. It's like I'm in a daze. Millie talks to me at lunch and helps me remember how to use the stove, and I join the *Dungeons & Dragons* game, but all I can think about is Rachel's face staring at me from that screen. I could've messaged her if I made an account. Should I have? It wasn't my phone, but I doubt she'd have minded.

"Dinah," a voice says.

For a second, I think it's a guard taking me to visitation, but it's only Millie. I roll the dice and kill a kobold. Normally, it'd at least be a little satisfying.

Finally, a guard walks up to me. "Pelletier, you have a visitor."

I jump from the table and mutter something to the group, but I have no idea what. It's finally time. I'm going to see her.

CHAPTER THREE

Rachel Evans, the most beautiful woman in the world, the love of my life, and the woman I swore I would never see again, sits at a table in the corner of the visitor's room. I haven't been in a visitor's room since the last time I saw her. If we aged, maybe it wouldn't feel like that was only yesterday.

I take the seat across from her, trying not to stare and doubtless failing. It's her. It's really her. I won't cry. I try to force myself not to, but tears well up regardless.

"Dinah," she says, choking back a sob.

"I'm here." I reach for her hesitantly, far more worried that she won't take my hand than that a guard will stop me.

She takes it fiercely, gripping me hard enough that it hurts. "I didn't think I'd..." She sighs. "I've missed you."

I wipe my eyes with my free hand. "I told you to move on. That you needed to have a real life."

Her grip only tightens. "I know. And I tried. But it's sort of hard when the woman you love is rotting in prison for you."

I stare at her. How can she still feel that way after having not seen me for twenty-three years? "I love you too."

She takes a shuddering breath, beaming at me as tears shimmer in those gorgeous deep brown eyes I gazed into my entire childhood. Why did I ever stop seeing her? I could've had these visits every week. Maybe more often. I could've had time to visit her, though that still would have required dealing with the parole board. I could've had a life.

"I'm sorry," I say.

She shakes her head. "You don't have anything to apologize for. I shouldn't have let you be here in the first place."

"Well, if I'd known I could've just run..."

She laughs, and it's the most beautiful sound I've ever heard. It's fuller than it used to be, but it's so similar. It's hers. "We had no idea what we were doing, and you sacrificed everything for me. And then, you tried to force me to move on. I'm the one who owes you an apology for failing to."

I squeeze her hand. "I suppose I can forgive you."

That earns me another laugh.

"How did you manage all this? I'm in minimum security, and last I checked, we didn't have that kind of pull."

"I found a very good lawyer."

So she *is* the one who hired her. I guess I already knew that, but it's so weird to think. She never had the means to hire an attorney. What is she even doing for work? "I met her."

"I've only met her a couple times, but we found where you were being held, and she was able to grease some palms or file the right appeals or something, I have no idea, but it got you here."

"And I'll be eligible for parole soon."

She was already beaming, but now her smile is so bright, it burns, but I can't look away. "I know. She walked me through everything we have to do for that."

"She wouldn't tell me much."

"I guess I get the honor. You're going to need to petition them to let you volunteer in town. There's a soup kitchen that we checked out, and there's no direct sunlight in the kitchen. They'll let you cook for them if you can get approval."

They really planned all of this. "I barely know how to cook."

"I guess you'll just have to learn, or maybe you can serve the food. Once you're approved for, uh, I think she called them temporary absences."

"ETAs, Escorted Temporary Absences."

She nods. "Right. Once you're approved for that, you may also be able to start visiting me. Which would be nice. And a little scary." Her smile falters, and her gaze drops to the table between us. "God, it's been so long."

"It has." I try not to dwell on all the things I'd do if I could visit her. It's hard not to think of what's under the silk blouse she's wearing. I can still picture her so perfectly. It's been a very long while.

"Usually, that's just for family, so we might have to get married." The words are rushed, almost panicked, and she still isn't meeting my eyes.

I cough. If I had fed since I'd been transferred, I'd probably be blushing. "I…we…what?"

She gulps and looks up at me, but her gaze seems to stop just short of my eyes. "Dinah Pelletier, I love you. I need you home. If marrying you will help with that—"

"You make it sound like such a chore." Joking about it makes it so much easier. Is she serious? I haven't so much as talked to her in two decades, and she'd up and marry me right away? As if I wouldn't leap at the chance.

"I know. I'm not trying to. It's just…it's a lot. I know I still want this. I know I still want you. But it's been so long and I just…" She sighs but manages something resembling a smile. "If I had my way, I'd get to know you again first, but it's still you, and if this helps you get out of prison, then I'm more than happy to do it. I love you. I'll keep saying it because I really do, no matter how long it's been or how much things may have changed."

Those damn tears won't stop coming. I really hope they don't get me in a fight. Even if I don't fight back, it'll still ruin my chances at parole. "Okay, I guess we can get married, if we absolutely must, you know, for the kids."

"We don't have kids."

"For the parole."

She looks down, and I realize I'm still holding her hand. I'm not sure I have it in me to let go. "I mean it, Dinah. I've had to go twenty-three years waiting for you. If I can make your release even a day earlier, I'll do anything."

I nod because if I open my mouth, I'm going to end up bawling.

"Mrs. Gudaitiene thinks that there's a good chance that, especially if we're married, you'll be able to be released on parole to live with me. She said it was possible that you could get full parole, and we wouldn't have to jump through all these hoops, but that it's a lot more likely that you'd only be able to get, like, a partial one, where you'd have to either be at a halfway house or staying with family."

"Well, I'm certainly not staying with family."

A twinge of something shows in her eyes. Pain? We were both kicked out after her parents caught us. She knows exactly how I feel. It's gone as quickly as it appeared. She can't stop grinning any more than I can. "I know it'll be sort of weird living with me. Though I guess, you've probably had some experience with roommates."

"Actually, I never had roommates. They don't really tend to do that in max, though now, I'm sharing a house with seven other women, so that's kind of weird."

"Oh." She blinks, her hand finally sliding free of mine. "I always assumed it was like on TV."

"Those are American prisons. Kind of different." I gesture at myself. "Note the lack of uniforms."

"Huh." Her fingers dance on the table. "Okay, then. Sorry for getting you roommates."

I chuckle, trying to sound casual. This is still so strange. "I wasn't complaining. The new place is very weird, but it's definitely an upgrade. I'm not used to being able to cook my own food or having any real freedom at all, and I still have my own room. The only difference is not having a toilet in it."

"Well, we have bathrooms in my house. You probably won't have to do your own cooking, though. It'll be nice getting to spoil you."

"You can cook?" That's different. The only thing she used to be able to cook used a spoon and a lighter.

Her fangs show in a bashful smile. I still don't know how she makes them cute. I never do. Though I stopped smiling with my teeth once I got here. I can't risk the other inmates finding out. "Yeah. I uh…sort of opened a restaurant."

"You what?" I blink. Is that how she afforded this lawyer? Is she, like, some big famous Gordon Ramsay figure?

"It's nothing fancy. It's mostly an internet café, but they needed food too, so I learned a few things. The point was, I'll cook for you. Let me finally take care of you, like you always did for me. And to do that, we kinda need that whole marriage thing."

How much else has changed? I guess I shouldn't be surprised. It *has* been twenty-three years, even if we still look the same age. "Then at least propose properly." Joking is so much easier than being honest about how scary and overwhelming this is. She doesn't know the person I've become. I've had to hide so much. I don't know if I can still be the girl she loved. I'm always just playing a part, having to hide who I am. How can I be open with her?

She snorts, but I simply keep watching her. "Not exactly the place I'd have preferred to do it."

"I'm still waiting."

She bites her lip again. She always does when she's nervous. Can she not propose in front of everyone? "I want to. And I think it's a really good idea. And I know there's basically no way that it won't happen. We sure had enough pretend weddings as kids." I'd almost forgotten about those. We'd taken turns being the husband since we didn't know there was another option, then. "But maybe we shouldn't just rush into things. I want us to at least have seen each other more than once before we jump straight from being broken up to being engaged."

I stare at her. "We were broken up? I mean, I guess we were, but…I never thought about it like that."

"You kinda dumped me."

Wow. The room shimmers, and I can't bring myself to meet her eyes. "I guess I did. I didn't mean it like that."

"You meant, 'go move on and have a life without me while still being my girlfriend'?"

I sigh and shrug. "Maybe."

"It's been a long time. And I know I still love you, I just…can I propose next week when I visit?"

I nod. So we're engaged to be engaged?

She grins, looking as excited as if we were already married. "Can I kiss her?" she asks, presumably to one of the guards.

He offers a grunt that seems to be approval, and she rounds the table, pulls me close, and presses her lips to mine. She tastes just like she always did, and she still smells of lilac. I'm catapulted back to every kiss we've ever had, and I can't help but think of all the ones we have yet to enjoy. She pulls away without bothering to gasp for breath. I suppose she hasn't had to put on as much of a show of being human. "I guess that's settled," Rachel says.

"We have a wedding and a parole meeting to plan and so little time."

"See if you can get an ETA for that, I'd really rather not get married in a prison."

"I'll try. Do I just send in the form, or do I need Mrs. Gudaitiene to start the process?"

"I'll ask her. Will you actually call me tomorrow?"

The one nice part of not talking to her was not having to fight for phone time. I'm new, and I can't risk any infractions. Maybe Millie will let me use her phone. "I'll try. It's hard to promise it."

"I get it. I just hate that I can't…"

I wipe a tear from her eye. I want to kiss her again, but we've probably already pushed too far for visitation.

She sits across from me again, still meeting my eyes. Hers are the most beautiful, deep, rich brown, the kind of thing a girl could write poems about in high school, comparing them to chocolate and mahogany and would never recite because they were dreadful. "The other big thing that the parole board is going to really need you to prove is that you're committed to getting better. They'll probably be drug testing you, and I don't want that stuff in my house anyway. Are you gonna be able to handle that?"

Images of the dozens of times I've tried to get high in prison only for it to wear off in literal seconds flood my mind, followed by the whole five minutes I managed after selling my TV when I was transferred here. "Yeah, definitely. I'm clean."

"For how long?"

Great. I should've expected follow up questions. This is all that's been keeping me going for so long. And it used to be the only way she was surviving too. She gave it up and went through all of this without me. I should've done it with her. If I hadn't pushed her away, then she wouldn't have had to go through it alone. And I wouldn't have spent decades jonesing and trying to cop enough to actually get a real high, knowing it would never work. "You know our bodies are too strong for that shit to even affect us."

"Dinah—"

"A few days."

She sighs, and my heart breaks at the look of hurt in her eyes. "You'll end up right back here if you use."

"Like it would stay in my system that long…sorry, no, not the point." The disappointment in her eyes is too much, and it doesn't seem to be going away. "I've only done it a few times since I've been in prison. I don't need it. I'll be fine."

"I know what it's like, you—"

"Rachel, I'm okay. I'll be fine. Trust me."

"I do trust you, Dinah, but I know how difficult it can be. Is there a program you can join in the prison? It helped me a lot."

I've gone to a few sessions and hated every second of them. It's all so creepy and cultish. "Yeah, I'll look into it. I'm sure it'll help with the parole hearing."

"Thank you." She smiles again. Heroin who? I could do anything if it'd earn me that smile.

"Are we done with all the big serious parole stuff?" I ask. "Will you tell me what's been going on in your life?"

"I don't think we're ever going to be done with the big serious parole stuff, at least not until the parole board has all died of old age, but yes, I would love to. But I want to hear about everything that's been happening with you too."

I shrug, trying not to fall right back to that image of me falling back on the bed, properly high for the first time in decades. "I mostly just play a lot of games and watch movies, work some. I was playing this role-playing game. It's like *Dungeons & Dragons*—which I'm actually playing now—at my old prison for a few years, though it had ended a few years before my transfer, so thanks for saving me from that boredom."

She shakes her head, her beautiful smile still there, her eyes lighting up with amusement and a fondness that I should never have pushed away. "You already made friends here?"

I shrug. "People love me."

"Maybe the parole board will too."

I flash a grin that I'm not quite feeling, but my fangs must be showing, so I quickly close my mouth. "I read a lot. I exercise some, but I don't think we can actually build muscle. I got really invested in *Passions*, but that's been off the air for a while now."

"God, I can*not* picture you watching soaps."

"We do some crazy things in prison."

Her fang digs into her lip. "So um…speaking of crazy things, have there been—"

"No. There was never anyone else."

"Wow." She blushes. I suppose I should be glad she's eating okay. I wonder how she's managing it? I hope she's not killing. "There were a couple women for me, but it never lasted more than a few weeks. I was so mad at you, then, but I still couldn't move on. You'd dumped me and tossed me aside. And you did it to protect me. But that wasn't your choice to make, and I was furious, and I tried to…I forced myself to move on, to show that I was over you, but I knew you were here, suffering for me, and I was out there free to enjoy my life, and it made it so hard to do so."

Jealousy burns in me but not enough. I should feel so hurt, but I wanted that for her. She deserved a real life, and I still managed to take that from her. "I'm sorry."

Her eyes are sad and don't quite meet my gaze. She crosses her arms and shrugs. "I had a long time to process it. After those brief flings, it never really amounted to anything more. It didn't matter how mad I was, I couldn't make myself be with anyone else when you were still here. And I knew you'd have never gone along with me breaking you out. Even as hurt as I was, I knew you were the one who was suffering more. I had time to build up my business and have a real life, and you were here. For me."

"Your what?" Right, I still can't get used to that. "You mean, your internet café?"

That smile comes back. God, she must really love it. "It was a long road getting there. I worked in a few restaurants over the years. First as a waitress and later in the kitchen, and I learned how the whole thing worked, and around then, I found out about the Community Center. Mrs. Gudaitiene told you about it, right?"

"A little."

"It's a place for people like us. They were all so sheltered from the world. They had no real connections beyond whatever else was there. I want to say that I was doing it to help them, but the truth is that I saw a business opportunity. Computers were not only getting cheaper all the time, but they were becoming more and more important to having a functioning life, so I started up that internet café where people like us could go and do whatever. Except porn. I tried setting up a private room for that, but it's just not worth it. You don't want to see the kind of messes they can make."

"Ew."

She nods gravely, her eyes distant, like she's reliving the horror. "I have a restaurant as part of it," she continues, her smile returning. "We just serve a few little things, but it's been moderately successful. There aren't that many places where a lot of them can order dinner. I've had to learn to cook some really strange foods, but it's been nice. I even hired on help last year. I could finally afford it."

"Wow, that's amazing."

She shrugs, but that smile is still there. She's so proud of this. It's her baby. And it's all she had to throw herself into while I've been gone.

"And what else? Tell me. I want to know everything."

"Well…" She trails off, watching me. "I was in rehab for a while. It took a few times before it really stuck. And then, I had to try to figure out how to even have a life. I was used to having you there to rely on, and suddenly, I didn't. Sorry, I'm not trying to guilt-trip you—"

"No." I shake my head. "It's okay. I get it. It was so hard for me to learn to function too." We'd always been two halves of a whole, but it's been so long. Can we really go back to how we used to be? Minus the drugs.

"I got my GED and made a few friends in the program and at work. God, I've never had to summarize my life before."

"Then don't summarize. Just tell me everything."

Her smile grows all the more. "I will. There'll be plenty of time."

I can't wait to take her up on that. I could have years getting to know her again, but I'm not patient enough for that. "We only have eternity. I'd rather not waste it."

She rolls her eyes, but she keeps beaming at me. Even if I'm not sure how we'll fit together, I can still make her smile, and that's all that really matters.

"Visiting hours are up," a guard announces.

Fuck. I look to him and back to her. How can I go another moment without her there?

She grips my hand tightly. "I'll be back next Sunday. Call me every day."

I nod. If I say a word, I won't keep from crying. I follow a guard out, trying to watch as she's led the other way.

They lead me back to my cottage. Almost the whole house is in the meager living room, watching something on the TV that I don't recognize. It must not have caught on in Alberta. Millie is with them, so I guess I won't talk to her about my pre-engagement just yet. All of this still feels so unreal.

I head up the stairs to my room, my mind drifting back to all those kisses and just how sexy she looked under that outfit. Some privacy might be nice.

I stop at the top of the steps, drawn from my thoughts. Something's off, but it takes me a moment to place it. There's a smell. There are always smells. And so much of it is food. Sometimes, I can barely even think when a woman in a nearby cell happens to reach that time of the month. Though, it does give me easy food that doesn't leave a mark.

But this isn't like that. It's still food, but, like, it's rotting. Blood that was left out to sit and sour.

I take a step, already knowing what I'll find as I approach the open door to the room next to mine.

I never caught the inmate's name, but her throat has been torn open, and blood coats her clothes, but there's none to be found on the floor. She was drained. I'm not the only vampire here.

I scream.

CHAPTER FOUR

I stare at the door to my cell. It's still a simple wooden thing that I could easily toss aside, but that would only make me look more guilty. This must have happened before, but murders this vicious likely aren't common in minimum security. I can smell the cops sniffing around the crime scene and hear them snapping pictures and muttering to each other. And I can still smell that lilac that I've been smelling since I got here. Death and lilac, just like when I saw her. I wish it wasn't only in my head.

I lean back in my bed, lacing my fingers behind my head. They're going to want to talk to me, and most likely, the fact that this is a replica of my MO is going to come up. I have a rock-solid alibi where there were several guards and a dozen visitors all looking right at me when the murder would've had to take place—I would have heard something if it had happened when I was still here—but when you move in a new girl who was literally called a vampire by the papers and an inmate is drained of blood the next day, they're going to ask some questions.

And if I cooperate, even if all I do is prove my innocence, the other inmates will think I'm a snitch. I can't go making enemies. I have my parole hearing coming up. And maybe my wedding. Is that seriously a real thing? Like, I'm getting married? To Rachel? God, that doesn't even make sense. It's like finding out that not only am I getting out of prison, I'm also winning the lottery a few dozen times in the process.

Why did she wait for me?

I shake my head. She gave me all the answer I need. Guilt-tripping myself isn't going to help. She wants to marry me. She waited for me because she loves me just as much as I love her, and there's no one else I'd rather spend my eternity with. So all I need to do is make sure that I keep my head down, avoid any fights, do some volunteer work, and earn my parole.

Which would be a lot easier if I wasn't the obvious suspect for a murder I didn't commit.

I could mind control the cops, but that would still involve talking to them. There are only seven—no, six, now—other women here. I could force them each individually to forget all about this once it's over, and we could have a nice happy year together until I'm finally released.

And then, I'd be barely any better than whoever did this, which has to be one of them.

Maybe I could try to mind control all of them, and if it doesn't work on one, I'll know that one's the vampire, and I can kill her?

Can you mind control other vampires? I've never tried. And I've never killed one. Would I need a stake? I've probably killed a few people before, given the condition they ended up in, but I only know for sure that I killed the one. I'm not sure I could bring myself to kill someone who wasn't trying to hurt me.

Though, if they're trying to frame me for murder, they are trying to hurt me.

But that doesn't make sense. They knew I wasn't here, so it's a terrible frame job. It has to just be a vampire who got carried away trying to eat. The thought sends a pang of hunger through my body. I haven't eaten since my transfer. It's only been a few days. I've gone longer before, but I at least knew that I'd get some blood eventually. Now, what am I going to do? They'll be watching us like hawks.

I could drink the first cop who comes to talk to me, then make them believe that I'm innocent and have them leave us alone. But can I stop myself from drinking them dry? I'm starving. If I kill another cop, there's no way I'm getting out of here.

Now that I'm no closer to an answer, the door opens. A stern-faced, uniformed man greets me. He's lean and lacks the paunch that tends to go with the uniform, and he moves like a predator. If I so much as sniff the air, I'll end up draining him. I know it as surely as I know that I don't need to breathe.

So I don't bother. Any breath could give me that whiff of food. His gray eyes narrow. "Not even a hello?" he asks.

I remain silent, only slightly tilting my head so he knows I'm still alive. I'd rather my murder not send the cottage into some sort of double lockdown.

"Is it Pelletier? Dinah Pelletier?"

This is going to get old fast. I sit there, not doing a damn thing, lest anyone think I'm a snitch, and I end up in so many fights that I can't stay out of the hole for more than a day.

"The fucking vampire?"

I go even more still, my eyes wide. I must look like a surprised corpse.

"Yeah, I bet you thought you were pretty clever getting all that shit removed from the internet. But some of us still remember. My father was on that case." His voice is loud enough that some of the other girls must hear. He's trying to paint me as the killer, but I can't react, I can't make myself look guilty, and I certainly can't make myself look like a snitch.

Not a word. I can't give in.

"I don't know how you did it. I've talked to everyone else. Even the guards confirm your alibi, but I know it had to be you. There's no other monster who would kill a poor girl like that. The look of horror on her face, I don't think it'll ever leave me. She was here for drugs. Was she your dealer on the outside?" He's playing it up, like this is all a show to convince the other women what kind of monster I am.

I didn't know the girl, but she couldn't have been old enough to be my dealer. He should know this. And they had all been men anyway.

"Was this some sort of revenge thing for ripping you off? You, what, killed her and stashed her in the freezer without anyone noticing and had an accomplice put her there while you were gone? I've checked all the knives and searched every other bunk. None of them could've done it."

He's grasping at straws, but he's also intentionally making it sound ludicrous. He's trying to prompt a reaction from me. Or from someone else. It's tough to tell.

"All right. I can't say I expected more. But you'll talk eventually. This whole luxury condo is on lockdown until I get to the bottom of this. There will be guards watching your every move, and you won't be leaving this room to find another victim." He walks over to my desk, tears open the empty bag, and flips through my books. "But I'm going to search every nook and cranny and make your life a living hell. You killed a good man, and now you've killed another junkie. You're moving down in the world, vampire."

There's an actual killer here, or at least one who's not so rusty at killing. He's looking in the wrong place, and he's so blinded by his father's stories of my villainy that he's not even trying. I should mind control him. My eyes fall on his throat. Talking still requires breathing. I'd smell him. I can't kill another cop.

"Stand up."

I do as he says and hold my arms out, but he doesn't go to pat me down, instead flipping my mattress over and taking a close look at the bed frame. I don't have anything under there. It's the bright side of being the new girl. I haven't had time to grab any contraband.

Wait, what about Millie's cell phone? Did he find it? If only I could ask.

No, I would've heard her being dragged off. There's no way they'd find that and not lock her up.

He shakes his head and stomps toward the door. "You can't move an inch without us watching you. I don't care how solid your alibi is, I will find out how you did this, and I will make you pay." He slams the door behind him, the wall shaking in protest as his boots echo down the stairway.

I need blood, or I'll never make it through this.

I close my eyes and listen to the other women. They're not talking to each other; they're all too scared and don't know who to trust. Their hearts are racing, they're sobbing into pillows, and someone is tapping away on a screen. Millie must be messaging someone about all of this. If I could only talk to her, then she could get word to Rachel and…

The thought ends abruptly. What would I have Rachel do? Run here and throw a bag of blood through my blocked-out window? That would hardly make me look more innocent.

I'm not looking to her for help. There's nothing she could really do from a hundred kilometers away. What I want is to talk to her again. She's finally back in my life, and I want to be able to tell her about everything and to know that she's there for me.

It was so much easier when I was ignoring her and not even in the same province. But then, I wasn't getting married. I suppose there's a bright side to having the woman I love back in my life.

❖

They let us out of our rooms to use the bathroom every few hours, not that I need it. We don't get to use the kitchen, as they bring us our meals. It's like being back in max but with a softer bed.

And I don't even have my TV.

We've been stuck like this for two days, and I'm halfway through one of the only three books I own that I haven't read, and I already read one of the others yesterday.

A guard approaches the door, and I feel myself drooling. I swallow it, but it's difficult. Human food can numb the hunger sometimes, but it's getting to be far too much. The knob turns, and a heavyset woman steps inside, staring at me, blood pumping through her neck, practically singing, calling to me. I can hear her heart pounding away, spreading it from head to toe. She drops a tray of food onto the table by my bed. "Eat up, you look like you're dying."

I leap to my feet, and she backs for the door. She said to eat up. I should take a bite. I can—

Her eyes widen in fear. She thinks I'm the killer.

"Thank you," I whisper, scared to do anything more. I take the food and sit back down, eyeing the revolting bread, meat, and mashed potatoes. My stomach rebels at the thought. Human food isn't enough anymore. I can't take it. I need to feed.

The poor defenseless dead girl flashes before my eyes. Is that what her killer was thinking? Did she die because the prison was starving out whatever poor vampire did it?

I'm sympathizing with a murderer. A few more days, and I'm not sure I'll even recognize myself.

The door opens, and I don't know if it's been a minute or a week. "Pelletier," a voice says.

I blink, trying to will the world into focus. It's that same skinny asshole cop from before.

"You've done a good job holding out." He sounds like he's enjoying this. I want to rip out his fucking throat. "I've torn this place apart. I don't know how you did it. They want us to start looking into guards."

Why is he telling me this?

"I know it was you. You're the monster who killed that poor thing, and yet, everyone is convinced that you have to be innocent."

I stare at him, trying to figure out what he's talking about.

"Fine. I guess you get to go free. As free as you can with a life sentence." He chuckles. "But I'll make sure you suffer for every second of it, cop killer."

Why does he sound so angry? What did I do to him again? Was it his dad?

The door opens again, and his steps thud into the hall. "Thank you for your cooperation, Ms. Pelletier. I'm not sure we could've solved this without you."

What is he talking about? I didn't do anything.

Wait. Something clicks in my brain. Those words have another meaning. He's not thanking me. He's...I look up, staring into the monster's massive grin as he closes the door behind me. "It was Michaels."

The other officers murmur something more, but I can't quite sort it out. Who's Michaels? Was that the guy I killed? If I could just have a drink, maybe this would make more sense.

"I didn't do anything," a woman shouts.

She sounds so familiar. What are they taking her in for? Is she the one who killed that girl?

"I've never killed anyone," she adds for good measure.

Who hasn't said that? Something in her voice jostles what's left of my brain. I see red hair, a smiling face, and a d20. He's framing Millie. But why?

He wants me to suffer. Maybe he knows that we're friends, maybe he just picked from one in six and got lucky. Either way, if he tosses someone in the hole, supposedly on my word, my life will be a living hell, and I'll never get parole.

And she'll be stuck in confinement for something that she didn't do.

And I won't have a DM. Or a friend in prison. Anyone to talk to. A way to contact Rachel.

If he didn't choose her on purpose, then he sure lucked out.

What can I do? She's so young, barely more than a kid. And she doesn't have an eternity to wait. If they think she's a murderer, she could lose her whole life behind bars, and it won't be a cushy place like this cottage.

I step toward the door, and the room spins. I could drink the guards. That'd stop them, and I wouldn't feel so weak. But then what? I don't think I could cover up the murder of, by the sound of it, two police officers and two correctional officers. That'd make the news for years. I'd be a world-famous killer, and any chance of people not knowing monsters are real would go out the window.

What does that leave? I take another step, gritting my teeth. Adrenaline is clearing my mind, but it's not enough. I need to think. There has to be something I can do. "Stop," I scream, and finally, I understand.

There is an option. And if it'll work here, maybe it'll work for the parole board, and that'll make my whole life so much easier.

"Shut up, inmate."

"She didn't do anything. Let her go and leave this place."

Handcuffs click on the other side of the door. Did I do it? Did it really work?

The room spins again, the colors shifting focus.

Did I save the day?

Darkness blots out what's left of the room, and the last thing I hear is a strange thud.

CHAPTER FIVE

D rink." The word seems to come from nowhere. It's as if I'm floating in an empty void, and someone is shouting for me to take blood. I know this feeling. It's just like when I first turned. The thirst was overwhelming. I couldn't stop myself. I don't remember anything leading up to it, but my teeth were buried in that man's throat, and I couldn't stop drinking, even as he screamed for his life.

Maybe if it had only been me, I would've taken enough, and he could've lived, but there were two starving vampires on him. I know I couldn't have done anything to stop myself, but I can still hear him screaming.

"Drink."

I won't do it again. I won't give in like that. I can't. It's already taken so much. I killed that man, and I've spent twenty-four years locked up to pay for it. I was nineteen and a newborn vampire. I had no idea what I was doing, and now, I don't even know the outside world. I won't do it again. It doesn't matter how thirsty I am. I can't fall for it. If I give in and drink and kill another person, especially in prison, that'll be it. I won't have a life anymore. Monsters won't be a secret. Hell, it could be all-out war between human and fiend. And it'd all be my fault. I don't care how badly I need it. I won't give in.

"Oh my fucking god, you stupid little whore, just drink."

That doesn't sound like my internal monologue. I blink, but the world is as unlit as before. Have I gone blind? Something hard is pressed against my mouth. It doesn't feel like someone's throat, so I take a hesitant sip.

It tastes like sex. Maybe even better.

I grab whatever it is—a mug, maybe—and pour the blood down my throat. It's almost the most intoxicating thing I've ever tasted. It's almost as good as heroin.

"Much better," the voice says.

I look around, blinking against the fluorescent light. Oh, I can see. Did I starve myself blind? I didn't even know that was possible. I'm in a bed in what looks like an infirmary. There are a few empty beds near me, and I can hear labored breathing from behind a curtain. I'm a vampire who just woke up in a hospital infirmary. This can't be good. What did they figure out? I wouldn't have had a pulse. Why didn't they just send me to the morgue?

And why did they give me blood?

I stare at the woman sitting next to me. For a moment, I expect it to be Rachel, or at least Mrs. Gudaitiene, but I don't recognize her. She doesn't smell human.

"You are so lucky that I live near here." She looks to be in her mid-forties, but who could say how many centuries ago that was? She's a vampire, I'm sure of it. She's pale and gaunt, weirdly pretty, with light brown hair, and she smells like a dead body before it starts to decompose or produce any of the other, less pleasant scents.

"What are you talking about?"

"This isn't my normal shift, but your lawyer warned me about you and told me to keep an eye on things. Nurse Laurence called me, and I took her shift and had to give her twenty bucks for movie tickets. God, that gold better be real."

"What are you talking about?" I repeat.

She groans, shaking her head. "Did you hit your head a little too hard? Anything left in there? I'm a vampire, like you. Some stupid little shit decided that she should go on a hunger strike and passed out, and if a human nurse had been the one dealing with her, they might've seen that she wasn't breathing, had no pulse, and was stubbornly still groaning and turning in her sleep like she was alive. You also probably would've tried to eat her, though as weak as you were, I doubt you'd have managed."

I lick my lips and stare at the empty mug. I'm still so thirsty. "I wasn't on a hunger strike."

"Then why didn't you drink? You were surrounded by plenty of humans, and you could've fed at any time. Someone else did, why didn't you?"

"I would've been caught."

"You could've used your powers. What are you even doing in prison? You can leave anytime you want."

Who the hell is this woman? "So you think I should just be a wanted criminal? How is that going to be any better?"

"You're a vampire. You're never going to have a normal human life again. You could be let out tomorrow, and you'd still be an ageless undead abomination."

I cross my arms, feeling like a petulant child as I say, "This way, I can still get married, at least."

She shakes her head, her brow creasing. "How have you made it this long? If you're too stupid to eat the other inmates, what's stopped you from starving?"

I don't dignify that with an answer. "Can I have some more blood?"

She pulls a half-empty blood bag from a mini fridge on a nearby desk and squeezes it into my cup. I hadn't noticed it was cold. It's strange, but I'm too thirsty to fight. I down it all, letting out a moan as I finally feel my body functioning again. There's blood running through me. I feel almost human. Better than human. "So you just use the prison's blood supplies?"

"Please, like they give us enough blood for that. I take it from inmates when they come here. Why the hell else do you think I'm a nurse in a prison? It gives me easy access to blood."

"You what?" I shout. "What happened to 'do no harm'? They're your patients. And they're innocent."

"The fuckers are in prison for a reason."

I grind my teeth. She just saved my life, but it's hard not to be disgusted by someone who treats the people in her care like a buffet. "You're supposed to be looking after them. And if they're in the infirmary, they're probably already missing blood. Can they really spare it? That's awful, how can you do that to them?"

She rolls her eyes. "They're food. We need to eat them to live, and I'm not even killing them in the process. It doesn't hurt them beyond a little prick. They're like cattle, and all I'm doing is taking some milk."

"That's…" I stare at her. Is it really that bad? It feels so wrong, but what do I expect her to do? I've done worse. I killed someone, and she's only taking their blood. But it's the blood of people she's supposed to be healing, not hurting.

She scoffs. "It's about the nicest thing a vampire can do. Why, what do you do? How have you kept your moral high horse while feeding off other inmates?"

I watch the inside of my mug. A droplet of blood slides down the side and coalesces at the bottom. I swipe it up on my finger and lick it off. "I don't feed on them. Often. Sometimes, it was necessary, but normally, well, prisons don't give enough women's supplies, so I'd buy menstrual cups and have them sent in and let other women use them for free on the condition that they give them back without emptying them. I sometimes made them not tell anyone, but people thinking I had a weird fetish was a lot better than thinking I was a monster."

Her lip curls back, showing bloodstained fangs. "That's disgusting."

Now she's the one judging me? Where does she get off? "It's nice having blood without the chunks."

She looks like she wants to throw up. That's about how I felt over her story. "You've been living off period blood for, what, years?"

"More like decades."

"How are you still alive?"

I shrug. It had seemed so natural to me. It smelled like food, and I didn't want it to go to waste. "It's worked so far."

"And left you a starving mess who passes out when she tries to compel someone. That's what happened, isn't it? One of the guards was freaking out about how they'd unhandcuffed some girl and walked out of the cottage for no reason. I made them all forget it. God, she better actually have that gold. I am not getting paid enough to cover up for your ineptitude."

"I…" She's right. I fucked up. I could've exposed us to the whole world, and it never would've happened if I'd just controlled that cop in the first place. I didn't trust myself enough. "I'm sorry."

"You should be."

The door bursts open, and a familiar fair one storms in. "Are you okay? Who did this to you? We'll sue the fucking pants off them. They can't go attacking inmates like this."

I blink, taking a moment to figure out what she's talking about. She thinks a guard assaulted me, and that's why I ended up here? I guess it makes sense. I probably had a concussion, if vampires can get them. I heard how hard I hit my head. I feel for a bump, but there doesn't seem to be anything there. It doesn't even hurt. I guess the blood fixed me up. "I fell."

"Oh, give me a break. I'm not falling for that. I didn't mean the pun."

I snicker. "Really, I fell. They were trying to arrest a different inmate. She's kind of my friend, or at least, she was. I have no idea what things are going to be like when I get back there. I mind controlled them. Apparently, I can do it to a group, so at least we know that'll work, but I hadn't had any blood, so I passed out and hit my head."

She looks to the nurse.

"It's true."

"All right, well…" She deflates. "Thanks for looking out for her, Moira."

She holds out her hand. "I didn't do it for you."

Mrs. Gudaitiene fishes a cloth bag from her jacket pocket and drops it into the nurse's hand. It jingles like it's full of coins. "Don't spend it all in one place."

"Well, I don't think Amazon takes gold, so you don't have to worry about that."

She reaches in another pocket and holds out a bag of blood. "I brought this for you. It's O positive, supposed to be a good flavor and good quality."

"I drank." I stare at the bag, my mouth watering.

"Put it in something else and put that in the fridge with your name on it. You need to be able to drink. We can't have this happen again."

"I'm sorry." I seem to be saying that a lot. I've been a vampire for twenty-four years. Why does everyone else know so much more than me? I've only met one other vampire before, and now I'm apparently around two. My throat goes dry. I left that vampire alone with the other inmates. More of them could be dead by now. I jump from my bed. "I should go back to the cottage."

Mrs. Gudaitiene's eyes narrow. She takes a step toward me but stops. "Are you sure that's a good idea? What happened? I wasn't given a very clear story."

I give her a quick summary, not wanting to waste any time. "I need to get back. There's a killer there."

"And you think you can stop her?"

I stare. Her blue eyes shimmer with concern, but she keeps her expression hard. As a lawyer, she probably has to learn to cut herself off from her feelings. She must meet so many train wrecks that she can't stop. I hope I'm not one of them. "Maybe not, but I'd rather be there to at least try."

"Hold on. Do you think you can spare a few more minutes without being a superhero, or do you have a cape to go change into?"

I stop mid-step, studying her. "Why?" I ask, unable to keep the suspicion from my voice.

"Well, for starters, you need a guard to walk you back and probably pat you down, though I suspect you can talk your way out of the blood being an issue. But more importantly, your fiancée has been losing her mind calling me since your cottage hasn't been allowing any calls. As I can't get any work done with her interrupting everything I try to do, could you appease her?"

"My fiancée?" Who…oh, right. Rachel and I are going to get married. She's not actually my fiancée yet, but we're planning our wedding, so I suppose it's close enough to make semantics difficult. I'm going to marry Rachel fucking Evans. My cheeks hurt from how hard I'm grinning, and I snatch the phone the second Mrs.

Gudaitiene holds it out. Wow, she really is calling nonstop. "Hello?" I ask, answering it.

"Have you…Dinah? Oh, it's so good to hear your voice."

I sink back onto the bed. Good is an understatement. It's like I've died and gone to heaven. "Yeah, it's me, babe. Sorry for worrying you. There's just a deranged vampiric killer loose in the prison. Nothing to worry about."

She's silent for a long moment. "It sounds like something to worry about."

"Yeah, but that's why I specified that it was nothing to worry about. Otherwise, you would have worried."

She groans. "Dinah, we're so close to getting you out of there. Don't get yourself into any trouble. I know you can't resist helping people, but—"

"I'll be careful. I'm not going to try to hunt down and fight a monster." Anymore.

"Fiend."

"That either. But these are good people who've just made some mistakes. I don't want to see them hurt, and if I can do anything to stop that, I want to."

"That's what you said when you kept giving our money to other homeless people when we were on the streets."

It hadn't happened that many times. We spent most of our money as quickly as we got it, so I never had the chance, but it was winter. "They were kids. I couldn't leave them like that."

"Yeah, and that was a night at the hotel we'd been saving for." She sighs, but she doesn't actually sound upset; she sounds almost proud and loving. "Please, just don't be your self-sacrificing self for a few months. Get to your first meeting with the parole board. We can compel them to make it all easy. You'll be able to go to our wedding, and you'll be basically free, even before they let you out on parole. Please, just make it that far without any trouble."

I sigh. I hate it, but she's right. I'm not a superhero. I'm just a very stupid vampire who's trying to get herself caught up in someone else's trouble. I have to keep my head down. I have to see her. "I'll try."

"I want you to promise."

"I promise, I'll try."

She groans. "I love you." That's code for "You're an idiot."

"I love you too." That's code for "You're the best thing to ever happen to me."

"You have to actually call me this time, okay?"

"The only reason I didn't was because there was a murder, and we were on lockdown."

"Then, don't let it happen again." She chuckles. "And you're okay?"

"I'm fine."

"Aren't you in the infirmary?" She sounds incredulous.

I grumble. "Yeah, I was just starving. I'm fine. Please, don't worry, babe. Really, it's okay." She worried like this when I first went to prison too. I've honestly missed it.

"I'm going to worry about my fiancée. You don't get a choice in that."

There's that word again. Heat wells in my cheeks. I guess there's enough blood in me to blush. "I thought we weren't actually…" I sigh. "I won't let you worry. I can just mind control…compel, if that's what we're calling it, a guard to let me use a phone if we're still in lockdown."

"That's more like it. And I looked into it, and there are AA and NA meetings there. Make sure you attend one. It can make a huge difference."

Oh, right. I completely forgot about that. The lockdown had been such a good excuse to avoid them. "Well, now, I haven't used in at least a week. I'm fine."

"Dinah, please."

She sounds so commanding. And even more worried. "Fine. I'll go to a meeting."

CHAPTER SIX

It's painfully easy to make them all forget the entire last week. Inmate Johnson had a freak heart attack. The guards took her to the hospital, but it was too late. We've all been in mourning and shock, but it's getting easier. Maybe they want to believe it, and that's why it takes so easily. Or maybe it's because I just had more blood than I've drunk in years.

I hate myself for it. I *hate* lying to them. They don't deserve it. But they can't know what I am. Mrs. Gudaitiene has made it abundantly clear how dire that would be. I don't entirely understand what it would cause, but I'm not willing to be the one responsible for it.

Anytime those two guards are on duty, we mysteriously don't have count. The other girls seem confused by it, but I don't want to compel them again, so I explain that they were the ones who found her, and they're probably too traumatized to come back in. For all I know, that could really be the case, but I suspect that my telling them to leave was more permanent than I'd meant it. They can't enter this cottage anymore. It's ironic. It's almost like they're vampires.

I've been on the lookout, but there hasn't been any sign of another vampire. All the other women smell human, and no one has been randomly murdered the entire time since we've been off lockdown. I'm still not quite sure how we managed that. Maybe Mrs. Gudaitiene pulled some strings, or maybe my compulsion made them all drop it. I hadn't said to, but I'm still not sure how it all works.

When Saturday rolls around, I know I can't put it off anymore. There's a Narcotics Anonymous meeting, and if I don't go, I'll have to tell Rachel tomorrow that I didn't keep my word. She needs me to go. She needs to know that I'm clean.

How can I start a life with her if she thinks I'm always looking for my next fix? How can I start it if I may actually be? It's been two weeks. She's at the front of my mind, except when I can't stop thinking about blood, but that doesn't mean it won't change. It's easy to go without when your life is great. I'm in minimum security, and I'm marrying a woman I'm absolutely crazy about. If there wasn't a crazed killer on the loose, I'd say things couldn't be any better.

But that won't always be the case, and I know I'll go right back to it. God, I miss needles. You can't get them in prison, and I've had to make do with snorting it.

Okay, there, see, that's the kind of thought I'm trying to avoid. Thinking about how I'm eventually going to crave heroin made me crave it. This is self-defeating. How can any rehab possibly prevent that? The more I want to make sure that I won't want to use anymore, the more I have to think about using, and the more I'll want it. It had barely even crossed my mind until I started thinking about NA again.

This is such a terrible idea.

I should just stay in and see if everyone is up for some *Dungeons & Dragons*. I could lie to Rachel and say I did it, except of course, I've never lied to her in my entire life, and I'm not sure I could start now. I could be honest and say I couldn't bring myself to do it.

That look of disappointment in her eyes replays in my mind. If I don't do this, it'll break her heart.

It doesn't matter how stupid I think it is. I have to give it a try. For her.

I walk out the front door, which still feels so wrong to be able to do. There's a fence topped with barbed wire still ineffectually blocking my escape, but being able to walk outside seems to go against the very idea of being a prisoner. The sun beats down on me, and the slight agony makes me want to go back inside.

But that's not all it makes me want to do.

Maybe I really do need this meeting.

I have to get a guard to take me over there, so apparently, I don't have total freedom, even in this weird minimum security…whatever the opposite of a hellhole is. Heavenbump? Purgatoryplane?

That last one works. It's still a prison.

"We'll escort you all back to your dorms after," the guard says once we're there. She probably thinks I'm new to prisons too.

I nod. I'm not talking to a guard in front of a bunch of other inmates.

It's outside. There are a few big picnic tables, with only one of them being under any sort of cover. My skin is on fire. This is literally torture. I take a seat under the umbrella and let out a shuddering breath. I'd be crying if I hadn't had years to train that out of me. What crazy person decided that we needed these meetings outside? What, do they think the sun helps people not want drugs? I could use a painkiller right now.

At the mere thought of injecting it, that familiar pain and relief washes over me. It's like it's almost real. It's so instant. If I just had some, then I wouldn't be hurting. God, I can almost taste it. I can smell it. That sweet sickly cocoa butter flavor.

I sniff again. I actually *can* smell it.

I glance around. I hadn't even noticed more people arriving. The scent is growing stronger. There are women clustered on every bench and a few in lawn chairs that someone must've brought out when I was imagining exactly what I shouldn't be thinking about.

The scent is overwhelming. I should leave. I need to get out of here. I didn't want to use at all; well, only a little before Rachel put this all back in my head. But with it literally feet from me, how can I resist?

I glare at the woman that the scent is wafting from. She's probably in her mid-thirties, with long curly brown hair and dull blue eyes. She looks high right now. She's almost asleep in her seat.

And she has more on her.

Why would she even come here? I should confront her. I can get her to leave. I can…great, and now I'm thinking about just how easy it would be to get it from her. I could compel her to give it to me. I wouldn't even have to give her any soup. I could sit through this stupid meeting and go back to my cell and...

And Rachel would never forgive me. She wouldn't want to marry me. She probably wouldn't even let me stay with her if I made parole. I would've broken my word.

But I've been here this whole time. She's been able to make a real life, and she hasn't been stuck bored and miserable in prison for twenty-four years with nothing to do but try to find a way to get high through my ridiculous vampiric tolerances.

Because I didn't want her to suffer like that. Because I knew it would be worse for her.

I can't blame her for my choices. And I won't break my promise to her. I said I'd stay clean, and I said I'd go to this meeting.

Another slight sniff has me nearly crying with need. It's so close. So easy. I could take it right now. It may even be enough to really feel something.

Can I both be clean and at this meeting? The two don't seem to go together. They may be mutually exclusive.

I should leave. It's the best option.

"I'm Britta, and I'm an alcoholic and an addict."

They've already started. Shit. I stay in my seat, trying to pry my eyes from the woman with the heroin.

She stares back at me, shifting in her seat.

I'm going to get in a fight at this rate. I must look insane. But I can't get the scent out of my head.

"That's what finally got me tossed in here," a woman says.

I take a deep breath, trying to steady myself, but all it does is flood my lungs with the scent. If I could get high off the smell alone, this would be so much easier. Except I don't want to get high. That's why I'm here.

I stand, trying to pull myself away from her, to do anything but think about how badly I need that hit.

Every eye in the courtyard turns to me.

We're still in the middle of a meeting. I can't just walk out. What would the parole board think of that? I'd look like I couldn't handle being sober. I'm trying to do what's best for me, but they'd think the exact opposite. But if I can mind control them, does it matter?

Assuming I don't pass out and give myself another concussion in the process.

I can't let them think that I'm running away, that I'm too weak to make it through a single NA meeting. Maybe I should try AA instead; at least people aren't as likely to have heroin there.

"I'm Dinah, and I'm an addict." The echoed "Hi, Dinah" should feel comforting, but it's creepy. It's like talking to robots. "I've been clean for…well, little enough time that I probably shouldn't be saying it in prison."

"Everything is private here," one of the women says. "And the guards stay out of earshot."

"I've been clean for about two weeks," I mutter, the words coming out far too quickly. It does feel a little good to talk about it, but it'd feel a lot better if it was to someone who actually cared, like Millie seems to, rather than to a bunch of people who're also here simply to look better for the parole board. "I've been using since I was sixteen. I'd been living on the streets for about a year after my girlfriend and our parents…separate sets of parents, this is not that kind of story." That doesn't even get a laugh. What is the point of this group again? "They'd kicked us out for being gay. And then, before long, I ended up in prison." For the cop killing, not the drug use, but they don't have to know that part. They'd probably respect me more for it, but I'd rather not draw the extra attention. "I've never really had to learn how to function as a person while clean. Next year, I should be getting out, and I don't know how to not end up back here."

I sit back down. I hadn't even realized I was feeling that last part. I knew I was scared that I'd fall back into old habits—or current habits, and that they'd make me lose Rachel, but I guess it's true. I've been in prison longer than I've been outside of it. I don't know what the real world is like. How can I possibly adjust to having freedom for the first time in my life?

Maybe that's the point of this purgatoryplane.

"I definitely get that," a nearby girl says.

"That's what happened to me too," the woman with the heroin says. I stare at her. "This your first meeting?"

I could talk to her. I could get her alone and make her give it to me. I close my eyes to pry my gaze from her and nod. Who thought this meeting was a good idea?

More people talk. "I had the chance to use the other day," one of them says. "I thought I'd give in. I couldn't reach my sponsor. But I think God stepped in."

I'm glad just hearing the word doesn't burn me.

"So you still seeing her?" I blink and turn to the source of the voice. That woman is sitting next to me now and staring at me as hungrily as I must've been looking at her earlier. Except, I don't think she's after the drugs I don't have. "Most of the actual lesbians in prison don't look half as good as you."

I should tell her off. That scent is so overwhelming. I want it so badly. But I could never so much as pretend to flirt with someone else. I'm marrying Rachel, and I'll do whatever it takes to reach that point. "Yes, we're still together. We're actually getting married soon."

"Oh." She looks disappointed. I am too. I need it bad.

"Sorry," I mutter, looking away from her, trying to look at anything that won't make me want to use.

"That was really brave of you," someone says. It's not the same voice as the painful temptation, so I turn to look. It's an older woman with gray coloring her cornrows. "I've never mentioned my sexuality in one of these groups. People can be pretty weird about it."

I shrug. "I didn't mean to say most of what I said."

She chuckles and takes the apparently now empty seat next to me. I guess the other girl took the hint. But it still smells so close, and it would make all of this go away. "Yeah, the first time can be kind of scary. Do you know much about the program?"

I shake my head. Talking is breathing, and that scent is still so overwhelming.

"Well, if you're looking for a sponsor, I've been clean for thirty years. It can really make a big difference having someone you can rely on."

"I can rely on myself."

"No, you really can't."

I stare at her. She doesn't look like she's insulting me; her brows are knitted in concern.

"It's one of the first things the big book teaches us. You're powerless before your addiction. It's why you have to put your faith in a higher power. And it's why having a sponsor can make such a big difference."

Oh, I get it now. They're a cult.

Her eyebrow quirks. "You look kinda freaked out."

Nothing about this has been what I needed. I'll tell Rachel that there has to be another way. She can't be upset with me. I actually went. I even stuck around. "I'm just not sure that this is really for me."

"It is if you want to get clean."

They're really driving home that cult aspect. "I'll think about it. I just want to go…" I was going to say to bed, but the sun is still up, much to my suffering. "Have some food. I'll be back. We can talk about that sponsor thing then." I hate lying.

"Hey, no pressure. It can be overwhelming. Just take your time."

Right, because that hadn't all been pressure. I force a smile and stand, walking right into the sun. How does enduring all this pain and insanity help anyone stay clean? I want it so much more than I did when I left the cottage. I keep the smile plastered on as we're all led away until I'm safely back in the cottage.

I go right to the fridge. I shouldn't waste it. I need to wait, to save it, but I feel like I've been roasting alive for the past few hours, and if I can't get high, I can at least eat for once. I pour half the bag of blood into a mug and microwave it. I don't care if anyone sees me at this point. I just need the pain to stop.

CHAPTER SEVEN

Why does she always have to look so beautiful? I take the seat across from her, thankful that I don't have to breathe as she's already taken my breath away, and I'm so glad I didn't say that out loud. She didn't bother with the top two buttons of her blouse, and even with barely anything showing, it's enough to heavily draw my gaze. It has been far too long.

"You look better." She's beaming at me. "You finally got some food?"

"I did." We could just run out of here. No one would be able to stop us. I could press her up against a wall and kiss my way down that neck to her collarbone and remind myself of exactly what the shirt is covering. God, I hope I get that ETA. "Though, I still need to work on finding a more sustainable source here."

"Can't you just ask your roommates?"

I shrug. "I'd rather not risk it. There aren't enough of them for that."

"Dinah, you have to eat. You can't sacrifice yourself for everyone."

"You know me better than that. I absolutely can." I flash her a grin, but she crosses her arms, looking annoyed.

"Look after my fiancée."

"I'm not your fiancée yet."

She blinks, and her lip curls into a mischievous grin. "That's right. I didn't actually propose yet. Though, if I'm going to go to all the trouble of marrying you, I need to know that you're going to put in the work to get out of here."

That's not playing fair at all. It's cruel. "Fine. After you propose."

Her smile only grows as she stands and gets on one knee. "Dinah Pelletier, I love you. Please, I want you to be mine. Marry me."

Tears run down my cheeks, and I have to blink a few times to make the world come back into focus. "Yes. Of course I'll marry you."

She kisses me, and the guards don't say so much as a word. We don't need to breathe, so we could keep going forever, but eventually, it would look suspicious, so I finally pull away, but she just plants another quick kiss on me. "I've waited a long time to be able to call you my fiancée."

I must be blushing. My cheeks feel like they're on fire. I'm not used to having blood in me. "All right. I'll…compel one of them."

"Thank you."

I feel dirty. It's not like it's the first time, but I've been so good about it for so long. I've been careful not to hurt people like that. But she's right; I'm hurting myself in the process. When that didn't affect anyone else, it was one thing, but now that's her life too. "How have you been?" I ask, holding her hands as we sit again, not wanting to be any farther from her. "Is work still going okay?"

"Yeah, it's been pretty great. We honestly do food more than internet these days, but fie…*people* are always happy to have a nice meal, and there are still plenty of them who need some help with using a computer and don't have or can't use a phone. Oh, I, uh, I never told you what my café was called, did I?"

I tilt my head, trying to recall. I hung on her every word, but I also kept picturing her naked, so it was possible I missed something. "I don't think you did."

She takes my hand, those deep brown eyes gazing into my soul. "Dinah's."

A lump forms in my throat. She keeps telling me that she hasn't stopped thinking of me, that she hasn't moved on, either, but I never thought she'd have done something like that. "I love you."

She grins. "And I love you."

I should probably tell her about yesterday. I really don't want to ruin the moment, but I can't keep anything from her, especially when we're talking about how much we love each other and how she named her business after me. "I..." It didn't used to be this hard to talk to her. She's been my best friend since kindergarten. I told her everything, all the time. She was there for me, and I trusted her, and she never judged me. The only other time I was at all scared was when I didn't want to tell her that I had feelings for her, but she beat me to that, so I never had to. But now, I have to tell her I hated something that she seems to care about. Have we really changed that much since I've been in prison? "I went to NA yesterday."

Her face lights up. "That's amazing. How did you like it? I know it can be tough, but it really makes a huge difference."

I don't want to make that light go away. I hate making her sad. "I don't think it's for me. It's outside in the sun for starters, so that wasn't a great first impression."

"Ow." She winces in what I hope is empathy.

"But I just...I don't think it will work for me."

"You don't think you can quit?"

"No, I can definitely do that," I say, panicked, needing to reassure her, for her not to think I'm beyond hope. "Babe, for you, I can do anything. I don't need it anymore." I'm shocked to find that I'm not lying. I don't. I haven't used that much since I've been in prison, and I resisted yesterday. I can do this. "I even had the chance to do some yesterday, and I didn't. I'm clean. I know how much that means to you. No, it matters to me too. I want to have a real life with you, and I know that I can't do that if I'm strung out. I'm not going to use, but it's just..." Cult-y seems so insulting. "I had enough religion in Hebrew school."

"It's not about religion." That same odd look shows for an instant. "It doesn't have to be. I..." She sighs. "I guess I'm the one who changed here."

"Huh?" She's been having the same thought about how different we are now. I gulp, trying not to let my fear show on my face. Is she having second thoughts?

"I was bothered by the higher power stuff too, especially when one of them tried to hand me a Bible, and well, I had a burn scar for a week, no matter how much I drank. But it really worked for me. Knowing that there was someone out there and trusting them with my recovery made it a lot easier. Maybe that's because I used to always trust you the same way."

Being compared to Him feels weird. "You looked after me just as much."

"It never felt like it." She sighs. "I want to know that you're clean. It's not that I don't trust you, it's that I know how difficult it is to not have a structure. It took me so many tries. I was in and out of rehab for years after you stopped talking to me."

Ow. "I'm sorry."

Her lip trembles, and tears well in her eyes. "You should be. I could've been here. We could've been supporting each other this whole time."

"I just—"

"Wanted me to have a life. I know. And I did. But I could've had you too. Please, if you're not going to NA, which I get, you don't need to be in the sun. I'm not asking you to torture yourself for me—"

"You could've said that before I went."

She gives me a pained smile. "I didn't know that it was outside. I wouldn't have insisted if I knew that was the case. If I set you up with a sponsor—not even a sponsor, just someone to keep you accountable who isn't also in love with you—will you at least talk to them?"

"I'm not sure how that's different from a sponsor."

"I just mean you don't have to be in the program. I'm not going to force you to do something you don't want to do. I know how much these sorts of things bother you. But having someone to talk to about it, who is only that, can really help."

It's a reasonable compromise. I thought she would resent me for hating her program, but I should've known better. She's worried about me, and if I can assuage that fear by talking to someone occasionally, I can manage that. "Okay, yeah, I'll do that."

"Thank you." Her lips press against mine. I could kiss her forever. I cup her cheek, kissing her back until we finally pull apart, and I can gaze into those eyes again. I can feel the guards' gazes on me. This is an easy way to pass contraband. She sits back across from me, smirking, and I can't help but think of where else she could kiss. And taste.

"I think I just forgot how to think."

She chuckles. "Yeah, you do that a lot."

"Hey," I shout, a little too loudly, judging by the increased eyes on me.

She grins. "Just saying, it is kind of what got you here in the first place."

"I didn't know we had superspeed," I mutter.

"You sure it's not just that you always want to sacrifice yourself for everyone, even if it's completely avoidable?"

I cross my arms.

"Babe, I know. I'm sorry if it's a sore spot. It kind of is for me too. Thank you for thinking of me and making me run. I just wish you would've followed."

"I thought I had to buy you time." It's definitely guilt in her eyes now. She blames herself for me being here no matter how many times I tell her it was my choice. "Okay, let's not have every conversation end up so dramatic. I put in my application for ETA. I'm trying to volunteer at that place that Mrs. Gudaitiene recommended and also for family leave. I don't know if you count as that yet, but I was hoping maybe I'd get lucky." Why does she only look guiltier now? "Babe, please, it's okay. I won't be in here much longer. You don't need to feel bad about it."

"It's not…" She sighs. "Do I need to talk to anyone? I don't really know what the process is like."

"You should probably ask Mrs. Gudaitiene. God, that name does not get easier to say. I've talked to a few other people about it before, but it never seemed real, so I didn't pay that much attention. I knew I'd never get it. But now, here, maybe it's possible. If only that asshole wasn't around."

"Who? Is someone giving you trouble?"

I shake my head. "No. It's not an inmate. One of the cops who was investigating that murder." Wow, these conversations do always have to stay so heavy. Can't we just make out and say we love each other a million times? I miss those days. We were even sober for some of them. "He says his dad told him about me."

Her eyes widen. "He what?"

"He called me a vampire too, but I don't think he knows. It's what the newspapers called me. I heard enough of it from every inmate when I first got there. I'm sure he, and apparently, a bunch of others, are all going to testify against me and say that I'm a danger to society. I haven't gotten in any trouble in years, so that should look good, at least, but it'll be hard to beat a bunch of police officers making me sound like a monster."

"Fiend…well, okay, not that kind of usage. Sorry. Didn't you find out that you can compel a whole group? Aren't you gonna do that?"

"It doesn't mean it'll work."

"Or is it that you want to do it all fair and square because you're terrified that they're right, that you deserve to be here? You were always such a goody-two-shoes. Did you stay behind because you wanted to protect me or because you wanted to pay for what you'd done?"

Twenty-three years without talking to me, and she still knows me too well. "I wanted to protect you."

"*And* not punish yourself?"

The table is smooth, polished wood. I study it intensely. I doubt it's mahogany or pine, but I don't know any other woods. Oak? Cherry. I *do* know other woods.

"Dinah, have you really stayed here this whole time because you wanted to make yourself suffer for hurting one person?"

I shake my head, still not meeting her eyes. "No. I don't think so."

"Okay…" She doesn't sound like she believes me. I don't think I do either. "You didn't have any choice. I know we were scared and confused at the time, but I've met other…others since. It's like that for all of us. We can't control ourselves when we first wake up. It's impossible to resist."

"I don't even remember being turned. We went to bed and woke up, and all of a sudden, I was feeling like that."

"Calling it a bed seems like a bit of a stretch."

I grumble. "I don't know how any of it happened. And then, I'd done that. How can I forgive myself?"

"So that *is* why you're here?"

I drop my gaze back to the table, trying to think of any other woods I know. "Not entirely."

She takes my hand and brings it to her lips, gently kissing each knuckle. "You did nothing wrong. You had no control. It happens to all of us."

"I still should've been stronger."

"Is it my fault? I did it too."

I stare at her. How could she even think that? "No, of course not."

She cocks her head, raising an eyebrow and giving me the most incredulous look. "Babe."

"I…" I stammer, looking for any rationalization as to how only I can be responsible for something that we both did.

"Then accept that neither of us are at fault. It's part of becoming one."

I shrug, sagging in defeat. I still killed someone, but she's right. She's always right. But how can I just forget that I did that? "Wait, what if that's it? What if the vampire…" Right, we're in public. I sit up straight, glancing around, trying not to look too suspicious and rolling a one. "What if he's the one who did this? I'm back in town, or close enough, and suddenly, someone starts trying to make it look like I'm repeating my offense. I hadn't even thought of that before. It could be whoever did this to us."

"Jerome? I really don't think so."

I blink. I shake my head. I screw my eyes shut. I stare at her. "What?"

She looks like she can barely hide her amusement. "I met him about fifteen years ago. I almost became his sponsor, and we started talking about the stuff he'd done, and this story came up about these two kids he turned when he was trying to get high off their blood and drank too much."

You can get high off blood? Why did I never think of that? It would've lasted so much longer. I'd actually have it running through my system. I should…never try that, and be very careful not to drink from anyone who's high because I'm not doing that again. "And you just now mention this?" As opposed to when?

"As opposed to when?" Okay, maybe we haven't changed that much.

"You're right. I never gave you the chance to tell me. So he just…"

"Killed us and then felt bad about it and turned us? Yeah, sounds like something you would do."

If I was as high as he must've been, would I even think to? I didn't think to bring back that cop, but I also didn't know I could. No, I'm not letting myself think that I'm a worse person than the guy who killed me. We all must have limits, and even my guilt can't go that far. "If it's not him, and all the other inmates are human, I checked, then who could it be?"

"A guard? A really weird suicide?"

A guard would make sense, but I would've smelled them. "I don't know."

"Then don't focus on it. You're not the prison superhero."

"Everyone keeps telling me that." I glance at the far wall, admiring the drawings of superheroes that so many inmates' kids must've made. Though, apparently, they can keep their kids here, so maybe it's nieces and nephews. I'm never going to get over how weird minimum security is. "Okay, you're right. I'll focus on getting approved for my ETAs. I'll be on my best behavior. I'll do everything I have to do. I need to see you."

"Naked," she adds.

I glower.

She grins. "You hadn't finished your sentence."

"It wasn't what I meant."

"Is it not the case? I know how much I've missed it."

I really hope there's not enough blood in me to blush. "I'll talk to Mrs. Gudaitiene and see if there's anything more I can do."

"And compel the parole board and someone for food?"

I sigh. It's not like I haven't done it before. And I'd be doing it for her. "And compel them."

"That's all I ask."

And that I stay clean. And that I not try to keep everyone safe. And that I not blame myself for the murder I committed. She's asking quite a lot. But she's worth it. "Maybe I can compel the warden or something and see if I can get some early ETA."

Her smile makes my heart thud against my chest, pumping absolutely nothing. "I'll empty some drawers in our dresser for you. You'll be home in no time."

Home. It's such a strange thought. I haven't had one of those since I was fifteen. Now, I can finally have one with her. Yeah, I can compel a warden for that. There's nothing I couldn't do for that.

Chapter Eight

A fter a few weeks, they finally add Rachel's friend—
acquaintance—reformed addict—whatever they are, to
my approved call list. I'm able to get a meeting with the warden
after a day's wait, only for her to say, even while compelled, that
it needed to go to the parole board because I was a murderer, but
adding a phone number still took two weeks. Prison bureaucracy is
ridiculous. I should've asked the warden to add the number.

I know I could've borrowed Millie's phone and made the
call myself, but it's hardly a great first impression if I'm using
contraband. She could tell the parole board. Plus, I've been terrified
to talk to her.

"So you finally call." Wow, not even a hello. I should hang up
on her for being rude.

"They only just approved you. I literally couldn't have called
earlier."

She chuckles. "Well, it's nice to meet you, Dinah. I'm Mia.
Rachel has been asking me constantly if you've talked to me yet.
It'll be nice not having to cover for you, since I wasn't sure if you
were lying to her, and I didn't want to blow it." Her voice is so dry.
It's like everything she says is both a joke and completely serious at
the same time.

"I would never lie to her."

"Oh yeah, I totally get it. I've never lied to my wife, either."

Okay, a snarky lesbian. I guess I can see why Rachel would
want me to talk to her. "You're in AA with Rachel?"

She laughs even harder. "Oh, fuck no. I can't stand that shit. She and my wife are friends from the weird nondenominational church at the Community Center, since they apparently like not being set on fire but still insist on going to services. I really don't get it."

Finally, someone who can actually speak sense. "I didn't know she went to a church."

"How long have you two been talking again? Do you know that much about her?"

I wish I hadn't been thinking the same thing. We used to know each other so well. I feel insulted at the implication that I don't know my own fiancée. But I'm the one who chose to stay away from her for the last two decades. "I think I still know her."

"Seems like a thing you should be sure of before you marry someone. I mean, if Olivia had sprung something on me after we were already married, I don't know what I would have done. Like, okay, the murder, the neuroses, the boatloads of money, that I could've lived with. But the devout Catholicism? If that was sprung on me, I probably would've flipped. I still can't believe I managed to get over it with ample warning."

Is Rachel that religious? She'd been rather repulsed by her family's church stuff as a kid. She was always so miserable when they sent her to Bible camp. Though, that might've been because I wasn't there. "Rachel's a devout Catholic?"

"No, this isn't an allegory for your relationship. Olivia is talking to her priest right now, and I'm in her thankfully well-tinted car making fun of her."

"Oh. I thought you were trying to teach me a lesson."

"A little. But mostly making fun of my wife. And I know she can hear me through the window."

Is she actually mature enough to be my sponsor? Then again, I'm probably not one to judge there, am I? "If you're not in the program, why does Rachel think you should be my sponsor? Or not sponsor, whatever we're calling it."

"Well Rachel said 'accountabili-buddy,' but I'm never using that word without making fun of it, so we can go with friend. I had a drug problem for a long time. I lied and pretended it was to treat my manic depression, and maybe it helped some, but that wasn't really it. It was to try to ignore reality. I quit, like a damn grown-up, without the help of some stupid group and giving myself over to a higher power. Because God is dumb. Okay, she's glaring at me now. I feel better. But, yeah, it sounded like that was more your style, and as I'm the only former junkie she knows who isn't in her cult, she thought I could help you."

"Is she actually in a cult, or do you just mean AA?"

"No, I meant AA. I guess Judaism can be a little cult-y, but I wouldn't call it a cult. I'm not that mean. I only say those things about Catholicism."

Rachel's Jewish? That's...what? How on earth did that happen? Was it like her café? She wanted to get closer to me, so she joined the religion that I left? That doesn't make sense. I need to talk to her about it, but how do you ask someone why they're Jewish? "Did I pick a bad time to call? Would it be easier to talk when you're not trying to antagonize your wife?"

"I didn't think you got to pick that much in prison. I assumed we had to talk now and hope it could happen again at some point."

"It's pretty free here. I could probably manage."

"No, it's fine. I'm done annoying her." She sighs. "How long has it actually been since you last used? Rachel said it was a few weeks."

I adjust in the chair. This is still so awkward. "I told you, I'm not lying to her. It's been a few weeks. I did some when I got transferred, before I actually came out here. I haven't since."

"That's not bad. It took me ages before I could go anywhere near that long. I told Ollie that I'd quit, but I messed it up so many times. I didn't even tell her about all of them. But she had me seeing a therapist, and she believed in me. The big secret that makes the whole thing so much easier is to not let that shitty twelve-step ideology get in your head. If you give in and get high, it doesn't mean that you're back to square one. You haven't thrown everything away. You made a single mistake. You just keep going, not using."

Does that mean I could try drinking that girl and really get high for once? I groan. "That makes it easier to do it, doesn't it?"

"Sure, maybe it makes it easier to give in and do it on one particular occasion, but it takes a lot of weight off. If any setback means you've lost *all* of your progress, well, that's a terrible way to look at things and is why their relapses tend to be so bad. I'm a damn doctor, and if anytime something went wrong with a patient, they had to start all over, I don't know how I'd treat anything. 'Whoops, you missed your dose, guess you have to die now.'"

She's a what? No. I can accept so many things, but this crazy woman is a doctor?

"Well, I say doctor, but that's just for fiends. I'm actually a vet."

That makes more sense. She's a mob doctor. My world is no longer crumbling around me. "How did you manage to become a doctor as a junkie? I couldn't even stay out of prison. And I was on the streets before then."

"Weren't you on the streets when you started? Also, I did uppers too, and that helps. It's a lot easier to make your way through veterinarian school on legalized meth. Not that I'm saying you should do it. Because I'm supposed to be keeping you from doing drugs. Why did Rachel trust me with this again?"

I was asking myself the same question. "Yeah, I was already homeless. The heroin just made it easier to put up with. Maybe if I hadn't been wasting all our money on it, we could've managed something."

"Kinda sounds like you're blaming yourself for both your choices. Don't do that."

"Gee, thanks."

"I mean it. Self-hating bullshit is only going to make it harder for you. I get enough of that from the Catholic who burns herself when she crosses herself. Yes, I see you doing that. Stop it. You know Father Gregory and I both said you don't have to. Sorry, Dinah. Had to bitch at her. But you too. Rachel chose to start shooting up right there with you. You can't change the past. All you can do is move forward from here. You want to be better for the woman you barely know—and yet, are marrying for some reason—so do that."

Could she stop saying that? "I don't barely know her."

"You didn't know she was Jewish."

I stammer something that doesn't seem to include words. I do know her. I've known her my whole life. My idiotically forcing us apart can*not* have ruined things with us. I won't let it. She's still her. "Maybe there's more to learn. Maybe I don't know her as well as I used to. But I'm going to spend the rest of eternity making up for that."

She's silent for long enough that I'm a little concerned. She doesn't seem capable of shutting up. Is it a mania thing? I knew another inmate who had it. She stole my heroin. "That's the most reasonable thing I've heard you say. Being different from your partner can't make or break things. Unless they're, like, a Nazi or something. But what really matters is being willing to put in the effort to make the relationship work. I don't know Rachel very well, and I barely know you, so I'm not overly invested in this, but if you care as much as you say you do, I think you can make it work. You just have to put in double the effort because you also need to make yourself quit for real."

"I have quit."

"How many times in this conversation have you thought about using?"

Have I? I guess I was earlier. "Just once or twice."

"This is the other issue with twelve-step programs. They focus so much on using that it's hard to think of anything else. Are you quitting for you or for her?"

I stare at the black screen of the TV in the living room. I wasn't using when she said she wanted me to quit. Had I meant to be? I hadn't had time to find a new connection, but I was planning on it, wasn't I? Hell, I keep planning on it. "For her."

"Yeah, I quit my first time for her too. And my second. And my third. I didn't keep using because it's some innate moral failing that makes addicts incapable of stopping, the way they seem to treat it. I used because I wanted to. And I stopped again because I wanted to. You can want to do it for her, you can put in all the extra effort for her, you can even swear you'll never do it again for her. That will all help. And you'll have her, and I guess me, supporting you. But it's your decision to stop using. And it'll be your decision if you start again. So in the end, it has to be up to you."

I'm not entirely sure that all made sense. How can I do it for her while…I guess I get it. "What if I still want to use?"

"Then don't lie to her. Or do and wait for her to catch you. Just make sure you don't put the heroin in the blood until you drink it. If you have it in while it's still in the fridge, she'll drink it, and then you'll have all kinds of issues. Not that I'm speaking from experience."

I could find that girl right now. She's probably high. If she was high at NA, I don't know why she'd ever not be. I could get one last high and finally feel it like I used to. I wouldn't have to keep chasing that euphoria that I never get any more. And then, I could quit. I wouldn't be leaving it on such a sour note.

The door opens, and Millie grins at me. "Hey. Um, that guard asked me to give you this. I can't believe he's still not willing to come inside. That's so weird. Oh, you're on the phone. Sorry." She puts her finger to her lip, shushing herself, and hands me an envelope.

I know I'm in the middle of a phone call, but this has to be about my ETA. I tear it open and read it. I can't even process the words, and I seem to be tearing up, so I have to blink a few times and try again. "I'm approved. I can volunteer. And I can see that therapist. And…I can have my wedding. They approved all three. The only thing they didn't approve was the overnight to go see her. Fuck it, I don't care. That's enough. I can go home. I can see her."

"That's amazing," Mia says.

"And this is a good sign. I didn't even compel them. This means the parole board may actually let me out next year. I've been on my best behavior. I didn't know it was that good, though. This isn't just a fantasy. It's real. I can do it."

Millie grins, her crooked teeth showing. "Holy shit. Really? Sorry, I know I said I'd shut up."

I shake my head. "No, it's totally fine. Holy fuck. This is… wow."

"I'll let you go," Mia says. "Just think about what I said."

I smile back at Millie. I want to celebrate, but I don't know how the hell we'd do that. I probably shouldn't drink, even if we had any. Maybe a celebratory game of *Dungeons & Dragons*? "I don't need to think about it. I'm going to be free. I'm not doing anything stupid that could get me back here again. I'm doing this for me."

"Now that's a good answer."

"Thank you. I'm sure I'm going to regret it at the next minor setback."

"You can always call me."

I nod because I apparently don't know how phones work. "Thank you."

"It's no problem. I'll let you go, but unless I'm with a client, I pretty much always answer my phone. I don't really have much of a social life."

"I will try not to abuse that. I think you might actually be able to help me."

"I'm glad to hear that." She sounds genuinely happy. Or at least, something approaching it. "Now, go figure out your wedding plans."

She's right. There's a lot to do there. "Hey, Millie, want to look at wedding dresses with me?"

CHAPTER NINE

The gate rolls open. It's not the first time I've left a prison. I was transferred only a few months ago. Plus, I'm still in custody, so it shouldn't feel so different, but every other transfer was to another prison or the courthouse. This one is different. The van pulls out of the sally port, past the open gate, and onto the road.

They didn't handcuff me, but I'm in the back of a van, so I'm having to go more off sound than what I can see through the tiny rear window. I looked up the address on Millie's phone, but I'm still not super clear on exactly what I'm volunteering for. It's supposed to be a soup kitchen, though there wasn't anything showing it from street view. Would it be something that's normally shown?

I tap my foot on the metal floor and nervously toy with the seat belt. I don't know what they have planned. I don't even really know how ETAs work. Will the guard have to stay with me and watch me the whole time? That would make sense; it is called an *escorted* temporary absence, after all. He's just going to stand there and watch me make soup? I guess there are worse gigs.

It's so strange. Until I moved to this prison, I wasn't even trusted to make my own dinner, and now I'm going to be making it for everyone. And what about after that? I'm not sure what sort of parole I may make, but I'm genuinely starting to believe that I'll make it. I'll have a parole officer, but what's that like? Are they going to be as in my life as guards have always been, or will I only have to check in once or twice a week? I've known people who came back to prison. I just never had the heart to ask them much about life on the outside. I knew I wouldn't see it anytime soon. Now I need all that knowledge, and I don't have it.

The van pulls to a stop and shakes as the guard gets out, boots thudding on the pavement until he opens the back door, and I get my first glimpse at free air in two decades.

I step out of the van, standing next to him as I stare all around. It's a normal parking lot but weirdly empty. But there's no gate. There's no guard tower. I could walk away, even without superspeed. I'm not free yet, but it's so close, I can taste it.

I take a deep breath, savoring the scent of the air. It's vile. Full of car fumes and piss and more than that. There's the distant smell of people, vampires, and other things that I can't quite name. They don't have the woody scent of fairies or the dull solid scent of vampires. It's something else. And there's spices and meat and metal. It's people and buildings and food. It's not that different from prison, and yet, it's nothing like it.

And there's that familiar lilac scent.

I open my eyes and can barely contain my excitement when I see Rachel moving toward me. What is she planning? This isn't a jailbreak, is it? "Hey, Officer, you're going to forget everything you see and just follow along, okay?" She doesn't wait for him to answer, instead running right up to me and throwing her arms around me. "Fuck, I've missed you so much."

"I…but…" I hug her back. I'm even more confused than I was before, but I don't care. I need this so badly. I can finally feel her here, and I don't have to worry about a guard deciding it's too much and tossing me in solitary. "I've missed you too."

She finally pulls away and runs her fingers through my hair. I've missed her touch more than anything. "How's it feel to be out?"

"Like I only have a few hours." I chuckle, leaning into her hand. "It feels amazing. Am I not doing community service?"

"No, we are. This *is* actually a soup kitchen, but since they didn't approve our date, I thought maybe I could make this into one."

"That sounds amazing." I rest my hand on her lower back. It's been so long since I've really touched another person. Even hugs aren't too common in prison, but this level of intimacy is unheard of. I'm worried I've forgotten how.

She presses against me, kissing along my jaw. "God, I didn't think it'd be this hard to just go inside. I mean, the soup kitchen. We should actually be volunteering. There has to be a record of it."

"Yeah." I breathe her in, that wonderful lilac scent that never seems to go away, even years after she's died.

Her lips press against my throat, and I shudder against her. Her hands move lower, her nails digging in as she grips me, pressing our bodies flush together. "We should really go inside."

She keeps using that word. It is so hard to think she means the building. I barely even remember how, but I want it so badly, I can almost feel it.

Footsteps thud behind us, and I finally manage to pull away. A couple of people are staring at us, though the guard doesn't seem to be managing. He's not quite slack-jawed, but his eyes aren't focusing on anything. She did quite a number on him. I feel a little bad. I'll have to make sure he's okay after I tell him what to remember. Though, then he may freak out, and I'll have to erase his memory again.

"We should..." Rachel says.

I nod.

She takes my hand, and we head toward the building. We've been in these people's shoes before. Maybe I can get lucky and, well, get lucky later, but I'm not gonna make people wait for food so I can awkwardly make out like a teenage girl in front of a hypnotized correctional officer. I already regret this decision. Her hand in mine isn't enough. I need to feel all of her all over.

We find someone with a name tag: an older woman with food stains all over her apron and sleeves, an extremely tired expression, and who smells like sweat and tears. The guard gazes vaguely in her general direction. We probably can't count on him. "We're here to volunteer," I say.

"I thought there was only one of you."

Right. I probably shouldn't have walked in holding her hand. This must look so suspicious.

"Sorry, I'm volunteering separately," Rachel says, her fingers trailing along mine as she slowly pulls away. "Not through the prison."

She looks between us and shrugs. "Whatever. We need a cook in the back, and one of our servers is just about to leave, so one of you can take over."

I was only with her for a few minutes, and already, they're splitting us up. It's agonizing. And we won't even get a honeymoon after our wedding. "We have time," Rachel says, her eyes on mine. She looks just as hurt by the news as I am. "I run a restaurant. I can cook."

"Perfect. Aprons are in the back."

I spend hours serving food to people and only get the occasional quick kiss from Rachel. I'm working my ass off, making nothing, and I get to see Rachel and help out people who're in the exact same situation I used to be in. The only part that hurts is the scent.

It's not because the people smell. Some of them certainly do, but I've lived in prison for long enough that I'm more than used to that. The issue is exactly what tends to come with homelessness. When you're sleeping on the streets, you cling to anything that'll make it more bearable. It's exactly how I ended up on heroin in the first place.

There's a residue of it on so many people here. I could sink my teeth into any one of them, and I could feel it again. And a few of them seem to have more on them. Rachel hasn't left the kitchen, even to give me a kiss, since the last couple guys came in. Other people keep bringing out the food.

She can smell it as strongly as I can.

"Are you okay?" I ask when I have the chance to slip back to the kitchen. There wasn't anyone in line, so I doubt I'll get in trouble.

"Yeah," she says. "I haven't had to deal with that in a while. Well, there are a few drug dealers at the Community Center, but they tend to keep their stuff in better bags than whatever these people are using. How about you?"

"I…" Do I still want to use? I made my decision, but as Mia said, a single slipup wouldn't mean the end of it. But it would mean the end of Rachel's trust in me. "I can't stand being near it. I am losing it a little. But I'm more okay than I thought I'd be."

"Sometimes, it's easier when it's early. Or maybe you're just better at this than you thought you were." She kisses my cheek. "Are you sure you can keep going?"

I want to shake my head. To say no. But I don't think that'd be true. It's hard. I hate it. But I don't mind paying back all the meals I took, and it brings me all the closer to being with her again. Plus, any time it gets too bad, I can just do this. I lean in and press my lips to hers, needing so much more but savoring the chaste kiss as I head back to work and do my best to ignore the scent.

I don't bother breathing, and it makes it all a lot easier. Before long, we're finally done. Everyone else looks exhausted, even the blank-faced guard, except us lucky vampires.

Rachel and I walk into the night, the guard trailing us. It's almost serene. There are people talking somewhere behind us, and several of the other volunteers are smoking off to the side. I wish there was a lake we could look out over or something, but we're in the middle of the city, and there's nothing but graffitied buildings on either side. I want the end of the night to be romantic and perfect, to speak of what we have ahead of us, but I suppose it's not like we ever had perfect to start with. Maybe ending the night between a soup kitchen and a homeless shelter is the most appropriate way to do it.

"The next time we get to see each other outside of the prison, it will be our wedding day."

She shakes her head. "Your therapist is at the Community Center. I'd be insulted if you didn't stop in for food."

I can feel myself grinning. That will be amazing. I'll get to see her restaurant. And her. "I hope it's not the same guard. Having to forget that much can't be good for someone."

She laughs, lacing her fingers between mine.

"What is this Community Center like?" She's only hinted at it before, since we always had witnesses. I suppose we still do but not to the same degree.

"It's a hollowed-out mall full of shops run by fiends. And one crazy human who you're going to be seeing."

"My therapist is a human?"

She shrugs. "If she even counts as that. I don't really know her, but I've had a few other people from AA recommend her before. She's supposed to be pretty good. Maybe I could make you something special for when you're done? It's not like I have to follow my menu. Is there anything you've been wanting?"

I look her up and down, trying to hide the lewd expression I'm sure I have. "There's only one thing I really want."

Her giggle is adorable. Her smile is so comfortable and natural, like we're actually used to being around each other again. "I want it too. You have no idea how badly."

"No, I'm pretty sure I can imagine."

She kisses along the back of my hand before resting her cheek against it. "I wish you didn't have to go back."

"I'm not running away when I'm about to make parole."

"I know. It'll be worth the wait, but it doesn't make it hurt less."

"Maybe I could borrow Millie's phone tonight, and we could—"

She looks up from my hand, her smile growing far more lascivious. "Yes. God, I could use it."

I pull her to me, kissing up her neck until I find her lips, needing to taste her, to feel her. Are conjugal visits a real thing? The warden could probably approve that without needing to talk to the parole board. I could set up another meeting.

She sighs as we pull away, looking forlorn. Tears well in her eyes. "My car's this way." She gestures behind her. It's time to leave, isn't it? "You could always come with me."

"I will. Soon."

"I know." She sighs again and turns to go, only to turn back around. "Oh, I almost forgot. There's a cooler in my car with something for you. Walk me there?"

She's finally accepted that I'm too useless to fend for myself. That's true love. I follow her to the car and receive yet another good-bye kiss before she hands me the bag of blood. "I'm sure they'll search you when you get there."

"I honestly have no idea. This prison is weird. But I need the drink anyway." I bite into the bag, letting out a moan that sends her hand to my thigh as I drain the bag.

She licks the blood from my lips, her hand sliding up farther, feeling me through my pants. We could climb into the back seat and just have a quickie, couldn't we?

I turn to find the guard staring blankly at me. It's a bit of a turnoff. "I should fix him."

She nods. If she says another word, we may just do it in front of him. She kisses my cheek and opens her car door. I don't breathe again until her car pulls onto the road. I lick my lips, making sure she got all the blood. It's not like I can check my reflection.

A car honks, and my heart pounds. I didn't think I could have a heart attack. I turn to glare at whoever did it, but it's not just some asshole trying to give me a hard time. It's a police car. The window rolls down and proves me wrong. It is, in fact, an asshole. The very one who tried to arrest Millie. His shark-like green eyes settle on mine.

I stare back, trying not to let the fear show. I sniff the air and catch the same collection of scents. There are people nearby, meat, the scent of vampires still so close, mingling with Rachel's lilac, so many spices from the soup kitchen, fresher urine than before, and something swimming through someone's veins that I'm not going to let myself focus on. No breathing, then. Maybe that'll make me look scarier, and he'll leave us alone.

"It's you," he says, all but snarling as he climbs out of his car and slams the door behind him. The other door opens, and another officer stumbles out. He's much larger and more cop-looking. "You escaped from prison. What, were there not enough people to kill there? Turn around, hands behind your back."

"I didn't escape," I say, trying not to take in any air with it. "I'm on ETA. Officer..." Not only did I not catch the name of the guard who came with us, he's not present enough to do anything.

"It's Marsden."

"I wasn't asking your name. Officer...Landrey!" I knew I knew his name. "He's right there. He's escorting me." I point to him. Why couldn't he do the talking? Every time I speak, I catch another breath of it. Rachel's lingering scent is comforting, but this cop is not. If he ruins my chances at parole, I'll never be out of there. That heroin is sounding so much more appealing. Landrey is in his uniform, so he should stand out, but he looks more like an ornament than a guard.

Marsden stares at me. "You...the fucking vampire was approved for ETA? That's bullshit."

"He has all the forms with him. You can ask him. Right, Officer Landrey?" I ask, trying to stir him from his hypnosis.

He says nothing.

Officer Marsden stares into my eyes. He's taller than me, despite being rail thin, and he looks hungry. His hand rests on the gun at his side. "You'd best stay on your best behavior. I don't want to get called back to that prison. It's depressing."

"You should see a normal prison."

He glares at me.

I stare back. No more breathing. That vampire scent was so close. Did Rachel stay behind when she saw the cop car? I don't want to look away from him. I have no idea what he could pull.

"I'm watching you," he says, climbing back into his car.

The other officer looks between me and the closed car door, then quickly wiggles his way back inside. They drive off slowly, and I can feel his eyes lingering on me. What is that asshole's problem?

I look around as soon as he's gone, but I don't see Rachel anywhere. "We had a normal day at the soup kitchen, you watched me serve food and be an upstanding member of society, and you'll be your normal self and can do as you please."

Officer Landrey blinks and rubs his eyes. He peers at me, and for a second, I'm worried he's forgotten what we're doing, but he mutters, "Where's the van?"

I lead him across the parking lot, and he seems to be less confused by the time we reach it. Is it safe to let him drive? I suppose a crash won't kill me, but I don't want to be responsible for his death.

What alternative do I have, though? It's not as if I can offer to drive for him. He opens the back door, and I climb in, hoping that Rachel didn't break his brain. By the time the van stops at a light, my fears have lessened. Maybe he's going to be okay.

We reach the prison, and I'm feeling a lot better. Seeing that cop again stressed me out, but it wasn't enough to beat out both my first taste of freedom and of Rachel. He doesn't have anything on me. I didn't kill anyone. Recently.

When Landrey helps me out of the back, I want to ask how he's doing, but I have too many years of not talking to guards ingrained in me. I'm back in the prison, and I'm not willing to take any risks. I leave him looking around and hope the confusion on his face is only my imagination as I head back into my cottage.

Where I have a date planned. I need to ask Millie if I can borrow her phone. Tonight is still looking up. I knock on Millie's door, and it swings partially open.

I take in a breath in surprise and know exactly why. There's that same scent of rotten food. I push the door open the rest of the way and find her there on her bed, her phone still in her hand. I don't think I'm going to be borrowing it tonight. I don't steal from the dead.

I rush to the bathroom and hurl blood into the toilet. Who the hell could've done this?

Chapter Ten

It's almost reassuring to be in a proper metal cell again. I know how to handle being in this place. I know the rules, the feelings, and I don't have to share a bathroom with anyone else.

I can hear the other girls pacing about their cells, frustrated and restless. They've had too long to get used to going outside, working on the lawn, eating whenever they want, and having the freedom that inmates don't tend to have. At least we still have TVs. I was lucky enough to have Rachel deposit some money in my account, and it arrived just the other week.

We've been kept in administrative segregation in the main building of the prison since the second murder. A different cop came in to take our statements. The other girls all talked because minimum security teaches you absolutely no decency, but none of us seem to be suspects at this point. It's honestly shocking. I'd been sure that I'd be in maximum security for murders I didn't commit and staying there, not held for my safety until I get to go back out on ETA.

It makes absolutely zero sense. Who could've done this? And why? I wasn't here, the other girls are all human, and Millie wouldn't hurt a fly. She was the closest thing to a friend I've had in years, and she was snuffed out like it was nothing.

Will it happen the next time I'm gone?

No, this wasn't my fault. I've met with Rachel in visitation a dozen times, and no one died. Except the one time. And the one time I went out for ETA.

But why would this happen while I'm gone? If they're trying to frame me, that doesn't make any sense. Are they trying to send me a message? What the hell is the message? Don't leave my cell? People are tasty and delicious? They're a very poor communicator, whatever they're trying to tell me.

What if it isn't about me at all? Almost no one still knows what I did. It could be a coincidence. We're a bunch of defenseless women who can't even keep knives with us and with only a meager fence keeping out hungry vampires. It would explain why the killings don't make any sense. If it's simply someone feeding, it's not my fault.

Except, I could've been here to stop them.

But I can't put my entire life on hold to be the prison superhero. Rachel's right. I deserve to have a life. I have to believe that. I'll be gone in nine more months. I'll walk out that gate and never come back.

Leaving these girls to be killed by a hungry monster they have no way to stop.

I pinch the bridge of my nose, trying to keep from crying. Rachel deserves to have me with her. If it's between her and these women, I'll pick her every time. I love her. But doesn't that make me just as bad as this killer? I'm leaving them to him.

I groan and pull the blanket tight about me. I don't feel the cold, but it's the closest thing I can get to a hug right now. It'll be okay. They're all being kept safe here. Maybe the vampire will take a hint and go elsewhere.

Yeah, that's exactly it. The guards moved their prey, and now there's nothing they can do. They'll move on and find hunting grounds that aren't so secure.

And then, there are other innocents that I'm grateful are being hurt instead.

I need to not blame myself. Would I even stand a chance in a fight against another vampire? Rachel is the only one I've met, and I've certainly never fought her. Humans weren't much of an issue when they attacked me, but a vampire who knows what they're doing and is willing to hurt people is something else entirely.

Maybe I have to hope that there's someone out there more capable of doing this than I am. I'm not a superhero. They're right. I'm just a stupid junkie who keeps getting in way over my head, and I need to learn my lesson and keep my head down, like I've always told myself.

It isn't a satisfactory answer. It doesn't stop anyone from dying, and it makes me feel so much worse, but it's the truth. I can't bear the weight of the world on my shoulders. Hell, I couldn't even handle looking after myself. It's what got me here.

That therapist is going to get an earful.

❖

The lights come on, but the doors don't click open. This isn't max; we're sequestered for our protection, not everyone else's. Which means we can't gather in the range and play together. I chew on the fruit and bread I was given with dinner, as that's all the breakfast they give us, and I'll have to leave in an hour. It's a long trip, and even if food doesn't do much to me anymore, I'd hate to leave on an empty stomach.

I don't know how they managed to get approval for me to see a therapist back in Toronto, but I'm not going to put up a fight about it. I'll get to see Rachel. That's more than worth having to spend a few hours in the back of a prison van.

A few minutes into the trip, I'm already starting to change my mind. Did cars always feel like this? I've been through a few prison escorts and my arrest when I was nineteen, but I don't think I've been in a car for more normal reasons since I was fifteen. Were they always this bumpy?

You'd think being dead would make it easier.

I try to get comfortable in the beaten-up leather seat and focus on the fact that I'll be seeing Rachel soon. Is she going to come out and hypnotize the guard for me?

No, she'll be at work.

Shit, I really don't want to do it, but this is a place full of fiends. What if someone eats the guard? What would I do? I don't think I can just go back to the prison and be like, "Sorry, he was murdered."

Would I get in trouble? I wouldn't have had anything to do with it.

Maybe I could get him to wait in the van? Would monsters come out and eat him? I have no idea how any of this works. I don't even know what this Community Center is like, other than that it's in a mall and apparently has drugs, therapy, a café, and a church.

I suppose that's probably not that weird for a mall. Most of them already sold drugs, in my experience, and some must have had churches and therapy. So it was mostly the fiend—one of these days I'll remember the word—angle that's so weird. Either way, it's probably not a good idea to drag a human into it. Other than the therapist that I'm not going to get over.

The van finally comes to a stop, and I'm no closer to being at peace with the idea than I had been at the start of my rambling diatribe. At least it passed the time.

The back door opens, and the guard helps me out. Can I really do this? What if he ends up as confused and blank-faced as…I stare at the guard's face. It's the same guy. This can't be good for him. I'm going to give him a magical brain tumor or something.

I glance around, hoping Rachel is going to come out and save me from having to do this, but I'm in a nearly empty parking lot in front of some run-down buildings, with only a couple cars almost as beat-up as the van and one surprisingly nice one. "Is this the right place?" Landrey asks. It probably looks rather suspicious to him. I can smell so many creatures moving about inside. It's far more than that soup kitchen. There're dozens of them, smells that I couldn't place but can feel the heat from, with food and metal and so many more confusing scents all piled on top of each other.

At least no one will see me talking to a guard. "Couldn't tell you. I've never been here before."

"Then how did you end up with this therapist?"

I sigh. His questions aren't going to get any easier to answer. "Wait in the van, keep the doors locked, and don't let anyone but me in."

He blinks, his eyes going fuzzy as he tilts his head. Did I break him? Is it too much? Can you compel someone too many times?

What if they can develop a tolerance for it? He seems to look right through me, blinks a few more times, closes the back doors, and gets back in the driver's seat. A few seconds later, I hear the doors lock.

Is he okay? There has to come a point when I've scrambled his brain too much. He looks no worse for wear. I hope he's not the one to take me to my wedding.

I look around the lot and head toward the dilapidated building. Is this seriously the place? It looks, well, like an abandoned mall, but the door opens easily, on well-oiled hinges, and inside, I find the source of all those smells.

Dozens of tables fill the hollowed carcass of the mall, with beings of so many shapes and sizes that I wouldn't even know where to start. There are hooves, horns, fangs, claws, tentacles, and even a few that look almost as human as me. So this is where Rachel spends all her time.

I breathe in the air. Lilac. She's here, just like she said she would be. I want to run to her, to hold her and maybe find someplace more private, but I have an appointment that I'm already running late for.

That doesn't mean I can't take another lingering whiff of her aroma, though. I know I've smelled lilacs so much since I came back to Ontario, but this isn't all in my head; this is her. She's so close, and I'll see her after my appointment. It's not like Landrey's going anywhere.

Except, I don't know where the therapist is.

I probably should've asked that.

I try to smell my way to her, but all I know is that she's human, and unfortunately, so are the pies, so there're quite a few traces to sift through. I try asking the goat-man selling the Sweeney Todd delicacies. "Do you know where the therapist is? Uh, a Miss…" Shit, what was her name? "Rosseau-Lester?"

"There's only one therapist here." He chuckles. "Yeah, her office is in the back wall." He points with a surprisingly human hand. "There's a door there. Should open right to a sitting area with a receptionist. If it's topless women instead, that's the massage parlor, and you went one door too far to the right."

"I'll stick with the therapist." I feel kinda bad not having money to buy any of his baked goods. I can't remember the last time I had a good cinnamon roll. What was I, twelve? No, I got one after busking that one time, so I think I was seventeen. Maybe I could ask Rachel to buy me one. "Could you save me one of those cinnamon rolls? I don't have any cash on me."

"They sell out fast. A friend of mine tends to buy them all." He glances at the table. "I'm sure I can manage to save you one, though. Just try not to take too long. Kara will lose it if she knows I'm hiding some from her."

I thank him and hurry to the back. The door I open sadly does not lead to a bevy of busty demons and instead only to a terrifying, humanish, gray shape in a poofy pink top.

"You must be the two o'clock. Only fifteen minutes late." The creature chuckles. Her voice is high and pitchy, more valley girl than flesh-eating monstrosity. Maybe I don't have room to judge, but I'm still adapting to this whole thing.

"I'm sorry. Does it help if I have absolutely no control over it and have to deal with prison bureaucracy to get me here?" I can't quite bring myself to look into her dead, milky eyes, so I settle on her stony gray forehead.

She chuckles again, and it's playful and friendly and does not belong coming out of the mouth of something like that. "She's ready for you. You can head right on in." She flashes sharp, jagged teeth in something that vaguely resembles a smile. I try not to look like I'm skirting her as I cross the room to open the door.

"You must be Dinah." The voice comes from a woman who looks to be around thirty, sitting in a plush desk chair with a laptop in her lap. She has green hair and an unconvincingly reassuring smile. "I'm Liz. It's nice to meet you." She shifts the laptop to the side and stands, holding out her hand.

I take it, probably too firmly. "I'm Dinah. That is to say, yes?"

With a warm laugh, she points vaguely toward a leather chair and a couch. "Sit wherever you want, just make yourself comfortable."

I study her for a long moment, but that genial expression doesn't change no matter how fake it looks.

Once I've sat, I realize what it reminds me of. It's the same way I smiled when I had to learn to not show any fear in prison. I've never actually seen it on myself, but I know how it felt, and that's exactly what she looks like. I could beat anyone who wanted to fight me, but that didn't mean they knew it, and my obvious nerves got me in quite a bit of trouble early on. As a human surrounded by monsters, she doesn't have that advantage. She must've had to learn to completely hide her feelings no matter how intimidating her clients are.

A framed photo on her desk showing her in the arms of some gargantuan furred zombie thing makes me question that. She might just not know that monsters are supposed to be scary, and this is a normal therapist smile.

"Is there anything specific you wanted to talk about?" she asks.

That I'm utterly terrified of rejoining the real world when I've been away from it for longer than I was ever part of it? If I was ever even part of it, considering that I was either a child or a junkie for nearly all of that time, neither of whom have much in the way of responsibilities or a life. Or maybe that I'm utterly convinced that I'll return to find another inmate dead, drained of blood by a vampire? That the first friend I'd made in years was killed just a few weeks ago? How about that I haven't had the nerve to talk to my fiancée about her having found religion while I've been away? "Not really."

She sighs, and the expression falters for the merest instant. "You're worried about how this could affect your parole, aren't you? You think if you're open with me and reveal what's going on in your head, I'll tell them you're a threat to society and shouldn't be released, right?"

Is she actually a good therapist, or is the issue that obvious? I've only ever met with prison shrinks before, and they seemed as uninterested in talking to me as I was in talking to them. "There's nothing to tell." Unless she's secretly a fiend and can read minds. Can vampire minds be read? I do not know enough about how any of this works.

She snickers. "Okay, how about this? You're a fucking vampire in a black market where there's a literal slave auction right outside my door later today. I am not concerned with you re-offending. I'm concerned with you being healthy. If you want to eat people, more power to you. I hear we're delicious."

I stare at her. "What?"

The smile grows more genuine and quite a lot cockier. "I work in the Community Center. It's not some wholesome place. I'm not here to change fiends to not be fiends. I'm here to help them function better because a whole hell of a lot of you have some serious trauma, and there's no one else catering to this market. I've already written a letter to your parole board saying that you've made tremendous progress and are planning on continuing to work with me upon your release and that I think you pose no risk of re-offending. You can read it if you like, but I'm sending it in tomorrow. What you tell me will not leave this room. Now, you can either take this hour and spend it trying to work through whatever issues you may have, or you can sit here and not say a word. Either way, the parole board will still get that letter. Just don't bullshit me and waste my time. If you don't want to talk, I have client notes to do."

She's a very odd person and should probably be the one in this chair instead of me. Or maybe we both should be. I suppose I do have quite a few things I want to talk to her about. "I don't know where to start," I admit.

"Well, much to my great jealousy, I find a lot of vampires have trauma around being turned. Would you like to start there?"

I shrug and study the fractal patterns of the carpet, marred by stains here and there, some of which are clearly blood. What happens here? "Apparently, my girlfriend—my *fiancée*—is friends with the guy who turned us. I never knew how it had happened, but she met him years later. He's in AA with her. From everything she's said, he's turned his life around and had only turned us because he'd accidentally killed us and felt awful about it. Maybe if I had been awake for it, I'd be more upset with him, but it's all so abstract that it's hard to know what to feel about it. Though, I guess I wouldn't be in prison if he hadn't killed me."

"Huh." She sounds genuinely surprised. "That's still pretty traumatic, but..." She shrugs.

"I suppose other vampires must have more upsetting stories?"

"Usually. So how did he get you sent to prison?"

"Rachel, my fiancée, and I woke up and ate a cop. I knew she'd face a lot more problems than I would—she's black—hell, they'd probably just shoot her outright, and I didn't know that wouldn't kill her, so I told her to run. I figured I'd be a distraction. She fought me on it, but we were scared and confused, and I told her I'd be right behind her, so she finally gave in. I think she still blames herself for my arrest when she doesn't blame my tendency to fall on every sword I meet, as she puts it."

Her brow creases, and she types something. "Tell me about her. How long have you been together?"

"That's kind of a difficult question."

She tilts her head, watching me. "Why's that?"

"We never really broke up, but I kinda, sorta, stopped letting her visit or call me about a year into my sentence because I wanted her to have a real life and not spend it waiting for me."

"Ah." She types something more. I hate that. I feel like a lab rat. And I don't even get any cheese. "There's that sword again, eh?"

"At the time, a life sentence seemed like it would be a long time. We were nineteen—"

"Oh wow."

"Yeah..." I trail off. What's the point of any of this? I already know what I've been through.

She taps a pen on the bottom of her laptop, pursing her lips. "What were you doing before prison?"

"Killing a cop?" I laugh, and she rewards me with a small smile. I feel like I'm not adequately winning at therapy. "We were on the streets ever since both our parents kicked us out." I'm not even gonna try that joke again. She does not appreciate my jokes. "When we were fifteen, her dad, um, caught us. And he told my dad. And none of them took it well. So I guess we've either been together since we were twelve or for a few months, if that counted as a breakup."

She nods slowly, still tapping her pen. "I know what that's like." She gestures at the picture of her and the scary monster. "We were like that too. We didn't actually get together until much later, but her parents reacted about the same. And then, she ate them." She laughs harder than she did at any of my jokes. "Did you ever get back in touch with yours?"

"I didn't eat them if that's what you're asking, but, no. My mom tried to visit a few times." It had actually slipped my mind; it was so inconsequential. "She tried again a few weeks ago. A friend of mine had just been murdered, so I wasn't really thinking much about it, but I turned her away just like usual."

"Uh." She shakes her head. "I'm sorry?"

"It's okay. I don't want to deal with her."

"I meant the murder. What happened? Are you okay?"

I sigh. "Weren't we talking about my relationship and upcoming nuptials?"

"Are you not ready to talk about this?"

How do I even talk about it? I still don't know if it was my fault, and I can't bring myself to accept that it wasn't. "A vampire keeps killing women in my cottage, although now, we're all in administrative segregation, so not in a cottage anymore. She was the first friend I've had in years, and she was so sweet and not at all ready for prison, and some vampire ate her. I'm terrified that I'm going to return to the prison, and another one of them will be dead. It only seems to happen when I'm gone, and I don't know why. I don't know if they're trying to frame me, send a message, or if they're just hungry. All I know is that it keeps happening."

"I'm sorry." She sounds more human. Not the weird fucked-up monster who didn't care about murder or the neutral therapist with the friendly facade, but a normal concerned person. "That sounds terrifying."

"I don't know what to do about it."

"Is there anything you *can* do about it?"

I shrug and study the carpet. "Probably not. That's what I keep trying to tell myself. I can't be the prison superhero. But I don't know how not to be."

"Well, you're not going to be in prison for much longer. I think it's only a few months before your parole hearing, right?"

I nod.

"You'll make it, and then you'll be gone from there. If the vampire is after you, I suppose you'll find out soon enough, and everyone else will be safe." I hadn't thought of that. "If he's not, then you're not responsible in any way, and you don't owe them anything."

"But I could stop the vampire!"

"Can you?" she asks. "From what I understand, you're not a soldier or any sort of fighter. Have you ever fought a vampire before?"

I shake my head.

"I was almost killed by one once. A few times, actually. They don't always take therapy well. They can be kind of terrifying. If you're not trained and experienced, all you're doing is throwing your life away to accomplish nothing. That isn't your responsibility."

I jump to my feet. "But they keep hurting people around me. Doesn't that make it my responsibility?"

"They have to eat. And so do you. Have you not been feeding on people in prison?"

I really don't want to go over that whole story again. As funny as it would be to finally rattle her, I'd rather not sit next to a wastebasket of her throw up. I sink back into the chair. "I haven't killed anyone, that I know of, since I was arrested, and I don't intend to do it again. Why should I let other vampires?"

"Because you're not in charge of them. You can change yourself. You can, hell, go to the group for people who don't want to eat people anymore and swear to never touch a drop of the stuff. You can't make other people do the same."

It's strange how she uses "people" instead of "fiend." Is she trying to emphasize that I am one? Or that the vampire killing these women is one? "You really don't think I should do anything?"

"Normally, I'd say that's up to you, but I'd rather not have a client kill herself for no reason, so, no, I don't think you should do anything. Accept that it has nothing to do with you, and focus on your upcoming marriage, which I do believe you were already freaking out about before we got sidetracked with this admittedly rather important tangent."

I sigh and nod. She's right. I tried to tell myself all of this already, or at least most of it, but I'd hoped an outside perspective would be less heartless. I should be better than that. But maybe she's right. "I'm scared I don't know her anymore," I admit, shocking myself with how naked the confession is. I didn't think it was quite that bad.

"It's been, what, twenty-three years? Twenty-two?"

"Twenty-three."

"Maybe you don't. And maybe you shouldn't be rushing into marriage."

"Then, I don't know if they'll give me parole. It's a lot more likely they'll let me out to be released to family than on my own, and I'm sure as hell not willing to see any other member of my family."

She nods. "Then do it. Marry the woman you love, and take the chance to get to know her again. Not too many people get to fall in love with the same woman twice. It can be magical. You already know that you're compatible, or at least, that you were. It's possible it won't work any longer, but it's also possible that you'll fall even more in love and that you'll be happier than you've ever been. And I'm sure either way, it'll be better than prison."

That is decidedly not the advice I was expecting. I was sure she'd tell me I was making some huge mistake rushing into marriage. "I love her. I know we still love each other. I've seen her every week for the last four months, and we talk on the phone as often as we can. It's still a little awkward and new, but you're right. It's an old relationship, with someone I've known as long as I can remember, but it's also a new relationship, and I need to treat it like that. We'll get to know each other all over again. Maybe I should start looking at it as something exciting rather than something scary."

She smiles at me, warm, gentle, and real. "That is the healthiest thing I've had a patient say in months."

"That mean I get a clean bill of health?"

"Not at all. I'd like the two of you to come see me once you're out. I think it could also benefit you to continue receiving private therapy, but I think, at the very least, a session of couple's therapy could be helpful."

I hesitate, meeting her eyes. "You think we need couple's therapy?"

"I think everyone could use some. It doesn't mean there's anything wrong with you. It's simply a nice way to work on things together."

"I guess that makes sense."

"Has anything come up yet that you've been scared to talk to her about?"

Can she see right through me? She must be a hell of a therapist. "Yeah. There's one thing that's been bugging me. I found out that she converted to Judaism. Wow, that sounds bad out of context. I was raised Jewish and lost the faith, if I ever really had any, and she and I had both been atheists when we were homeless and in the gutter. Okay, we never actually slept in a gutter, but it paints a picture."

"Very colorful."

"Apparently, she's found my old faith that I must've left somewhere, and she hasn't said anything about it to me. There's nothing wrong with it, exactly, but it's weird, especially since we've been planning our wedding. I thought it would come up."

She types something. Did I say something bad? Am I a self-hating Jew now? Would a therapist write that as a note? "You could always ask about it."

"I know." I groan. "But I feel like, if she wanted to tell me, she would. I just don't understand why she hasn't."

"Then ask her that or accept that she's not ready. Do you think you can handle that, or will it keep eating at you?"

I flop back in the chair, my head sinking into the overly stuffed back and leaving me staring at the ceiling. "I don't know. I don't want to push her. Clearly, there's some reason she's not ready to talk about it. Maybe she's reconsidering things herself. Or maybe—"

"Or maybe she's scared that it's too big of a change for you."

How is there a bloodstain on the ceiling? Who was in here before me? "Do you think I should press her or let her come to me with it in her own time?"

"How did you find out?"

"An acquaintance of hers told me."

She chews on her pen. "That can be tough. I always try not to tell a client what to do. Okay, I sometimes try. I think, if you can't handle waiting and it's going to cause issues between you, then you should ask her, but if you think that you *can* wait, then give her time so that she can talk to you about it when she's ready."

That makes sense. "Yeah. You're right. I can wait. I trust her."

"I would certainly hope you do, given that you're marrying her."

I snicker and find that I'm smiling. Getting that off my chest helped a lot more than I'd expected.

"I think we've made some great progress. I should have a client waiting for me, so please schedule an appointment for when you're out, and I'll let you…fuck, go back to prison. That sounds awful. How long do you have before you have to go back? There's plenty to do around here."

"Yeah, I'm seeing Rachel."

Her smile returns. "Good. Then take that time and enjoy getting to know her all over again."

I shake her hand again and thank her genuinely. "This really helped."

"I'm glad."

Waiting in the reception area, there's something eight feet tall and with massive red horns poking out of his red forehead on the top of his red face over a surprisingly nice black suit. "I think she's ready for you." I manage to keep from stammering. This is so much scarier than prison.

He smiles at me, showing yellowed teeth that look made to grind bones to dust. "Thank you." His voice is friendly and jovial and does not match anything about his appearance.

I can make an appointment once I'm out. I don't want to be around these terrifying things a second longer than I have to be. I hurry out to find Rachel exactly where she said she'd be, behind a counter, handing someone a plate of food in her café. I take a seat a few spots down and wait for her to finish talking to him.

"How can I help you?" she asks as she moves toward me, stopping mid step as she faces me, her fangs showing in a bashful smile. "Dinah."

"What's your specialty?" I ask.

Her smile only grows. "Our roast beef panini gets a lot of praise. And our poutine is to die for."

"I'll have both. And..." What do adults drink that isn't alcoholic? Ordering a soda sounds so childish. "A milkshake?" Definitely doesn't sound childish.

"Coming right up." She leans in, tilting my chin up until our lips meet, and I breathe her in, lilac and desire. How long do I have again? "It's on the house." I can feel her cool breath on my cheek as she speaks.

Her cooking is the most delicious thing I've ever eaten. Even the blood she slips me and the cinnamon roll she buys me on the way out can't compete. But nothing comes close to getting to spend even this meager time with her. That's the woman I'm going to marry.

CHAPTER ELEVEN

No one is dead when I return from therapy. An additional no one dies over the next several weeks. I wake every morning, scared to breathe for the knowledge that one of them must have been killed, only to smell them all still living, to hear them moving about, talking to themselves, watching programs, and simply being alive.

Finally, when I accept they're alive, I get up, have whatever little breakfast they gave me the night before, a muffin or some fruit, and I read or watch TV until I have to head to work. I was finally approved for a job and was lucky enough to get work in the kitchen. I've been hoping I'd be able to help out at Rachel's café once I get out. Or my café, if one's to believe the name.

As soon as I finish my shift, it's back into solitary for my own protection. It's more constraining than maximum security, but the guards are a lot more polite about the whole thing, and they don't tend to bother us for kiting notes to each other.

None of the other girls seem to be any more over Millie's death than I am. She's mentioned often in the notes, though they did eventually let me take over as DM, and we've been continuing our campaign each evening through even more notes or in the range when the laxer guards are on shift.

One morning, on a Tuesday where I don't work, and for once am lucky enough to have the next day off for my wedding, the phone in the officer's station rings for what has to be the three-hundredth time in a row. It's between two metal doors and nearly thirty feet away, but it feels as if it's growing louder every time. One of the officers answers it again and tells whoever it is to stop calling. Is someone prank calling a prison? That seems like a poor decision.

I turn the volume up on my TV, hoping to drown it out, but I hear the first of the doors open, the one into the range leading to our rooms. A few seconds later, my door opens, and a guard peers in at me with a strangely pleading look. "Call your mother," he says.

My jaw drops. "What?"

"I can't get any work done. She's been calling for three hours straight. I've threatened to call the cops on her, but I'd really rather not. Please just call her."

Why the hell would she be calling me today? "You can call the cops."

"She's…well, I don't exactly know what's bothering her. She won't actually tell me anything."

"Yeah, so call the cops. She can't bug you from prison."

He looks around the prison we are very clearly in.

"Okay, maybe she can. But she probably won't be in your custody."

"Please just call her."

I groan, raking my fingers through my hair. I haven't talked to her since I was fifteen, and I have no desire to start now. "She's not on my approved call list."

"I'll let you call her anyway. The warden can chew me out all she wants."

I'm not sure I'd believe that, even if I had it in writing. Even the nicest guard isn't going to stick their neck out for an inmate. Wait a second, I'm talking to a guard. This isn't me. My mother is already rattling me. I turn back to the TV, wrapping my blanket tightly about me.

"Pelletier, please. I can't even think. The phone will not stop ringing. I can't make you call someone, but I'll…I don't know, not search your cell for a month?"

That has my attention. I don't have any contraband, as it's not worth it since I'm clean, but being searched is so annoying, and they always end up damaging something, at the very least tearing a page in a book. But I still don't talk to guards.

"Two months," he says. "And by that point, you'll be leaving here in just over a month, so you'll be so busy packing up that any search would just be looking at your mostly empty cell and going 'Yep, that's empty.'"

I sigh.

"How about I go back to my desk, and I will write down her phone number, and if you just so happen to see it and decide to dial it, then I will separately and unrelatedly not search you for a while."

What work is she even keeping him from? All the guards do is talk about music and random women they've screwed. It's like having a frat house right outside my door.

"I guess we'll see," he says, leaving my door open as he walks back to the officer's station.

They're going to think I'm working with a guard.

The phone rings again. And again. And again.

"Dinah, just answer it," Paige says from the cell next to mine. "I don't like talking to my mom, either, but that phone isn't going to stop, and I can't focus on my shows. It's as loud as these damn toilets."

It is nowhere near. "I'm not doing a favor for a guard."

"Then do it for me," she pleads. "I just want to watch my soaps."

It rings again. "Fine," I mutter.

A cheer sounds from the other three cells.

I roll my eyes and stomp down the metal steps to the central area where the guard station sits and where there are passages to the other two ranges and their sets of cells.

On top of one of the phones is a scrap of paper with a string of numbers hastily written on it. I'm going to get in so much trouble. You can't call someone who isn't on your approved numbers.

I pick the phone up and dial. There's a long silence as it waits for her to accept. "Finally, you call. I've been worried sick," my mother says.

I glower at the wall. "Stop calling the prison. I don't want to talk to you."

"I've been visiting you every weekend for years, only to be turned away each and every time." It has been months, not years, and not even every weekend. "You don't even care what's happened to your poor mother."

"No, I don't. Good-bye."

"Wait! Wait, wait, wait," she pleads.

Why the hell should I? God, if anything would push me back to heroin, it's her. I smell the air, certain that someone has to have it, but there doesn't seem to be any nearby. "No. You have no right to expect anything from me. Stop calling, stop visiting, I don't care."

"I'm dying."

She's dying? I narrow my eyes. Despite the deaths I've had to witness this year, it's hard to imagine her ever dying. I assume when all the vampires are nothing but dust, it'll still be her, annoying the Grim Reaper as he collects the last soul. "I don't care."

"What a heartless daughter I've raised. Fine, I'm not dying, but I knew you wouldn't talk to me any other way."

"I'm not talking to you this way."

"Di, please."

"No. I don't care. You had your chance, and you blew it. Good-bye."

She sighs like somehow, I'm the grating one here. "I know you're getting married tomorrow. I just want to be there to see my baby girl on her big day. Where is it? No one will tell me. Please, let me see you."

She wants to see my wedding? My wedding to a woman? The same woman she kicked me out of her house for being with? "No. Fuck you."

"Di," she shouts. "I know I've said and done some things—"

"Oh, like what?"

She only sounds more exasperated. "You know what, Di."

"No, I don't. Why don't you tell me? What have you done that you regret?"

I can imagine the petulant look on her face, her stomping her foot and whining about how she's being held to account for her own horrid deeds. "I didn't approve of you and Rachel being together."

"Is that how you put it?"

"I've come around to it. Why else would I want to be there to see you two get married? I always liked her. I used to give her extra hot chocolate when she came over."

"No, you gave me less because you didn't want me to be fat."

She huffs. "It's my last wish, please."

"You're not dying. You don't get a last wish."

"Well, we can't all be immortal," she mutters. "I'm dying in a certain sense. Think about it. You'll be around for centuries, and you never would've gotten the chance to say good-bye. Don't you want that now?"

What? My mouth goes dry. She...knows I'm a vampire? But how? She hasn't seen me, and she hasn't talked to me. I was called a vampire in the papers. Did she take it literally? What on earth is she thinking? Don't they record these calls? She can't say something like that. "I'm hanging up now."

"Please just let me see you. Let me apologize."

"You haven't tried yet. Should I be expecting one?"

Another huff. Another petulant stomp. She's not getting her way, and it's driving her insane. "You know I never wanted this for you."

I roll my eyes. She can't even *try* to apologize, can she? Did I really let myself believe that she'd changed? I should've hung up already. "What did you never want for me? Marrying the woman I love?"

"No, well...no, I suppose I didn't want that." At least she can admit it. "But any of this. I never wanted you to go to prison, or to be a...you know."

Junkie? Vampire? Homeless person? Lesbian? "I really don't know."

"Vampire," she whispers. I sit in the chair by the phone, staring at nothing. She'd already made it clear that she knew, but how? "I wanted you to have a normal life."

"And you did a shit job of that," I snap. "Don't call here again."

"Dinah, please. I..." Say it. Say you're sorry. Come on. It's two words. "I just want to see you get married. You can't make a mother miss her daughter's wedding."

"I don't have a mother. Good-bye." I set the phone on its hook and walk back to my cell. To my great shock, the guards' phone doesn't start ringing again. Maybe she finally learned to take a hint.

Chapter Twelve

I can scarcely believe it's really happening. Rachel and I, along with Landrey a few meters away, are sitting on benches in a courthouse. We have an appointment for about fifteen minutes from now.

It really is a fantasy wedding, isn't it?

I'm trying to mean that sarcastically. I'm on temporary absence from prison and getting married in a courthouse where my only guest is a brain-scrambled guard, and yet, it's still so much more than I'd ever hoped for. It's actually happening. I'm marrying Rachel fucking Evans today. I've only been dreaming about this since I was like ten.

She leans in, her lips pressing against my cheek as she wraps an arm around me. "Nervous?"

I shouldn't be. "Not to marry you. Nothing could scare me less."

"You keep looking at the door, so I wasn't sure. Are we too exposed or something? I don't know what new instincts you've picked up."

I shake my head. I'm not worried about anyone trying to attack us. We're immortal. It wouldn't do much if it happened. There's only one person I'm scared is going to walk through that door. "My mother called me yesterday."

She stiffens, pulling her arm back. Her fingers tap on her leg. "What did she say?"

"She knew about our wedding. And about what I am." It still doesn't make any sense. How could she have possibly known any of that? There's no way it's simply because the papers called me that. No one would assume it was literal.

Rachel gulps. "Ah."

I stare at her. She looks…I narrow my eyes. Why does she look guilty?

"We both go to the same temple." Her words are oddly deliberate. She's really been scared to admit that she's Jewish, hasn't she? Does she think that because I left the faith that I'd judge her for it? Is she right? Or maybe she's scared that we won't have as much in common anymore, and she's been trying to hide it? "I had mentioned I was getting married. I didn't think she'd do anything."

I should really press on that, but I want to let her elaborate on her own. I shouldn't make assumptions. What do I say here? She's been so scared, but at the same time, she told my mother about me. How could she even stomach being around her? "Why do you go to temple?" I ask. I already know the answer, but I want her to be the one to tell me, not Mia. She's going to be my wife in a few minutes, and I trust her to be open with me. Even after months of not telling me. Is there something that I'm missing?

"I…" Tears well in her eyes. She's so scared that I'll resent her for it. Is it really only because we were both atheists? I don't think I'm even capable of resenting her. "I'm sorry. I…when I was trying to quit, I was really struggling." A tear runs down her cheek, and I reach out to wipe it, but she slides away, taking a shuddering breath and shaking her head. There's something I'm missing. I guess I'm about to find out.

She closes her eyes and takes a deep breath. "I'd gone to AA and NA. I'd gone to rehab. I'd tried so many things. None of them were working because I couldn't view myself as powerless. I couldn't give myself to that higher power. It didn't matter how many times I tried or how much work I put in, I fell again and again and again. I kept relapsing, and I kept trying, no matter how hopeless it seemed. I wanted to have my life again. I wanted to build something up for you to come home to."

She really did all that for me?

"Maybe I needed to be doing it more for myself. I don't know. But one day, I was at this detox clinic, trying to force myself to be clean. It was probably a dumb choice. I can detox in minutes. I'm a fucking vampire. But it gave me distractions and a place to sleep, even if my superspeed withdrawal confused the people there." She sighs, more tears falling. I want to hold her, to make her feel better, but there's some reason she doesn't want me to. It seems like there's something that she thinks would make me not want to. "Your mom came to visit."

I stare at her and shake my head. "No." That doesn't make any sense. My mother blamed her for everything. Why would she…no, there's no way.

"She'd apparently been trying to see you in prison for months." Rachel sighs and seems to grow smaller, shrinking as far away from me as the bench allows. "You kept sending her away. And you'd started sending me away too."

"I…" Did I push her into my mother's arms? Wow, I hope not in the way that sounds.

"I'm not blaming you. For anything. I get it. You were trying to look after me, like you always have. And I wanted to look after you too. It's why I built up this whole life for you to come back to. Why I needed to get clean, why I own a business, why I contacted Mrs. Gudaitiene, and got you transferred here, working toward your appeal. But at that point, I wasn't in any place to look after myself. She came and talked to me. We both missed you, and we weren't handling it well."

"She had years to not miss me," I spit back. I hate how angry I am. We're about to get married. We shouldn't be fighting. But she shouldn't have hidden this from me. How could she possibly be okay with my mom? "She threw me out on the street for being with you. I was fifteen. I didn't know how to look after myself. I didn't know how to do anything. And she didn't care."

She nods, sniffling and wiping ineffectually at the constantly flowing tears. "I know."

"How? How can you be okay with her?" And how can I ever be okay with Rachel now that I know this? Not just that she befriended my mother but that she hid it from me for so long.

"I didn't have a lot of choice...no." She shakes her head. "I did. But I needed someone, and you weren't there. She wanted to make up for how terrible of a mother she'd been. Those were her words."

"It's sure not how she sounded on the phone."

She nods and sighs. "It took her a while to say it to me too. She'd apparently been looking for you for a while before you were arrested. She never managed to find you."

"She didn't look very hard."

Rachel sighs, wiping tears from her eyes. "But she found me. Desperate, scared, confused, and trying to find a way to build an actual life. She took me to temple, and I guess I found religion. I say it like it was an easy thing. I spent, like, a year studying it before I converted, but it took my mind off everything, off you, and it helped me finally be able to stop using. And she helped me get my GED, and she bought all the computers for me to start the café. I've replaced them since, but I couldn't have done it without her help."

I huff. "She's still—"

"I know. It took me a long time to forgive her and to trust her. But she was there for me through a lot, and I know she should've been there for you."

"But she wasn't."

Rachel shakes her head. "She wasn't. And she should've been."

"We...if she had just...fuck!" The room swims, and I try to blink away tears. "We wouldn't even be here. I never would've been..." I gesture toward where I guess the prison is, trying to swallow the lump in my throat so I can form a coherent sentence.

"I'm not saying you have to forgive her."

"I fucking won't."

"Dinah." She takes a deep breath and looks at me, hope in her eyes, but she doesn't say anything as her gaze drops back to her lap. "I'm sorry."

That's how she knew I was a vampire. It's why she knew about the wedding. "You told her. Everything." There's an unfamiliar rage in my voice. I've never sounded like this talking to Rachel before. I didn't even know I was capable of it.

Tears fall into her lap. "I did. It was kinda obvious when I wasn't aging and when I could barely enter the temple."

I hadn't thought of that. She was torturing herself for her faith. For me. "Then how do you go?"

"I tried a few times just ignoring the pain, but our rabbi's nice, and we were able to have some private conversations outside of it, and we had a little group for studying the Torah and debating it, which took some getting used to, growing up Christian." She chuckles, but it sounds broken. She's utterly terrified that I won't forgive her for this. Is she right? I know I can't forgive my mother for everything she did, but can I forgive Rachel for forgiving her? "I mostly go to the church at the Community Center now. We don't have a rabbi or anything, but it's easier, and there are a few other Jewish fiends, though it's more just a generalized religious room."

It's how she knew Mia. At least she finally came clean about all of that. Is that enough?

"Pelletier and Evans?" someone says.

We turn to them.

A woman in a neat suit smiles apologetically at us. "Sorry if it's a bad time, but we're ready for you."

Right. My wedding.

Rachel looks pleadingly at me, desperately. She still wants this. But why? Clearly, we're too different now. Aren't we?

"Babe, I'm…" Rachel swallows. "Can we please talk about this more later?"

"I…" She told my mother. "I don't want her coming around." Can I still go through with this?

She looks even guiltier. "She won't. I don't even have to talk to my rabbi anymore. I need *you*." We sound like she had an affair. "I love you."

That's not fair. It's so easy to see how it all happened, how they bonded over missing me, how it helped her quit, how it was exactly what she needed, but it was still the woman who kicked me out on the street, the very reason I became a vampire junkie in the first place. How can she move past that? "Yeah, we'll be there in just a minute," I say to the other woman. "Sorry, just a lot of emotions."

"I get it. I've certainly seen worse. It's in the room over there." She points toward a door and walks off.

"Babe?" Rachel asks. "Dinah, are we still…I know this is a lot. I know I should've told you and that it's been so long, but I know I love you, and I'm so sorry—"

"Rachel." I wish I knew what to say. This should be so easy. I'm marrying the woman I've been dreaming about marrying since I was a little kid.

"I understand if you can't forgive me, but if we're not married, the parole board might not let you leave. I hope that you're not just doing it for that reason, but I know that if we don't get married, then we won't have the chance to try to fix this, and believe me, I want to. I want to make this all up to you. I'm so sorry."

I take her hand and stare into her eyes. Those same brown eyes that I've been lovingly gazing into my whole life. That now look so heartbroken and terrified. I could never hurt her like this. I could never walk away. Not again. Not after I already pushed her away for so long. But can I forgive her? Can we really still have a chance when we're so unlike the girls we used to be? I know I love her, but do I only love my memory of her? I told my therapist that I'd try to get to know this new person, that it was a new relationship, and I understood that, but at the same time, I knew I was marrying the love of my life. But the girl I knew would've never forgiven the woman who threw me out on the street for being with her. "I hate that you did that, and we *are* talking about it more later."

"I know."

Can I really move past this? I know I can't get out of prison if I don't, but can I really still be with her after this? "I love you." I don't think it's a lie, but it feels so terrifying to say now, in a way that it never had before.

"I love you too." She says it so quickly, like she's scared I'll change my mind.

There's no way I can leave. She means too much to me. This is heartbreaking, but it may not have to be the end of us. Either way,

I'll never know if I don't marry her. I'll never have the chance to find out what sort of life we could make or what sort of people we now are. "I don't want her around. I'm not talking to her."

"I don't have to talk to her. I shouldn't have forgiven her. That wasn't...you're the one she fucked over, and I shouldn't have let her back into my life when that's supposed to be your life too. I was scared and needed help, and she was there and feeling the same way. I'm sorry."

I pull her to me, and she gasps and sobs into my dress, hugging tightly to me.

"I'm sorry," she says again.

It's still so amazing being able to hold her. "We're still getting married. We still have centuries to move past this and to sort out our lives."

A tear falls on my shoulder. "Thank you."

We splash some water on our faces, and she fixes her makeup. I was planning on using some too, but even with vampire speed, we're out of time. We hurry to the room and find the clerk just setting up. Even after everything, Rachel has never looked so beautiful as she does standing before me, saying that she'll be my wife.

She's wearing a drop-dead gorgeous white dress, though it doesn't have the train or any of the normal accoutrements, and I'm wearing the same dress Millie had helped me pick out. It's white, modest, and Millie had not been able to stop raving about the poofy sleeves. It had been heartbreaking to put it on, but judging by the utter adoration in Rachel's eyes, I look amazing in it.

Before we even reach the vows, I already want to kiss her. I'm not sure that I've forgiven her yet, but I think I can. I wish she'd have picked a better day to come clean, but I suppose my mother had to ruin that too.

I won't let her ruin my wedding.

I try to shake it from my mind and focus on the fact that I have eternity with the woman I love. What more can a girl ask for?

"I don't know what my life would be without you," she says. "You've been there for as long as I can remember, and I hope you'll be there forever." I wasn't there for twenty-three years. I should've been there for her. That's why she needed someone else. I could've left prison years ago and been there for her through everything. "I'd probably have died a long time earlier if it wasn't for you." If the clerk notices the implication, she doesn't react. "I want to take care of you as much as you've taken care of me or more. I want to provide you with the life that you deserve. You're the only one I've ever loved, and I think you're the only one I ever could love. You're my soulmate, and I know that we can be perfect for each other and make each other all the better for being there. And I pledge to do my best to do all of that, every single day." A tear threatens to spill, but she blinks it away, her eyes shimmering.

That kiss is so hard to resist. "You're my everything," I say. "You've been in every thought and every plan as long as I've known you. I've never seen a future without you, and now, I finally get to make that a fact. I love you with every fiber of my being, and I hope to keep reminding you of that and never let you forget it." Maybe I do forgive her. My pushing her away was so much worse. I did let her forget that I loved her. I can move past this. I just need to know that there can be a relationship past that, that there's still an us that works, even after everything. "All I want is to be there for you and with you, for the rest of my days, and I intend to make good on that."

Finally, we're pronounced wives, and I get to kiss her. I taste tears as I do it, but I know that we have each other. That no matter what happens, we'll make it through, just like we always used to. Because no matter what, I can count on her.

Chapter Thirteen

Yet again, I'm sitting on an uncomfortable bench in a government building, though this time, only in the second nicest clothes I own. Rachel bought me a silk floral dress. It looks professional and nonthreatening. That seemed to be important. I have to look like the innocent girl I used to be.

She and I still haven't really talked. She's visited every week, and I've called her every day that I could spare, but the conversations have been even more surface level than usual. We talk about our days and say we love each other a million times, but we can't go into any details when the call is probably being monitored, and neither of us have had the courage to bring up my mother again. I wonder if Rachel's really stopped talking to her.

I tap my foot, looking down the hallway, empty save for Landrey leaning against a wall. I feel bad for how much I've scrambled his brains. The man was the witness at my wedding, that has to mean something, even if he is a guard. It doesn't mean I'm willing to talk to him, but I should maybe brainwash him a little less. I guess he likes doing transport, or maybe no one else likes working with him.

At least if today goes right, he won't have to be compelled anymore. I'll be free.

I tighten my fists. I want to grip the bench, but I'd crush it, and that would be a terrible look. My nails dig into my palms, and a trickle of blood comes out. I'm not used to having that much in me, but Mrs. Gudaitiene gave me some before the hearing.

What the hell am I going to say?

How can I possibly convince them that I deserve to go free? I'm still a cop killer. I'm still a murderous monster, and someone just like me killed two women in my cottage with no explanation.

They finally let us back in the cottage yesterday. I can't help but worry one of them will be dead when I get back. Maybe whatever vampire was using that cottage as his personal deli has finally moved on. I have to hope so. We're doing a big finale for our campaign tonight if I make parole, and I want to give their characters the happy endings they deserve. If one of them is dead, I can't really do that.

I lean forward, looking toward the nearby door. I think it's the right place. How is it still not time? It feels like I've been waiting for hours.

And what about Rachel? If I'm going home, that means I'd be going home to her. She may even be here; hell, maybe she's talking to them right now. I'm still not super clear on the whole process. I know I make my case, but I don't know if I'm the only one who does. I breathe in and detect a faint hint of lilac and vampire. She must be here, but there are other scents too. I'm too nervous. Every time I try to focus on her, she tangles up with another smell. Is one of them my therapist? It smells a little like her, but I'm not sure. There might even be more vampires. There are quite a few humans nearby.

Will we really be okay? I've tried so hard to go back to the relationship we used to have, but as much as I've tried to ignore it, we're not the same people we used to be. My therapist said that I need to focus on getting to know her again and that if we both put in the effort, then it can be amazing. I thought it would be easy. It's Rachel. We've always been able to move past any change. But then I pushed her away, and she made a life without me, just like I wanted, and yet, I don't know that I can get over it.

I keep thinking I can, and it doesn't make sense not to be able to, but she forgave my mother. That wasn't her wrong to forgive.

But if she hadn't, then she might still be strung out and desperate, just like I probably would've been if I hadn't gone to prison. I'm a murderer. It doesn't matter how little I meant to do it,

I still did. Do I have the authority to judge her for accepting support and help where she could find it?

The fact that she's a murderer as well should really affect my judgment, but it doesn't. She's still her. And maybe, once we've had time to get used to each other, for real, without all the awkwardness of visitation and ETAs, maybe it can be like it used to be or even better. Our relationship has gone through so many forms, what's one more?

Finally, the door opens. I don't look up immediately, as I'm still panicked about the whole thing and need a moment, but when I do look, I swear I see that cop going around the corner. Right, his dad was on my case. I knew some police officers would be testifying that I shouldn't be freed. I don't know why I'm surprised to see him.

I stand and get a reassuring smile from a familiar woman in a pantsuit. Mrs. Gudaitiene must've just been talking to them. "They're ready for you."

I nod, trying to find my voice.

"Don't be so scared. Just be honest with them, and you'll probably get it. They don't like to reject parole if they can avoid it."

I needed to hear that. "Thanks."

"Plus, you know you can make them."

I try to laugh, but it barely comes out as a noise. I breathe in, attempting to calm myself. That lilac scent seems to be fading. Maybe it was only in my head. I hope she's here. Or maybe she already left, and it was only a remnant that I caught earlier. As much as I'm still struggling with what she did, I feel so much better when she's around.

I walk through the door and find a table with a chair facing a far longer table with a collection of people in nice clothes all studying me like I'm a particularly interesting rat in a maze. Do I get cheese? I'd like cheese. Or chocolate. Or blood. Probably not heroin, though. I mean, I'd like it, but I shouldn't. I should stick to chocolate.

I sit and look between them, trying to hide the panic from my face and almost certainly failing. Didn't I practice a speech? I feel like I had something planned. There were words in it. I bet they were compelling. Some of them probably included my name. Am I supposed to say that? Or maybe hello? Mrs. Gudaitiene walked me through all of this. Why don't I remember any of it? Am I really that scared? I've never had to give a speech before. I dropped out of high school a few weeks before I would've had to do my first.

"Dinah Pelletier?" one of them asks.

That's probably my name. Not too sure of anything right this second, but it sounds right. "Y…" I try to breathe and make a weird whimpering noise that can't possibly make me look better. I will not cry. I close my eyes before tears can finish welling. I won't make a fool of myself. I open them and stare straight ahead, trying to ignore the people watching me. "Yes. I'm Dinah."

"You're supposed to be forty-four."

"That's what the birthday card I got from my wife says." I'm joking. I mean, it's the truth, so I'm not really joking. But I shouldn't be joking to the parole board. Why do I joke when I'm nervous? It's not even a good joke. "Yes, I'm forty-four."

I can feel eyes on me. I still can't bring myself to look at them, so I'm looking at the wall behind them, right over their heads.

"Hmm," one of them says.

They're going to realize I'm a vampire. I have to do something. Wasn't there…oh, right. Okay, I know what to do. I was freaking out the last time I compelled a whole group too, so maybe that'll help. "I look exactly like I should for being forty-four. I've been on perfect behavior, and I deserve the chance to be free and to live with my wife."

The room spins, and I have to fight to stay awake. Why does it still take so much out of me? I'd thought it was because I was starving, but compelling a whole group must just do that to a vampire. I wonder if it gets easier with time and practice or if any vampire will always struggle with it.

"Right, of course. She looks forty-four. It must've been the fluorescent lights," one of them says.

Another mutters in agreement.

They all look old. There're gray hair and gray jackets, but I still can't bring myself to look them in the eyes. They're deciding if

I'm allowed to be free. It's too much. It's overwhelming. How can anyone be expected to go through this?

"She's seeing a therapist, she's a first-time offender, and her wife has vouched for her." So she *was* here? "I don't see any reason not to release her to her family."

Someone is going to argue. They'll stop me. I won't get to go free. I needed more blood. It wasn't a good enough compulsion. "Yes, I agree," another says. "She's been a model inmate, and she's ready to return to society."

"I don't see any reason she should remain in prison."

Wait, they keep agreeing. Are they actually going to release me?

"She looks forty-four," one adds. I may have fried his brain a little. I need to stop doing that. I should never compel anyone again. He'll get better, right? Will Landrey? I know I'm doing it for Rachel, but how can I really be a better person if I keep hurting others?

"Dinah Pelletier, tomorrow, you'll be released into..." Paper rustles. "Mrs. Rachel Pelletier's custody. Your parole officer is Officer Michael Jefferson. He'll be in contact soon with everything you should know. You may leave."

I can leave? That's it? I'm free to go, and tomorrow, I leave prison? There's nothing more to it? "Thank you?" I should sound more confident.

She waves me toward the door, and I walk back out, blinking and barely processing anything. I'm getting out of prison. I can have a life again. I can be with Rachel.

Holy shit. It doesn't feel real.

"Sounds like you made it," Landrey says, dragging me from my thoughts. "Congrats. I'll miss having an excuse to be away from the prison and making overtime."

He managed a full sentence. He may really be recovering. Maybe I'm not a monster. "Thanks," I mutter. I still can't bring myself to talk to guards.

He takes me back to the van and opens the back. "Sorry. You're still a prisoner until tomorrow. I don't feel like getting fired for letting you ride up front."

I should tell him that I don't mind, that I'm free, but I just nod and climb in and think about what I'll do with my freedom as he drives me back to what was never my home but is something I'm far more used to than a real home.

I don't know what Rachel's place is like. I don't know what her life is like. What can I do? Will I find a normal job? There's the Community Center, and I had wanted to help out at her café. How does one handle having free time? What does any of it mean?

By the time I'm standing in front of the cottage, I still don't have any answers. I've never known any real freedom in my entire life. And tomorrow, I have to find out how to deal with it.

Fortunately, the cottage doesn't have a new corpse in it, so I do my best to focus on the *D&D* game. I already planned everything out, and the girls deserve their proper finale, but it's hard. There's so much to worry about, so much to plan, but I've taken enough from people. I've hurt enough people. And I've let too many people die.

Their characters find their treasures, marry their lost loves, avenge their families, and acquire a pet dragon, and I'm starting to feel like even if I don't know how to run my own life, I can at least give other people something good.

Maybe I can do the same for Rachel. Are dragons real? I could probably find her a pet dragon at the Community Center. Not sure how I'd afford it, but I could work toward it. Everyone loves a good dragon.

Chapter Fourteen

The gate opens, and I step out into the sun. It hurts. A lot. My skin feels like it's bubbling beneath the surface, and every little movement makes me have to hide a wince, but I'm outside for a reason. I've walked out the prison gate, and I'm free.

I didn't think this day would ever really come.

I breathe in the air, tasting real freedom for the first time I can remember, along with that reassuring lilac scent. A familiar car sits on the road just in front of the prison, and leaning against the side is the one person I need to see. Rachel is grinning at me, her arms folded over her chest as she watches me, letting me take my time. The sun hurts her as much as it hurts me, so I'd rather not dally and cause her any more harm than I already have.

"Hey, babe," I say, walking to the car.

She throws her arms around me. "You're here."

"Thought I wouldn't be?"

She hugs tighter, and I feel a tear fall on my back. "I don't know. I was scared that maybe something would happen. Or that you'd…"

I pull away, looking into her eyes. "That I'd what?"

"Think better of it and run off?"

"Rachel." I sigh. We went months without speaking about it, but we finally get to be out on our own, and we can't keep from it any longer, can we? "Let's get in the car before we burn up." I've been stuck in the sun for a while before and survived, but the pain never gets any better.

She nods, looking worried, and opens the door. "Do you need help with your…" She stares at the small bag in my hand. "I guess not."

"I gave most of my stuff to the other girls in the cottage." And didn't even get any drugs for it this time. I feel ripped off. "I didn't have much to start with, and I doubt your place needs a tiny prison TV in it."

"*Our* place. Our house. It's not just mine, Dinah. I've been waiting for you this whole time and doing all of this for you."

I won't lash out. I won't ask how she was befriending my mother for me. I know why she did it. She needed help to get better, and I wasn't there. But how can she have forgiven her? I toss the bag in the back seat and climb in.

She gets in the driver's seat and pulls onto the road. Neither of us say anything for a long moment. "You want more of an explanation, don't you?"

"I don't know what more I can get. I understand why you did it. I'm just…I'm trying to get over it."

"Might've helped if I'd tried to at least talk to you about it these last few months?"

I shrug. "I could've brought it up too."

"I haven't talked to our rabbi or gone to our group or anything. I haven't talked to her at all."

She really did that for me? That should make me feel better. Why doesn't it? "I'm sorry."

"No. You have nothing to be sorry for. She's a monster. Or she was. I don't know. I hadn't seen you in years, and I didn't have you to talk to. I knew you wouldn't have forgiven her, but she was trying so hard to be better, and I guess I let myself believe that that was enough. That her trying to help me and to be a better person was enough to earn your forgiveness, when I knew full well that if my parents had done twice as much as she did to repay me, I would never have forgiven them. The truth is, I was scared and confused and looking for anyone and anything to cling to. I'm still glad I found my religion, and it did me a lot of good, hell, *she* did me a lot of good, but it doesn't make up for what she did to you."

Tears won't stop coming no matter how hard I try. "She had so many years to find me, and she didn't do anything until I was already in prison. She didn't even try to visit me until three years into my sentence."

"I know." She pulls to the side of the road and wipes her eyes. "Sorry, I just need a minute. I can't drive crying like this."

"She tried to tell me she was dying."

"Of course she did," she mutters. "You never actually told me much about that call."

"She guilt-tripped me about how cruel I was to make her miss my wedding. She doesn't actually care about me. She never has. All she cares about is getting the proper Mom moments to make her think she wasn't a wretched excuse for a parent. So she called the prison until they forced me to talk to her."

Her eyes widen. "Wow. I didn't—"

"What has she done to suggest that she's better? Because that all sounds like the usual her."

"She was trying to see your lesbian wedding."

I glower, crossing my arms. That being true doesn't mean anything.

"She seems to support us now, and she did a lot to help me, but maybe she was just trying to make herself feel better for kicking you out of the house and causing all of this in the first place. Your dad left her over it."

"He what?" That doesn't make any sense. If anything, he'd always been way more homophobic than her. I'd assumed they were joined at the hip, just as they used to be. Maybe that was why she'd been focusing so much on her religion.

"Apparently, it was before you were even arrested. After a few years with you gone, he couldn't take it. He kept blaming her for pushing you away. That she 'cost him his daughter.'"

"That doesn't sound like my dad."

"I'm not saying he would've been great or anything, but it's what happened."

"You haven't talked to him?"

"He uh…drunk driving. He crashed into a semi. The other driver wasn't hurt too much but he…the funeral was awkward. I don't even know why I was invited."

"My…" My dad died. "Why didn't you tell me?"

"I thought you knew. It was in the papers, and I figured they would've told you anyway."

I shake my head, staring at my shimmering knees. "He was a bastard."

"He was."

"Is that why you were so intent on rehab?"

She's silent for a long moment. Maybe she's shaking her head, but I don't look. "I was already clean at the time. This was only ten years ago."

"Wow." I'd assumed it was longer than that, but at the same time, that means my dad has been dead for so long, and I never even knew. Good. He deserves it. It doesn't matter how much he came around. I still remember how he acted. My mother wasn't the one calling me a freak; she was just the one saying I wasn't allowed in the house.

"I haven't talked to my parents at all. I saw them at the store once and super sped out of there, stealing a bunch of groceries. I felt awful. I went back and paid for them later." Wow, that's weird to hear given how much we used to shoplift. "I didn't…I should've thought about how you'd feel. Clearly, I can't forgive mine, so why did I expect you to be okay with me being friends with yours?"

"You didn't have me around to ask."

"I didn't." I can feel her eyes on me, and I know they're red and sad and angry, and there's every reason for all of it. "And I resented you for that, but I love you, and you were trying to do it for me. I wasn't being friends with your mom for you. I was doing it for me because she was helping me and paying for things I needed. If I thought you'd have been okay with it, I wouldn't have hidden it this whole time, would I? I went to temple every week, and I had a group with my rabbi, and I'd been talking to you for months, and it never came up."

"I wondered about that." Should I tell her that Mia told me? It would probably make her feel worse, and while I'm still hurt, I don't want to hurt her anymore. I want us to patch this up and finally get to enjoy our marriage. It's only a little bump, and then we can maybe have our life. The delay was only a few decades.

"I'm sorry. A lot of it was because I knew I'd end up having to mention your mom, and as much as I tried to pretend otherwise, I knew you wouldn't be okay with it. As you have every right not to be. And a lot of it was just that I've changed, and while I like the person I am now, I was scared that you wouldn't. I'm not the same girl you fell in love with, and I'm terrified that you won't be able to love the new me."

"Rachel." I finally meet her eyes, and I have to pull her to me. I hold her, rubbing her back. We're both crying too much to kiss. I wish I could say I didn't have the same fears. "I want to get to know the new you, but you're still Rachel. I don't care how much you have changed, there's no world where I don't love you."

She tries to pull back, but I offer the slightest resistance, and she stays there, clinging to me. "You're sure?" Her words are muffled in my shirt.

"I've changed too. I don't exactly know who I am anymore, but I can't pretend I'm the same kid I used to be. I've been in prison for the past twenty-five years. That's longer than I was anything else. Maybe you've figured a bit more out than I have, but I still want to get to know the new you and—"

"And I want to know the woman you've become and be there while you figure out who you want to be."

I finally release her and gaze into those eyes, then just give in and kiss her. She lets out a surprised gasp but kisses back, hugging me.

"Are you sure?" she asks when the kiss finally breaks, and neither of us bothers to breathe.

"I married you, didn't I? We'll take our time. We've both hurt each other, and we've both changed a lot. We know that now, and we'll figure out what to do about it."

"Okay." She sniffles. "I'm sorry."

I kiss her again. We'll be okay. I don't know what else will happen, but I'm sure of that.

She grabs a napkin from the glove box and dries her eyes, then takes me to my first ever home.

❖

The car pulls up in front of a house that puts the cottage to shame. There's an actual driveway, and it looks like something you'd see on TV. She kisses my cheek and giggles, back to her normal self. Her new self? "Let me show you the place. Maybe next weekend, we could start working on your driving lessons, and then you'll be able to go wherever you want. Or I guess you could just run."

"Couldn't that attract attention? I haven't used my powers very often."

"Only if you're seen." She grins and gets out of the car, and I have to chase her. "We're not using the garage?"

"You'll see," she says. "Come along. Oh." She tosses something at me, and I catch it before I've processed anything. It's a key. To her house. Our house. I've never had a key before. "Open the door."

It goes right in, and I turn it and get that clicking sound, like a cell door unlocking but softer. I turn the doorknob, and the door comes right open. We step inside, and I get my first glimpse of home.

"It's nothing fancy, and I still owe a bunch on the mortgage, but I thought it'd be nice for us."

We're standing in a hallway leading to a living room with a massive couch and the biggest TV I've ever seen and a kitchen running off it where I can hear a fridge humming and can see part of the stove showing around the corner. Down the hall, the other direction from the door, there's a bathroom, a doorway, and a set of stairs. Everything looks so nice. There's a little table by the door with a glass bowl that she drops her keys into. I don't think I can bring myself to do the same. I want to hold on to mine. "It's beautiful."

"Let me give you the tour," she says, taking my hand and showing me the living room and pointing at a collection of remotes. She explains what they do, but I'm so overwhelmed, I'm probably going to have to ask her again later. There's a table separating the kitchen and the living room that looks to be polished wood, with four chairs pushed in, and the fridge is even bigger than the one in the cottage, and that held food for way more of us. "The pantry is just over there." She points to a door opposite the fridge. "I don't know what you're eating these days, but I tried to stock up, and it's all yours, like everything is. I don't want you to think that you have to ask or…this is your home, Dinah. It was always meant to be. I need you to know that."

I take a shuddering breath, fighting back tears. I will not cry. "I know."

"Okay, well." She drags me down the hallway. "There's an office in here. I don't really use it for much, but I didn't need a guest bedroom on the first floor, and it seemed like a good place to put a computer. Do you know how to use computers?"

I shake my head. I vaguely recall having to use one in middle school, but it looked nothing like the one on that desk, and while I've seen them in movies and TV shows, people seemed to only have to type something really fast, and random stuff would happen.

"Okay, I can show you that, uh, I guess, after the tour?"

I nod. I knew the world had changed, I'd seen it, but it's so strange looking at it in person. Rachel owns a house. And a computer. And we have internet. Right, it is we. We own a house. That feels so weird.

"There's a bathroom right there, but I've never used it. I actually had to clean a cobweb out of the shower yesterday while I was panic cleaning." She laughs. "Um, well, this way." She leads me up the stairs and points to one room. "That's the guest room. If you don't think you're ready to—"

"Show me our bedroom." I squeeze her hand. I'm terrified, to put it lightly, but I'm not going to let her think for even a second that I don't want to share a bed with her. A lot has happened, and probably even more has changed than I realize, but she's my wife, and I love her more than anything.

She nods, her cheeks darkening. "Yeah, so, um, this is it." She opens a door at the end of the hall and shows me a huge bed with another giant TV across from it and a nightstand on either side with lamps on them. "This is us. This is our bedroom."

I kiss her hard, holding her to me, and she kisses me back. I want this so badly. I've wanted her for so long. I've needed this.

She pants, looking between me and the bed. "There was a little more to the tour."

"Can it wait?"

She whines. "Yes, but I wanted to show you your car."

"My what?"

Her smile grows slightly less lascivious. "It's just an old beater. I couldn't afford anything too pricey, but I wanted you to have something once you learned how. And you know, I'd rather you not wreck my car while you're driving it."

I want to see it, but there are other things I want to see more. I kiss her again. "You can show me in the morning."

Chapter Fifteen

A knocking on the door wakes me. At first, I expect it to be a guard, that maybe another inmate was killed, but no, I'm home. Rachel bolts up next to me, looking around. Maybe predator instincts make you about as jumpy as prison. Good to know.

"I'll get it," I say. It's my house now. I should get used to answering the door. I throw my shirt and pants back on and hurry downstairs. Who the hell would be coming around at a quarter to midnight?

Right, we're vampires. Does Rachel have vampire friends who stop by? Or maybe her Torah reading group? I open the door and peer out at a dark-skinned man with tired eyes and an ill-fitting suit. "You must be Mrs. Pelletier." He flips a paper in his hand. "Or rather, one of them. Dinah, right?"

I stare at him. Is he here for my soul? I don't know how demons work. No, he smells human.

"I'm your parole officer. Michael Jefferson."

"And you're coming here at midnight?"

He shoves past me into the house. I could stop him. I could kill him. But I don't. I watch as he marches toward the kitchen while looking around and scribbling on his paper.

"You can't just barge in here," I finally say, and the words sound completely impotent. What am I going to do, threaten my parole officer? I'd be back in prison before I could figure out what to even say I'd do to him.

"I can, actually. Maybe you should read the papers the prison gave you." He smirks and opens the fridge door. "Quite a lot of human blood in here."

"Uh." Do I actually have to kill him? What do you say to that?

"Who's this?" Rachel asks, coming downstairs wearing a dark blue silk bathrobe. She looks way too good in that. And it looks so soft and makes it all the harder not to touch her.

"My—"

"Parole officer," he says holding out his hand. "You can call me Michael. Or Officer Jefferson. Or MJ. I always tried to get people to call me that, but it never took."

She shakes his hand, staring at it, confusion clear on her face.

"You have a good supply of blood by the looks of it. Sustainable source? I assume you can just buy it?"

"What?" I ask helpfully.

He shakes his head, looking at me like I'm an idiot. "You were put away for murder, remember? I need to know you're not going to kill again. You're very bad at it."

"She would never," Rachel says, putting an arm around me protectively.

"She did. Most vampires do. So I'm glad to see that you're keeping her well-stocked and away from peoples' throats. Other than yours, by the looks of it."

I hadn't even noticed. There's a scratch on her neck where my fang grazed it.

She sighs but doesn't tell him off. Is it because she's as confused as I am or because he's my parole officer? "So you know—"

"About vampires? I mean, the papers did call her the Vampire. Very scary name. You shouldn't eat cops."

"Of course. I don't eat pork anymore," she says.

I try really hard not to laugh. I don't succeed, but I try, and I feel I deserve more credit for that than the look in his eyes suggests he's giving me.

"I'm here to make sure you don't commit more crimes. You're stronger than me, faster. It would certainly explain how those girls in your cottage died—"

"I didn't—"

"You had a good alibi, but you probably still could've done it. However, as you're not ripping my throat out right now, I'm going to assume you're not much of a killer. You don't act like one. You don't move like one. You act like a scared little girl who doesn't want to go back to prison. How old were you when you died?" He does not stay on one point for long.

"I didn't kill them. I swear."

"Okay. I came to the same conclusion. Nothing about your case suggests the kind of competence to fake that. So how old? Seventeen? Eighteen?"

"I was nineteen."

"A baby." He sighs, looking around. He opens the pantry door. "Fresh pasta. It's always too expensive for me. How much do you buy it for?"

Rachel shakes her head and holds her hand to it like she's getting a headache. "Like, four dollars a pound?"

"Hm." He digs past a few boxes. "Where do you hide your drugs?"

"I don't have any," she snaps.

He pops back out of the cupboard to look her up and down. "I get told that a lot. A lot of the time, I still find some."

"You want to see my twenty-year chip in AA?"

"Vampire too, then. Nineteen as well?"

"Yeah. It was the same time."

He nods, sucking his teeth. "There were two bite marks on the cop. I assume you were the other. Don't answer that. I'm not interested in digging up cold cases. So your girlfriend went to prison for you, and you felt guilty and are putting her up?"

"My wife. And no—"

"Okay." He starts going through the cabinets. "This is a really nice pan. It would cave my skull right in if you were trying to stop me. So that means I'm not near the drugs."

"There aren't any." She looks at me, and there's the slightest hint of doubt. She doesn't trust me yet. It hurts, but I suppose I don't trust her completely either.

I step toward him, hoping it buys me enough time to sort out what to say. "Sir. Mr.....MJ."

"Yes?" he turns, smiling cheerfully.

"I'm clean. She's been clean for years. We just want to have a normal life."

"I'm sorry, but you can't have that. You're going to have me in your hair for a long, long time. I'm gonna need you to piss in a cup, but I'm not even sure if the tests work on vampires. I've never had one before."

I thought maybe he was the special parole officer for fiends. If that's not the case, I'm even more confused. "Then what...how—"

"How do I know about you? Oh, you could've just asked. You're forty-four, and you look like you're barely older than my daughter, and you went to prison for drinking someone's blood. It doesn't take a genius to figure it out. The Community Center sells blood, right, so you're stocking up there or using one of the delivery places?"

Rachel sighs and takes a seat at the table, still lightly touching my back. "Clearly, you did more than put together that we're vampires. How do you know about the Community Center?"

"Oh, like the Honeydale Mall is some well-kept secret? Just because you kill or sell off any human that goes in there doesn't mean word never gets out. Oh, and slavery, also illegal. Don't buy any slaves at the market. Even if you're freeing them, it's still violating your parole."

Words completely fail me.

He opens another cabinet. "You can't have any weapons, and I know they sell those too, so don't even think about it. Oh, do you have a job yet?"

"I was hoping to work at Rachel's café."

"Babe, you don't have to do that."

"I want to help out."

"Well." She sighs. "I want you to have your own life. You don't need to work there for my sake. I have you here, that's all I need. Take the time to figure out your life."

He says, "So she is an employee? I need to know that she has a job. It's at the Community Center, right? That's hard to verify. I guess just say she's an employee, and we'll pretend I've made the necessary checks, as I don't feel like being on the auction block. It's uh...well, you know." He gestures between the two of them, as if she may not have understood why another black person would be bothered by slavery otherwise.

She sighs again, sounding increasingly exasperated. "Yeah. She's an employee."

"Family business. *Cute*." He jots something down. "How much are you paying her?"

"Fifteen an hour."

That's more money than I could've ever imagined. I was making dollars a day in prison. "Do I get tips?"

"Of course, babe."

He nods and writes that down. "Okay, see, now we're getting somewhere."

"How do you know all this?" she asks. "You're clearly human."

"I'm going to pretend that didn't hurt my feelings," he says, sniffling, I think as a joke, but he could start bawling, and I wouldn't be any less confused, so I give up on trying to read him. "I dated an incubus in college. Nice guy, we stayed in touch. He officiated my wedding. And the orgy before it. Weird ceremony."

She screws her eyes shut, rubbing her temple. "And this incubus told you everything?"

"Of course. Though it was still at the old Quaker building back then. I'm surprised it's been at the mall for so long. I know you need a big building with how many fiends have moved to town, but it seems like that'd ruin operational security. You keep on the move to avoid the authorities figuring out where you are. Now, any old parole officer might know exactly where a massive black market is where his parolees could be buying drugs, weapons, and human meat pies that I've heard are surprisingly tasty. I've heard good things about the croissants too. You can buy those. That's not against your parole. I'm not actually sure if the pie is. I guess it wouldn't be if the blood is fine to buy. So, sure, you can buy any of the baked goods."

Rachel holds her head in her hand. "We get it. She shouldn't commit any crimes."

"You shouldn't, either. If she's hanging out with criminals, I have to report that. I suppose she's working around criminals, but that seems unavoidable, so I can probably avoid remarking upon it. What's your café called?"

"Dinah's," she says.

He grins, nodding. "Oh, that's sweet. Wait, it's that internet café, right? James told me you had good poutine. I'm a sucker for some good poutine."

She nods. "I'm told it's quite good."

"I had some," I say, trying to help. "It was the best thing I've ever eaten."

"Including blood?"

"Well…"

"How did you get your blood in prison, anyway? I've been reading through your files, contacting inmates you used to know, everything I could think of. I was sure those corpses in the cottage had to be your work, but it had been twenty-four years in prison, and there hadn't been any other strange deaths. It seemed weird for you to be that sloppy so close to release."

How many times do I need to say it? "I didn't kill them."

"Okay."

"I never killed anyone in prison. I didn't hurt anyone."

"Except for those women you fought. They sounded pretty hurt."

Right. Them. I sink into a chair, dread filling me. "Yes. Except them."

I can feel Rachel's eyes on me. I never told her about them.

"Seemed like they attacked you, from the records I could find. Bad choice. Why would you attack someone known as the Vampire? I'm antagonizing you, and even I feel like an idiot. I can't imagine trying to punch you."

"I didn't want to hurt them."

"But you couldn't look weak in prison, I get it. Did you drink their blood?"

"No!" I leap from my chair. I've had it with him. "I didn't feed on people. I didn't hunt. I didn't kill anyone." It would mean so much more if he hadn't already brought up the person I'd murdered and the women I'd hospitalized or killed. I could ask him if they lived. He clearly has the records. But I don't think I could stomach the answer.

"So how did you feed?"

"Period blood."

His eyes widen, and he's actually silent for a second. "That adds up. And explains a few rumors I heard. I'd assumed it was just people saying you'd slept around."

"Never!"

Rachel takes my hand and tugs, and I find my head on her shoulder. "Have we answered all your questions?" she asks.

"No, not at all. You still haven't said where you get your blood."

"Sometimes, I buy it after work, and sometimes, I order delivery."

He nods and checks the fridge again. "Can you taste the differences in blood type? They're all labeled and mostly O."

"Yes, you can taste the difference," she says. "But diet matters a lot more. It's on the back."

He picks up a bag of blood, and I nearly drool. I'm too used to not eating. "Vegan. I guess that makes sense. We do mostly eat herbivores. Looks like someone hasn't eaten."

I try to wipe from my face whatever expression gave me away, but he tosses the blood at me, and before I can even think, my fangs have sunk into the bag.

"Babe, you can tell me if you're hungry," she says.

I don't answer, consumed solely by my consumption.

"Am I going to find anything I don't want to see if I search the rest of this place?" he asks.

"No," Rachel says.

He nods and walks down the hall, and I hear the door to the study open.

"Are you okay?" she asks.

I nod. "I'm sorry. I'm not used to having blood available."

She kisses my temple. "It's always in the fridge, and the number for delivery is saved in your phone."

"I don't have a phone."

"It's in the drawer of your nightstand."

I can feel myself blush; the blood is already making its way through my body. I press my cheek to her shoulder, nuzzling her, feeling so content to finally be able to touch her, even if a crazy parole officer is going through our house.

His footsteps thud up the stairs. "Is he allowed to search us like this?" she asks.

"I don't know. I don't want to ask for a different one, even if I can."

"Yeah, it's probably better to have someone who knows about us." Her grip tightens on my shoulder. "I thought sleeping with an incubus killed you. How does that work?"

"Maybe they can take a little at a time, like with blood?"

Her fang digs into her lip. "Maybe. I don't know, he seems like a liar, and it's making it hard to trust anything he says. What if they all know about us? The Community Center could be in danger."

"You could compel him." And cause irreparable brain damage to someone who seems innocent, despite his eccentricities. We're relying on it too much, but I don't know if there's a better option.

He walks back into the kitchen, grinning broadly. "You were right. Nothing I didn't want to see, except a few really outdated vibrators. You can do better."

She groans.

"So I think I got everything I need. I'll leave you be."

"Tell—"

He stuffs his fingers in his ears. "No," he says firmly. "I hear that cadence in your voice. I'm not gonna be hypnotized."

I swear she growls. It's kinda hot. She bares her fangs at him. "What the hell do you want?"

"I can't hear you. Do you promise not to use that vampire mind control magic on me?"

She grumbles and crosses her arms but nods.

He takes his fingers out. "Okay. I already have my report, and I don't want to change it. I've had enough supernatural whammies on me in my life that I'd rather not go through another one. I'm sure you can understand."

She huffs and looks away. "Your story doesn't make any sense. Incubi are demons. They don't make friends with humans. They screw them to death."

His expression grows wistful. "Yeah, he sure did. Actually sent me to the hospital. He swore off sex 'cause of me. He could only watch the orgy. It was kinda sad."

"What?" Exasperated is putting it lightly. She sounds pissed.

"Like I said, he's a good guy. And he tells me every interesting thing that happens there. Don't worry, I don't tell any of the other officers. I think a few other parole and police officers have probably put it together, but you don't go into law enforcement if you have a head fit for anything more complex than bashing it into a wall repeatedly. Most of them could probably look at an ogre and assume it's just an ugly guy in body paint. They don't want to know what all is out there, and they don't care to learn. However, that doesn't mean you should rub it in their faces. Try not to attract attention, or you might get worse than me going through your pasta. Is it from the Community Center?"

"Yeah, there's a Monaciello there who makes them and some amazing pasta sauces. The marinara in there is his too."

"Damn." He grumbles. "I've always wanted to check it out but not quite as badly as I want to not die. Maybe I'll ask James to bring some next time I see him. And some more of those croissants. I could eat a mountain of them."

"But you're done here?" she asks. I think she's well past wanting answers and on to wanting this crazy person to leave and never come back.

He shrugs, not looking at all offended. "For now. I'll see you next week. I try not to schedule it. I like being a surprise."

"So I've noticed," I say.

He grins and takes out his wallet, producing two cards. "Here's my business card. Call if you have any questions or if you want to go out of town. I need to know what you're up to, not quite at all times, but a general where you are and what you're doing is a good thing for your parole officer to be aware of. Don't eat people, don't do drugs, oh, and let's do that drug test." He shakes his head, chuckling. "Can't believe I almost forget."

"Okay. You know it won't give you anything, even if I'd just done some."

"Did you just do some?"

"No."

He shrugs. "Cool, then nothing to worry about. Let's go get that negative so I can log it."

I don't have the energy to fight anymore. He doesn't even try to watch, and at least that finally gets him out of our house. When he's finally gone, Rachel and I collapse on the couch, still shaking our heads and at a loss for words. How long do I have to put up with him?

Chapter Sixteen

I wake up at five on the dot, exactly like I have for the last twenty-five years. It's when they'd hit the button to unlock the doors in max, and apparently, despite being an undead creature of the night, I can't shake that programming.

This is a far better morning than any that I could've had in prison. The arm of the love of my life is draped around my body, and as I open my eyes, I find her lips pressed to my temple. "Good morning," she says.

"Were you watching me sleep?"

She kisses the top of my head. "I woke up a little while ago." She sighs. "I was scared you being here was only a dream. I've been waiting for it for so long, dreaming that I'd be able to share my life with you the way we had always planned, and I'd always wake up, and you'd still be in prison. So when I found you still here in the morning, I guess I didn't want to close my eyes again and have you vanish."

I take her hand and trail kisses along her fingers. "I know what you mean. I woke up thinking you were there a lot of times."

"I wish I had been."

"I don't think they'd have let us share a cell."

She hugs me tighter.

"Do you have work today? Or do we?" She was a little unclear on if she is actually going to let me work for her. I don't understand why she wouldn't. I spent all that time in the kitchen making sure I'd be as good as I could be, but I guess it was only a few months, and I'm probably not good enough for a professional kitchen. I could learn on the job, though, and it'd be so nice to be there with her.

"We don't."

"Oh, right, Saturday. Had to close it for the Sabbath?" My mother wasn't all that practicing. She did marry a Christian, after all. I heard horror stories from other kids about not being able to do anything on Saturday.

She chuckles. "No. I'm not Orthodox. I'm having Cherry run it because I want to spend time with you."

"Oh, so does that mean…" I slide her hand down my belly and press it between my legs. "That you can still push buttons?"

She chuckles again and very convincingly demonstrates her button pushing capabilities. I whine pitifully. "I already said, I'm not Orthodox."

Shuddering, I glance around the room until my eyes settle on the vibrator still on her nightstand. "Can you use tools?"

She rolls her eyes. "If you want to have sex, we can have sex. I think I've made it pretty clear that I've missed it as much as you have."

"Yeah, I kinda noticed how worn out your vibrators were."

Her fangs graze my neck, and her finger presses harder. "Have I answered your questions adequately?"

I have missed her so much. Obviously, years on my own have left me rather desperately craving sex, with no real release beyond my own hand, but it's far more than that. Feeling her everywhere, smelling her, tasting her, it all reminds me that she's real and that I'm really here. That even after I pushed her away, she still came back, and we still managed to have our life together.

"I had thought we'd talk, catch up more without any interrupting eavesdroppers and see what we'd like to do with our day." Cool breath puffs against my ear and neck with each word, tauntingly, making me anticipate what she'll do next. "Though if you have other urges in mind…" The pressure redoubles, and I want to scream.

"I..."

"Can't even form words?"

I nod.

She pulls her hand away and licks her finger. "I'm only teasing, we absolutely can—"

I kiss her, trying to turn the advantage my way the best I can. She's been flustering me since I got home, and I'd like to, for once, be the one leaving her at a loss for words.

Her hand rests on my back, and she gives my lip a sharp nip as we break the kiss. I'm going to constantly be covered in cuts from her fangs. "Were you serious about wanting to work in my café?"

"Of course I was. I've been learning to cook, and I know you spend a lot of time at your business, and I wanted to make sure that I could help you."

Her fingers trail through my hair. "You've been doing everything at the whims of other people or the state or however it works for so long, I don't want you to keep doing that. I want you to find what you want to do. I've never heard you express any interest in cooking, and you're my wife, and it would feel weird having you as my employee. You know I'd play favorites."

"Well..." She presses me to her as I try to pull away to look into her eyes. "Do you not want me to?"

"It's not about not wanting you to. I want you to do what you want to do."

"I want to be near you. I want to spend time with my wife."

"And you can do that without working for me."

I try again to pull away, and this time, she lets me, but it's not worth it for how sad she looks at the loss of me pressed against her. "So I'd, what, just hang around your café and do nothing?"

"You could. You could use a computer all day, getting caught up on the world and technology, and I could give you lessons and free food and blood sausage, and we'd talk whenever I didn't have customers to deal with."

She makes it sound wonderful, but I'd be so useless. "I want to contribute."

"You don't have to."

"And you don't have to provide for me." I huff, sitting up.

She pulls up and cups my cheek. "You have been in prison for twenty-five years for me. You stayed and let me get away, and I'm not sure I'll ever forgive you for that. But I know that you deserve a real chance at life now. I can pay for things. My business gives me enough money. There's basically no overhead on the actual main source of my profit other than the occasional computer repair and internet fees. The food is just extra income. We make plenty. I'm not loaded, but I can afford to have you as my kept woman." Her eyes close, and she groans. "That was a poor choice of words, wasn't it?"

"No." I hadn't even considered the comparison. I suppose I was kept in prison and all that, but she's overthinking things. "I'm not sensitive about prison. And I don't mind working. Plus, I'd be making way more than a dollar an hour, so that'd be great."

"Babe…wait, a dollar an hour, really? God, you were a slave."

I make a noncommittal noise. It had felt like a lot of money after I hadn't had a job for the first year.

"What would you like to do? If you could do anything?"

"And working in your café isn't an option?"

She goes from looking regretful to annoyed. I seem to have that effect on people. "Dinah, I'm serious. I don't think that's your dream job. I can look after us. I've wanted to look after you for so long. Please let me."

Well, when she puts it like that, how can I say no? "Okay."

"So what would you like to do? If you want to stay at home and watch TV, that's fine, but I figure you probably want more than that."

Heroin? Right, no, not doing that. Though, if I could be doing anything, that would be up there. "What are my options?"

"That's my point. Anything."

I stare at her. Anything? Obviously excepting drugs, but what does being able to do anything even mean?

"What did you like doing in prison? Was there anything you did for fun?"

"Besides heroin?" Shit, I said it out loud that time. "Sorry, I mean, no, not really. I read, I played *Shadowrun* or *Dungeons &*

Dragons, I watched TV, and I did a few different jobs that I basically only liked for giving me a break from having nothing in particular to do."

Her brow furrows. "What did you like about *Dungeons & Dragons*? That's, like, improvisational storytelling, right?"

"Yeah, sort of."

"You could take an improv class."

She's really grasping at straws, isn't she? "I tried that once. It got a little offensive. One of the other women, I think her name was Richards, kept doing bits about a Jewish vampire. I'm honestly not sure if they were directed at me, but they were really bad. Like terrible. 'Oy vey, I want to suck your blood, but I don't think it's kosher. Let me get my inhaler first.'"

Her eyebrows shoot up, her expression incredulous. "Wow."

"Yeah, the swastika tattoo didn't help, either."

"Oh." She blinks and shakes her head.

"She bitched at a Native woman for being an immigrant and was stabbed about twenty times."

Her eye twitches, and she opens her mouth, then closes it, shakes her head, opens her mouth again, and sighs, before finally shrugging.

"Yeah, she died, so I suppose it worked out."

"How many people have you seen stabbed?" She sounds so shocked. She killed someone with me and buys blood and works at a place that apparently has a slave auction. How does stabbing bother her that much?

I rub my chin, trying to recall. "Like, actually seen or just been around for? 'Cause I think I've only seen three, no, five. I've seen five people stabbed."

"Oh." Her voice is high and broken.

"Babe, we're vampires."

"Yeah, but...I didn't know it was that bad."

I chuckle. "In maximum security? Yeah, I mean, it wasn't that bad. There was only real violence maybe once a month or so. But sometimes, someone pissed someone off enough, and they got shanked."

"How on earth do they expect to rehabilitate people by putting them in that environment?"

I shrug. "Maybe they don't. If you're in max, you're probably considered too far gone for that, and those who make it down to medium or minimum, well, now they're being rehabilitated."

"Did that work for you?"

I tilt my head. "What do you mean?"

"Are you rehabilitated?"

"I wouldn't kill anyone."

"Yeah, and you wouldn't have in the first place if you'd had any control over it. But did prison make you a better person, or did it leave you twenty-five years delayed in life, with a crazy parole officer who digs through your stuff, no idea what you like doing, and the ability to casually refer to people being stabbed like it was nothing?"

This is really bothering her. "I'm sorry."

"No, I'm not upset with you." She grabs my hands, leaning in, looking terrified. "None of this is me attacking you."

"It sounded like it."

She sighs and presses our hands to her cheek, leaning against them. "I know we've both changed a lot. I keep learning that over and over again, but I didn't think you were stuck someplace that might be changing you for the worse. Not that you're worse, I only mean in a way that's worse for you. It's no wonder that you were still using drugs all the time when that was the environment you were in. You were bored and scared and—"

"I wasn't scared. I can handle myself."

"And that's all the more terrifying."

How is that scary? I shake my head and scoff at the idea. "It's not scary. I'm fine."

"Yeah. You shouldn't have had to be. You're the sweetest, kindest, most wonderful person I've ever known, and you had to make it in a world where people casually stabbed each other. That officer talked about you fighting people. You weren't stabbing anyone, were you?"

Does she really think I'd do that? I pull my hand back. "I wouldn't—"

"You're right, I'm sorry."

"No, I would never. They attacked me, and I fought back. And I'm a vampire. I did a lot more damage. And I learned to start acting like I was ready for a fight, and eventually, people stopped trying to fight me."

Tears stream down her cheeks, and she does nothing to stop them.

"I would never have started anything. I wouldn't have stabbed anyone."

"No, I know."

"Then why did you say it? You..." I swallow. No, there's no way. She wouldn't think that. "You do know I didn't kill those girls, right?"

"Of course." She reaches for my hands, but I pull back, staring at her, not knowing what to believe. "Dinah, it came out wrong. I didn't think you would've done anything, but I didn't know what you might've had to do to survive. I wasn't accusing you of anything. I know you're not a killer."

"Okay."

This time, when she reaches for my hands, I let her have them. Her thumbs rub slow soothing circles along my knuckles. "I was shocked. I didn't know it had been that bad. If I had, I'd have broken you out years ago, consequences be damned. I don't think you did anything wrong. It doesn't change how I see you. I know you didn't hurt anyone when you had any choice in the matter. You're still a good person. I'm sorry if I made you feel like I didn't believe that."

"It's okay."

"No, it isn't." She rests our hands in her lap. "I never want you to feel that way again. I love you."

I nod. If I say anything, I'll start crying. Maybe I needed to hear that. I hadn't realized that I'd told her so little about prison. Maybe it's the same reason she hadn't told me about my mother. I didn't want to change how she saw me, and when it seemed like I had, I think it broke my heart a little.

"You're free now. That place..." She finally releases one of my hands so she can rub her eyes. "You don't have to go through anything like that again. I won't let anyone hurt you."

"You can't guarantee that."

"It's not something that happens to most people. It doesn't happen to me. We can have a normal life now."

It's sweet, and I know she wants it to be true, but how am I supposed to believe that? "What's a normal life, Rachel? Living in suburbia with families who love us? Because we saw how that ended. Being a vampire housewife to a woman who works in a black market? I don't know what normal is."

More tears fall, and she grabs a tissue from the nightstand, dabbing at her eyes and nose. "You deserve a normal life," she blubbers.

"I appreciate that you want to give me one. I'm only saying that I don't know how to have one."

"Then let's figure it out," she says, her voice still nasally. "Together. We can try out other things. You can find a game in town. You can find a job you'll actually like. Spend the eternity that we have together to figure out who you want to be, and I can join you. I haven't ever really given myself a chance to relax and have hobbies or anything before. I was so focused on building us this life. We can take dancing classes and experience all kinds of new technology as it comes. I haven't tried out anything VR, and I know that's supposed to be the new trend. We could test it out, and I could add it to the café."

Exploring the future with my wife? That wasn't exactly a normal life, but it had a hint of it. We could see everything that comes, together, and have all these years to figure out who we want to be. Maybe I lost twenty-five years, but what is that to the infinite years to come? "All right. We can explore stuff together."

"And you can explore things on your own too. I've found a few things I love. Running my business makes me happy, I like cooking, and I love caring for you. Maybe that's the real reason I don't want you to be my employee. At least for a little while, I want to take care of you. I got you your parole and that less stabby prison." She shudders. "Let me make you dinner, and let me keep a roof over your head and blood in your veins while you take all the time you need to figure out what you want to do?"

How could anyone say no to that? "Okay. I'm not giving improv another shot, though."

"After that horrific experience you had with it, I don't expect you to."

"I'll find a *Shadowrun* game or something, I'll look into classes on whatever sounds interesting—"

"But not technology. I'm teaching you to use it."

I can feel myself smiling. I was crying and heartbroken a few minutes ago, how am I already so happy that I can't keep from smiling? "All right. I'll rely on you to teach me how the last few decades of technological advancement went."

"Perfect. It's literally my job."

How many ancient monsters has she had to teach how to use the internet? I probably shouldn't mention that Millie already taught me the basics. The thought brings up the bloodless image that's still seared in the back of my eyes, so I try to focus on the present. "It'll be amazing. And I can learn…uh…" It would be so much easier if I knew literally anything about the world beyond what I've seen in fiction.

"You like playing characters, right?"

I nod, narrowing my eyes. "I'm still not doing improv."

"Try community theater. You could be in a play."

Butterflies flutter in my belly at the thought of being onstage. The parole board was traumatizing. I don't know if I could do that again. "Maybe I should try a book club."

"I thought that was a good one." She was really set on this idea, wasn't she? Should I try it? She's always known me so well, but it's been a long time. Maybe she doesn't really understand me anymore.

How can I explain how terrified I was? How much baring my soul to a roomful of people shook me to my core to the point that I didn't even remember I was supposed to compel them until I'd already made a fool of myself? Was I better at expressing myself when I was younger? I feel like I never struggled to open up to her when now it seems so difficult. Did prison teach me to stuff everything down? I'd never noticed.

She slides closer. "I bet you'd be a great actress. I could have flowers sent to your dressing room."

I blush. I'm still not used to the feeling. "Babe…"

"Tell me, what is it?"

I've seen so many sitcoms deal with stage fright. I didn't even think to picture the parole board in their underwear. "Maybe acting wouldn't really suit me."

"Why?"

"I don't think I could do a crowd," I finally say, forcing the words out in a discordant rush.

She watches me without saying anything until she finally laughs and says, "It's community theater. I don't think it'd be much of a crowd."

"The parole board was only a few people, and it was already too much."

"Believe it or not, the audience of a play aren't there deciding whether you get to leave afterward."

There may be a few differences that I hadn't considered. "It was still scary." I sound so weak. I want to take it back, and the impulse terrifies me. I really don't know how to be open with her anymore. I'm trying. My old impulses must still be there if I'm telling her any of this, but it never used to be this difficult.

"You don't have to if you don't want to, but it sounds like all you've really done is watch other people play characters, read stories where you can essentially put yourself into characters' heads, and be characters in games all about telling stories. I thought maybe exploring fiction in another way would be fun."

There were plays in prison, but I never considered auditioning. I watched a couple productions, and they were rather painful. Would these be as bad? Probably if I was in them.

"You could take an acting class while you're taking all these other ones. There's one on Wednesdays."

Is she right? She's always known me better than anyone, but that was before we'd spent so long apart. If she's wrong, that may scare me even more than if she's right. If I like acting, it means she still gets me to the point that she knows things about me that I don't know. With anyone else, that'd terrify me, but with her, if that's gone, it would mean even more has changed than I feared. "All right. I'll take an acting class. Maybe I'll like it."

CHAPTER SEVENTEEN

How did you like our first acting class?" Rachel asks, grinning at me, looking far too sexy in the loose-fitting tank top and yoga pants.

What had I thought of it? I'd been struggling to keep up the whole way. It was a little too close to improv classes, but the lack of a Nazi did improve things far more than one would suspect. "I'm not sure we really did anything. I don't feel like I know how to act. And I'm really not clear on why we went to the Community Center instead of a local class for humans." It's still kind of terrifying being around all these creatures. I'm a vampire, so it probably shouldn't be, but in a lot of ways, it's scarier than prison. At least there, I knew for a fact no one could really hurt me.

"Babe, did you forget we're fiends?"

"I know! But, like, if I did end up liking it, and I'm not saying that I did, wouldn't it make more sense to be taking classes with humans since that's what most theater productions are going to involve?"

"There's the occasional play here."

That's hard to imagine. Is there anything the Community Center doesn't do? I suppose community theater at least makes sense, given the name. "I didn't think you'd take the class with me," I say, brushing it off. She's had a long while to grow accustomed to being a fiend and being around them. I haven't.

She tugs on my hand, leaning against me. She'd been away at work for only a few hours before coming home to pick me up for the class. "I'm not sure I'm quite capable of letting you out of my sight just yet. I've missed you, Dinah."

"I've missed you too. But your work is right over there." I point toward the café a few feet away. "I can handle doing stuff on my own. You've gone to every class you signed me up for so far. If I'm taking them here anyway, you can look after your work, and I can visit you."

"I trust Cherry. She's been working for me for two years and hasn't let the place burn down yet. I'd rather spend time with you, and we can check out those VR things, and we could figure out what else you might be interested in."

She worries so much about me. I suppose I worry as much about her, but it's strange having people around who care about me. "We already established that we have eternity. We don't need to rush from one activity to another trying to find the perfect one for me. I can enjoy the moment with you and enjoy being free, other than a weird parole officer who I'll have to deal with for the rest of my life." Or until I have to fake my death and take on a new identity. It probably won't be too difficult, given that there's a stand selling fake IDs right across the aisle, but I've clung on to my life for too long to give it up simply because parole is more annoying than I expected.

"Okay, you're right. I'm sorry, I'm probably pushing you around and running your life like another prison guard."

I shake my head and kiss her cheek. "No. I mean, maybe a little, but it's not the same. I'm not saying I don't appreciate this. I've loved spending so much time with you. Even if I did manage to burn both the recipes in our cooking class. How was I cooking professionally for six months? Did I poison the inmates?" It had been a lot more supervised. I'm not used to having to run my own life, and yet, I keep telling her off for trying to do so. I know she's only looking after me, but I don't want her feeling like she has to control everything. And maybe I want a little more freedom than that. "There doesn't need to be such a rush."

She sighs but slowly nods. "Okay. You're right. I suppose I've never slowed down myself. I've spent the last twenty-five years trying to build a life for you to come back to, and I never really found out who I was either beyond the business running, Judaism, and AA. And I'm not saying I don't love my life, but maybe I was a little hopeful that we'd find something we both loved together."

"We will. But we can't rush it."

"You're right. We need to slow down and smell the..." She breathes in and turns toward a nearby stand. "Blood sausage. I'm starving. Are you?"

Eating because I want and need to is still strange. I always barely scraped by on blood and ate to look human. Now, I can do either whenever I want, and it always tastes way better. "I could eat."

She leads me to a stand with a number of interesting smoked meats. "Do you have the—"

"Venison blood sausage like you like." The massive tree of a man—man of a tree?—whatever he is, hauls out a cooler from under the table. "Bring the cooler back when you can."

"I always do." She fishes in her purse to pull out her wallet and produces a couple twenties. I have no idea if that's a good deal for what we're getting. It could be a fortune. Prison has given me no real concept of money beyond what I can buy with ramen.

Past the stand, there's an open door to what looks like a casino. I can see the corners of what I think are a few poker tables and maybe a roulette wheel, but at one of the tables, there are fiends chatting. I've heard a lot of women loudly playing poker and bragging about their hands and winnings, but this sounds nothing like that. Someone says something about shooting a zombie, and I'm increasingly confused. Are zombies real? Was my therapist's receptionist a zombie?

The telltale sound of dice rolling on a cloth table takes me back. They're not playing poker or planning an assassination; they're playing a game. Rachel is still talking with her butcher or smoker or whatever he is, so I creep toward the casino, peer through the door, and see horrifying monsters with a few rulebooks, character sheets, and dice scattered about the table. Fiends. I keep saying monsters. It's hard to think of them otherwise when they're still these terrifying things. I know in theory that I'm one too, but I've only ever been around humans, and they don't tend to have rows of jagged teeth or massive, bone-crushing tails.

"We have the casino booked for the next couple hours," one of them says to me, sounding a bit embarrassed. Her top half is humanlike, but her bottom half is a snake tail wrapped around the chair. Finally, a monster—fiend, why is that so hard—that I actually know. A lamia. She's in *D&D*. I'd always assumed they weren't real. She mostly smells like a person, though her blood smells off, like it's not warm enough, and there's an odd musk. "Sorry. It's just, like, three hours each week." She thinks I'm here to gamble.

"No, I…" I don't want to be rude and barge into their game. "I heard people—fiends—playing a role-playing game and just wanted to see what it was." I move toward them, and none of the scary fiends try to eat me. Can they eat other fiends? I don't know how any of this works. I had an army of kobolds eat a dying dragon once in a campaign, but that's probably not the best thing to go off of. One of the other fiends at the table is covered in moss and smells of rich earth, and the other has a fishlike green face like the *Creature from the Black Lagoon* and a scent to match. The books interest me a lot more, so long as none of the fiends wants to eat me. Unless the books are mimics. Are mimics real? What if the books are the ones that'll eat me? How did I not think to ask if mimics are real?

None of the books move as I look at them, but the cover of one proudly reads *Deadlands*. "I've only played *Shadowrun* and *Dungeons & Dragons* before, so I wanted to see what you were playing," I say, feeling their eyes on me. I've never had so many monsters staring at me in real life. I feel like I should have to roll for initiative. But they're probably not *actually* going to try to eat me? I hope.

"Oh." The fish-creature grins at me. I think. Its teeth are showing, and its cheek fins are tilted up. "Most of the people here seem to find these games a little insulting."

"Maybe if a single picture of a lamia was wearing a shirt," the lamia mutters.

Fish-guy laughs. It's not all that threatening. It's warm and jovial. Maybe he won't eat me. "Did you want to join us?"

I can feel myself grinning, but I look over my shoulder. Rachel must be looking around for me by now. We've barely been this far away from each other since I got out last Thursday. "How often do you do these games?"

"Every Wednesday."

I could do that. Acting classes, then *Deadlands*, and Rachel would be right here at work, and we could hang out until we go home. Or I could skip acting classes if the game starts early. "Can I join next week? I guess I probably should come up with a character, but I don't really know the system and—"

The lamia's tail flicks, moving from the chair and revealing a purse that had been covered. She pulls out another copy of the book. "Just bring this next week. We'll see you at three, okay? Unless you'd need it at nights. You're a vampire, right?"

"Three's fine." Why am I so excited? I knew I liked this stuff, but part of it was only to kill time in prison, wasn't it? I'd never played before I went in. But then again, when would I have had the time?

"All right. I'm Phoebe, by the way. And this is Aldo," she says, pointing at the fish. "And Ife." The moss-covered guy—Ife, apparently—looks at me. He's small and has very sharp teeth.

"I'm Dinah," I say. "I should go find my wife, but I'll be here next week. And I won't forget your book. Thank you."

Phoebe chuckles. "It's no problem."

I wave, still grinning, and hurry back, finding Rachel looking panicked. "Where were you?"

"Babe, I'm okay."

"It's hard to track you down. There are so many vampire smells."

I could always follow the lilac for her. "I found my people," I joke, holding up the book. "I have a game after class next week."

"You'll take the class again?" She sounds so excited. "I thought you didn't like it."

"It wasn't that bad," I mutter. I liked taking it with her, and it's fun getting into character. I just wish there was more of that and fewer icebreaker games. "I thought it might be nice to have more stuff to do around here so you could work, and I could still—"

She kisses me. I'm not sure I did anything to deserve it, but I'm never against that. She pulls back, still grinning. "I've been so worried about you. I'm glad you're managing here. And even making friends. I know how scared you still are by..." She looks around.

"Yeah, I'm working on it. I'm a fiend, so I might as well get used to others."

"I'm proud of you." She beams down at me. "Let's go eat."

I follow her to her café. Our café? I don't know if I'm involved in that one, but it is my name. "Mind heating a couple of these up for us?" she asks the creature behind the counter, who I assume is Cherry. She's nearly eight feet tall and has sharp tusks and smells like iron. Not exactly what I expected when I heard the name.

"No problem, boss," she booms.

"So venison, is that a kosher thing?" I ask, trying to focus on the food instead of the tantalizing book in my hand. I'll have time to study it later. I don't want to waste my time with Rachel.

"I keep telling you, I'm not Orthodox."

"You're in a study group with your rabbi. I think assuming you eat kosher isn't unreasonable."

She rolls her eyes. "Dinah, you were in Hebrew school, you know blood isn't kosher. If I had to live off a kosher diet, I would starve to death. I just don't eat pork or shellfish."

I vaguely recall learning that. I never paid that much attention. "And your rabbi is okay with that?"

"She knows I'm a vampire. It'd be pretty strange if she wasn't."

I've never actually met a woman rabbi. I wonder if she still has the beard. "Some people are sticklers for rules. Wait, she knows you're a vampire?"

"Yeah, why else do you think she makes so many accommodations for me? She was even looking into running services here occasionally, but you can imagine it's not exactly the safest idea. Humans don't tend to do well here."

"What about my therapist?"

"Most people aren't as crazy as her."

Not exactly what you want to hear about a therapist. "I told her we'd come in for couple's therapy. We should schedule that."

Her brow furrows. "Do you think we need it?"

Things have been a little weird since I was released, but we seem to be managing. Liz acted more like it was to make sure we were headed in the right direction than anything else, though, and maybe that would be helpful. "I don't know. I think we're all right, but it could still be good."

She shrugs. "We can schedule something if you want."

Do I want that? This whole freedom thing is going to take some getting used to. "Not right now." Something sizzles, and I can barely keep from drooling. I'm starting to see what she meant about stopping and smelling the blood sausage. It's rapturous.

Her phone buzzes in her purse, and I check my pocket to make sure I still have mine. I've lost it, like, three times already. She glares at the screen and presses a button on the side before shoving it back in her purse. "Would you be up for meeting my rabbi?"

"Was that her?"

"No." She sighs. "That was your mom for the hundredth time since I told her I wasn't talking to her anymore. At least my voice mail is already full."

She can't take a hint, can she? At least she's not being quite as bad as she was at the prison. I feel so selfish, but I'm glad Rachel is ignoring her. "Why did it make you ask about your rabbi?"

"Oh no, that was about the couple's therapy thing. It wouldn't be the same, but it made me think of it. I would like her to know who you are. I said I'd stop going there for service, and I have. I'm not trying to get out of that."

"I never said you couldn't go there."

"But your mom goes there and clearly won't leave me alone. I wanted to prove that you could trust me. But Rabbi Becker is still my rabbi, and it would mean a lot if you would be willing to meet her. If I'm not going to temple anymore, I'd like to at least be able to show her why. That I finally got you back."

She's as set on self-sacrifice as I am. "You can still go to temple. I'm not trying to stop that. Just don't make me go with you."

"Dinah…"

"I'll meet her. I'm not saying I can never go with you. I know how important this is to you. You needed something, and apparently, religion did it for you in a way it never did for me. There's nothing wrong with that." Do I really mean it? I've felt weird about it since Mia told me, but I could never quite sort out my feelings. Maybe I've had enough time to. I was scared that it would mean we wouldn't be like we used to, but I'm starting to understand that's not important. What matters is that we put in the effort and support each other. So how could I not do this for her? "She'll meet us outside, right?"

"Yes. She's not so big on the whole self-flagellation thing. She never appreciated me putting up with the agony to sit through a lecture."

I did it to go to NA in the sun, but that was for her. I can't imagine doing anything like that simply because I wanted to. "Yeah, we can go after we eat."

"I doubt she'd be free on such short notice. Plus, there's the group tonight, but that's not until later, unless they moved it since they don't have to cater to a vampire anymore. I'll try to set it up for next week. Maybe after your weird game."

"It's not…" I guess I can't say it's not weird when I don't know anything about *Deadlands*. The cover is an undead cowboy, so I suppose it's a bit weird. "Are you nervous about it?"

"You meeting her? A little, but that's not why I'm putting it off. She really is crazy busy, and I'm trying not to rush us so much. I know I've been overdoing it. We have forever, as you keep pointing out, and I should slow down and enjoy things." She takes a bite of the sausage and seems to adequately enjoy it, judging by the look of bliss on her face. "Besides, we still need to look into VR stuff. And take those other classes."

"Ah yes, definitely slowing down."

She chuckles. "I've been a workaholic for a long time. I'm not sure how else to live."

"You should bring that up at AA."

She glares at me, but she still looks giddy, so the joke didn't go too far. "I could always drag you to a meeting, and you could bring it up."

"Nope. I'm good."

Rachel rolls her eyes. "Have you been talking to Mia?"

When was the last time I called her? It must've been the week before I got released. The cravings haven't been as bad since I got out. It's strange; there's the hint of it in the air, and I know I could grab some easily, and part of me, of course, wants to, but I know what I'd be throwing away, and it makes the thought a lot less tempting. "Sometimes. She was a big help in prison. I really wanted to use when I was freaking out about parole."

"And you didn't?"

I sigh. "I would've told you." Wouldn't I? I've gotten so much worse with my feelings, but I don't think I'd ever actually hide something like that from her. Even if she's hidden stuff from me, I think we learned our lesson. "I've been clean since I told you."

"I'm not judging. I trust you." She squeezes my thigh and gives me a gentle smile. "You've come so far."

I'm still just some awkward dork who has no idea how to function, just like when I went to prison. She's managed to put her whole life together. No, our whole life. She did a good enough job. I can't even be upset, but it makes it hard to catch up. "I'm managing."

She stabs the sausage with her fork, licking her lips. "Well, since we are trying not to rush, we can go shopping later. How about you tell me about your game?"

"I don't know anything about it yet."

"Then the other ones you've played. You haven't said much."

I didn't think she'd want to hear, but I suppose that's kind of silly. She's been so interested in finding out what I enjoy. I should've thought to tell her more about one of those things. "All right. But this'll take a while." I tell her all about the campaign I was running and how Millie started it and manage to avoid crying at the thought of her murder. Maybe it's only because she's asking so many questions and seems so interested or because we keep being given more sausage, but my story lasts for hours. The sun was still up when we got here, and the dusty windows aren't letting anything in by the time I'm describing everyone beating the Big Bad. Right when I'm getting to the conclusion and the beautiful send-off that I gave everyone, someone screams.

We both turn at the scent of blood, but it's not human. It doesn't even smell edible. The scent is followed by a sickening cry and the crunch of bones. A few seconds later, a woman is all but dragged to the door. She looks like a very broken version of the cover of my book. An angry vampire cowboy.

Blood coats her leather jacket, and she spins on the creature who brought her to the door, hatred clear in her eyes even from across the entire mall. If she says anything, I can't hear it, but I can see the murder in her eyes.

Is that what I looked like when I killed that guy? I can't imagine it. She looks like a monster. Far scarier than anything I've seen since I got here, and I'm in front of some sort of ogre or something.

Could she be the one who killed those women? She certainly looks the part, but why? I look to Rachel for any sort of explanation, but she only shakes her head.

"I've never seen this happen before. She must've killed someone here."

That answers that. Whoever she was, she committed murder, even if it wasn't the one I kept being blamed for.

CHAPTER EIGHTEEN

I have one last handful of chips and say good-bye to everyone. Our first session was a lot of fun, and I seem to already understand the rules. The crazy lady last week definitely changed how I view cowgirls, but mine is strictly heroic, and we've already managed to save the day from zombies, at least for now. The town is still likely facing extinction, but we'll try to stop that next session.

"You still have my book," Phoebe says as I start to leave.

Oh right. I was probably going to keep this forever otherwise. "Sorry." I hand it back to her.

"There's a bookshop that might have it a few stands that way." She points past the wall. "If not, you can order it online."

"I will. Thank you."

"It was fun," Ife says. "You seem to know what you're doing better than I do."

"I've had a few decades of practice." I chuckle. It's nice not having to pretend that was a joke. Maybe being around fiends isn't so terrible? I'm starting to think they might not eat me so that's a plus.

The other three gather their books. "I'll see you next week," Aldo says. "Unless you all wanted to grab dinner? It *is* six."

"I can't. I told my wife I'd meet her rabbi. Next week, though."

He flashes a fishy smile. It's going to take me a while to get used to this. He seems like a decent guy so far, if a little awkward around women. Not creepy or anything, just not used to us. Though

I suppose I have no idea how to communicate with guys, as I haven't had to in decades, but I'm not awkward about it as I don't care that much.

Phoebe slithers toward the door, and I follow. She turns, a smile spreading across her face that I manage to avoid flinching from. She's not that scary. She probably can't even eat me. At least without really crushing me first. "Hey, Dinah, I meant to ask, uh…" She chuckles, scratching the back of her head. "Some friends of mine and I do a weekly one-shot on Fridays. It's all girls now that Jackie left. Though, he was the only other lamia there, so it kinda ruined our lamia parody game the other week."

Was there a question somewhere in there? "I didn't know lamia could be boys."

"Yeah, no one does. Makes it a lot easier for some of us." She giggles. "But he certainly didn't appreciate some of the remarks. Honestly, it might be why he left. Guys tend to be a lot bigger creeps, but the other players acting like he was one of the girls, well, I know how awkward that sort of thing can be. But my point was, would you like to join us? We could use another player now. We just have a few drinks and do a dumb one-shot, taking the absolute piss out of it. It was *Maids* last week, but we were talking about doing *Vampire the Masquerade* this week, and I kinda thought you might enjoy riffing on those stereotypes more than we would. Otherwise, we might just do that *Firefly* game, since Courtney keeps insisting we watch it."

I think that made more sense. "I don't drink."

"Oh. Like, is it religious or more a…"

"The latter." It's weird thinking of myself as an alcoholic when I never had much of a problem with it. Mia insists that I just need to moderate and I'll be fine, but I'm not ready to test that anytime soon.

"We don't have to drink. I saw how nervous you were around Ife and Aldo. The game is great, but I thought it might be fun to relax and have a more casual one. I'll make sure they know no drinking this week."

She's considerate, isn't going to eat me, and seems dead set on being my friend. I could probably use more of those. She kinda reminds me of another redheaded GM I'd rather not think about. "Yeah. I'd love to."

She pumps her fists. "Awesome. It's at my place. I'll text you the address. See you Friday." We wave again as I turn toward the internet café and find Rachel instructing someone in how to use a computer. I listen in because I'm still a bit lost on it.

"Hey, babe," she says when she's done, her face lighting up. "How was your game?"

"Awesome. Killed so many zombies. Wait, can I say that? There aren't zombies here, are there?"

She shakes her head. "I don't think zombies are real."

"That's weird."

"They could be. I've just never seen one."

"Well, the Creature from the Black Lagoon is real, so I don't know."

She chuckles. "I'm pretty sure he's a siyokoy. It's a Filipino merman."

"That's disappointing. I thought I was friends with a movie star. Now you've ruined my *Deadlands* game."

"You're a dork." She laces her fingers between mine. "Are you ready to go?"

To meet her rabbi. Yes. I'm ready. There's nothing I need to do. It'll be fine. Or I could run and find those drugs. No, that's a terrible idea. "Maybe?"

"You don't need to be nervous."

"I really doubt that. What rabbi is going to like someone who just finished serving their murder sentence?"

"She's really not that judgy."

"Who's ever heard of a non-judgy rabbi?" I cross my arms, trying to grumble but am too scared for the noise to come out right. How am I going to manage this? I have no idea how to make people like me. The only thing I seem to be good at is role-playing games, and I can't roll a d20 to make Rabbi Becker like me. I should've dumped more points into charisma.

Rachel smiles at me. "It'll be okay."

She thinks everything will be okay. And sure, when I'm holding the hand of a beautiful woman who I share a house with and have eternity with, maybe that's a compelling point, but it wasn't as convincing when I was stuck behind bars. "If you say so."

"It will be."

I nod, trying to believe it and feel a weird buzzing on my thigh. Is she trying to cheer me up? I stare down, trying to figure out what it is only to remember that I have a phone now. I pull it from my pocket and see a number on the screen that I don't recognize. "Hello?"

"Dinah, where are you?"

"What?" I ask. Is this a threat?

"It's Officer Jefferson, your parole officer. Where are you?"

Oh, right. I should've recognized the deep voice. "I'm at the Community Center."

"And how long have you been there?"

"Four hours or so? Why?"

There's a long pause. "That should be okay. I'll get the phone logs."

"What?"

He sighs. "There was another murder. I'd like to prove that you didn't do it."

I blink. "You don't think I did?"

"We've already established that you're not the type, but it doesn't make you look less like the culprit when people keep dying around you."

"How was this person around me?"

Another sigh. "I can't give too many details. Just be careful and try to have witnesses as often as you can. And keep your phone on you so I can track your location."

"It's like being in prison all over again."

"Then you had a very nice prison." He hangs up, and I'm left staring at a blank screen.

"What the hell?"

Rachel looks at me worriedly. She must've heard everything. "He didn't tell us much."

"Who died?" I ask. "Could it have been another inmate?" I haven't talked to any of the girls there since I got out. There hadn't been a murder in so long. What if one of them is dead, and I didn't even fill out the form when they wanted to be able to call me? I should do that. "But then it wouldn't be around me. I don't even know anyone else." It better not be her rabbi. As badly as I'd like to get out of this meeting, I know that'd break Rachel's heart.

"We don't know anything yet. We can't make assumptions."

"Who the hell keeps doing this?" I can feel frustration building. I'd managed to move on and stop thinking about these deaths, only for it to start up again when I'm finally free. "I know I didn't do it, but it has to be someone."

"I don't know."

At least I know it can't be Rachel. She was with me when the first girl died. But it could be any other vampire in the world. Like that crazy girl who got led out of here last week. "What about that cowboy?"

"The one who attacked the slave auction?" She sounds disbelieving. Don't tell me she's defending that lunatic.

"That's what she did?" My jaw drops. "They kicked her out for—"

"Killing the auctioneer. Yeah."

She's still a murderer, but that doesn't exactly match the MO. I'm not sure what that stands for, but I've seen enough cop shows to know it's the term. "Wait, she was only killing prisoners before, and then the guy running the slave auction? What if she's after criminals?"

Rachel doesn't look convinced. "It doesn't seem likely, does it? Especially when it's someone dumb enough to kill a fiend in the middle of the Community Center but smart enough to break into prison twice without a single witness?"

That's a good point. That cowboy hadn't exactly seemed subtle. "Well, that's the only murderous vampire I've seen."

"I'm sure there are plenty here," Rachel says. "It might just be someone feeding. There are so many vampires in Toronto now. To think, we were considered endangered a few years ago."

"We were?"

"Yeah, we were hunted to near extinction in, like, 1900 or so after *Dracula* came out, but apparently, people keep making more of us."

I don't know how to feel about that. Vampires are horrible monsters, but I am one, and I was raised on enough stories of genocide to feel pretty uncomfortable with the idea of being hunted to extinction. "So you think it could just be anyone?"

"Maybe. I don't know. I think you should try to stay out of trouble and not investigate this. You're on parole."

I wasn't trying to solve a murder or anything, but… "I'm trying to be a superhero again, aren't I?"

"A little bit. And don't get me wrong, it's hot, but I don't want anything to happen to you. I just got you back."

"Okay." I sigh. Maybe my new hobby won't be murder investigator.

She rubs my shoulder. "I'll keep my ears open and let you know if I hear anything, okay? But promise me you won't go looking for trouble."

I nod. She's always right, isn't she? I wouldn't know how to stop a vampire anyway. I still barely even know what it means to be one. All I can do is not be around any murders and stay out of prison. And meet a rabbi. That sounds slightly less terrifying than meeting a murderous vampire. Barely.

Why did I agree to this? Not the temple part, I can maybe handle that, especially if I don't have to go inside and face that constant agony, but why on earth did I agree to let her teach me how to drive there? I have absolutely no idea what I'm doing, and I can run faster than a car anyway. It's unnecessary and silly.

"You have superhuman reactions," she says for what must be the fourth time. She's still not yelling it, but she's sounding increasingly exasperated. "How do I keep having to pull the wheel to keep you from swerving into a wall."

"I was just righting the car."

She sighs, taking in a deep breath. I took a few anger management courses when they thought I needed those. I know exactly what that means. It's stressing me out so much more and making it that much harder to drive. "I know this is your first time. I get it."

"This is why we have my car. Why did you want to start with yours? Can't you just take over?"

"We're on the highway."

I jerk the wheel, trying to stay between the stupid dotted lines. "And we can move so quickly that we could open the doors and switch seats long before it hit anything or anything hit us."

She sighs. "Babe, please, just calm down and—"

"I can't. I don't know what I'm doing, and I can feel how upset you are."

"I'm not upset."

"Sure you're not."

She grabs the wheel and narrowly avoids a concrete corner next to an exit. Another deep breath. "I'm not upset. I'm maybe a little frustrated."

"A *little*?"

"Dinah, I'm not upset with you. Please look at the road."

"I thought I was." What am I doing wrong? All I have to do is point the car and step on the gas, but it keeps veering off from where I want it, and nothing seems to change that. "I don't want to learn to drive."

"It's okay. If you don't want to drive anymore, you don't have to, but we still have to finish this trip. I know it's scary the first time, but we're both immortal, so worst-case scenario, my insurance can cover the damage."

Or we kill someone. Like my dad, apparently. I still can't believe he's dead. I can't say I exactly care, but I'm definitely shocked. "Fine."

"And I will stop sounding so upset. I know I'm stressing you out."

There are so many things I could bite back with, but I can see that she's trying, and I'm clearly the problem here. I swerve to keep from drifting into a truck and am greeted with a sustained honk and shouted curse words that I can easily hear over the road and everyone else's radios.

"Is it hard to focus?"

"I can focus. I just don't know what I'm doing."

"Just grip the wheel at nine and three, like on a clock, and hold it steady. You don't need to breathe or anything, so I know you can hold still."

Was that not what I was doing? I try to picture a clock and adjust my hands but have to slam on the breaks to avoid hitting a car and get another honk for my trouble.

"That's better," she says, but I don't think she means it. She knows she's stressing me out, and she's trying to make me feel better. It's not working. I hate driving. I never want to do this again.

She leans into me, and I start to let go of the wheel so she can take over, but she covers the fingers of one of my hands and holds them in place. "Just like this," she whispers into my ear. I might be a little less anxious now. She guides my hand, and I just have to focus on the pedals and the feel of the wheel in my hands, our hands. It's easier. And not as scary with her helping me do it instead of silently judging me. Her hands turn mine, and she says, far too seductively, "Slow down."

We take an exit, though I have to hit the brakes a few times to get to what seems an acceptable speed, and rather than letting me get out and have her take over, she guides me the last few blocks to her synagogue.

"I can park," she says.

She doesn't have to tell me twice. I don't want to be behind the wheel of these death machines ever again. I leap from the car and let her take over. I feel like my heart should be racing, but it's silent in my chest. Was there not adrenaline running through me? Then what the hell was the matter with me? Am I really so scared that I don't even need my heart to start back up to mess me up?

She grins as she climbs out of the parked car and pulls out her cell phone, which reminds me yet again that I actually have one. I'm never going to get used to that. I should work on being better about calling Mia and my parole officer. "I'll let her know we're here."

"And somehow in one piece."

"You did fine." She kisses my cheek. I don't know how she could call that performance fine. I could've killed someone. "Hey, we're here. You said…yep, all right, see you in the shade." She pockets her phone and points to the side of the building. "There's a covered sitting area right there." We hurry to it to get out of the sun. In the car it wasn't as bad; her windows must be strongly tinted, but out in the open, it's like bathing in razor blades. Though still less painful than trying to drive.

She drops onto the bench of a picnic table. "It's a beautiful place, right?"

I shrug. I'd assumed it was the same temple I went to as a kid, but this doesn't look at all familiar. My mother changed synagogues? That seems so unlike her. And one with a woman rabbi? I guess she was never that sexist. She only had something against women when it involved me dating them. It still seems strange, but I suppose I could be overthinking it.

A woman, disappointingly lacking a beard, in a sharp suit and with a bouncy bob, hurries over to us, grinning broadly. She smells like summer. "Oh, Rachel, it's so good to see you. It's been months. And this must be Dinah."

I try to return the smile. I make a genuine effort. But I suspect it must look forced. I'm nervous, I've never been comfortable with religion, and I just had to drive a car.

"This is her. She's—"

"She's finally out. Oh, that must be so amazing. I can only think how I'd react if my Rebecca had been in prison. I don't think I'd have slept a wink for years. Of course, I suppose that would hardly affect you." She chuckles, and it's warm and genuine, and did she say she had a wife? My mother is seeing a lesbian rabbi? Not as in dating, that would be even more shocking, but she has a lesbian rabbi? What?

Rachel's grinning so hard that she must know exactly what's going through my head. Like she probably always does. She could've told me any of this, and I'd have probably been a lot more excited to see her. Unless this is her trying to convince me that my mother has changed. "I'm sure she'd be running the joint in no time."

"Only if that's decided by who makes the best brisket."

"Being a good cook does make you pretty popular in prison," I say. "Especially if you can do it with limited or weird ingredients. Everyone was always on good terms with anyone who could turn ramen and chips into a gourmet meal. Or anyone who was a good enough farmer to have fresh peppers and onions to add. They don't exactly rule the prison, but they don't have a rough time."

She turns to me with a pensive expression and slowly nods. "I wouldn't have thought of that, but it makes sense."

"Anything's better than having to live off the food from the cafeteria."

"And I suppose you were one of those popular people?"

I shake my head. "No. I still barely know what I'm doing in the kitchen any better than I do behind the wheel." Or with electronics. I can't even type. I know I keep pointing out that we have forever to figure things out in this changing world, but she's so far ahead of me, and I thought her lessons would let me catch up, but I feel like I'm only further behind.

"Well, so long as none of the others had any sharp wood, right?" Her laugh feels more forced this time. "But I suppose I'm glad to know my wife could survive prison." She sits by Rachel and leans in. "How is everything in paradise now? I trust you're doing better with her back."

"Yeah," she says, and she sounds like she means it. I suppose I shouldn't be surprised, but with how frustrated that driving lesson made her, I was a little worried. "It's honestly been amazing. I'm trying to get her all caught up on the world, but she just wants to work at my café."

"Free labor can be very helpful."

"I'd pay her," she shouts, giggling and swatting the rabbi. I never would've gotten away with that in Hebrew school. "But I'm trying to look after her while she figures out her own interests. We had our acting class earlier."

"That sounds fun. Have you taken salsa yet? Rebecca got me a few classes as an anniversary present, and it was a delight. And led to some fun afterward." She wiggles her eyebrows.

"You're so shameless," Rachel says. "I'm trying to make a good impression on my wife."

"And yet, you didn't let me perform the ceremony. Besides, she's been in prison, I'm sure my lewdness is only making it easier for her to adjust."

"She's not religious. I felt like a religious ceremony would be unfair to her."

How did I not even think about that? I can be so selfish. "Babe, you should've said. I know I don't believe in this stuff, but it matters to you." Though, then again, she hadn't exactly told me. And I'd barely even been willing to go through with the wedding. She'd forgiven my mother. But it's passed, it's been months, and I can't dwell on that. I love her, and I'm glad I went through with it.

She stares at the table, her fang digging so hard into her lip that a drop of blood slides out. I kiss her because I want to remind myself how much I love her because she absolutely deserves it with that bashful expression, and because I've never been one to let blood go to waste.

"Do you want to do another ceremony?" I ask.

"We could do it right here, right now. Renew your vows before me and Him."

Rachel shakes her head, still beaming so much that I can scarcely believe she means no. "If we're doing another ceremony, I want a real one with my friends and with yours too."

"I don't have—"

"So we'll do it for our one-year anniversary. Or ten. Or a hundred. I'm already married to you, and that's all I need, so if we're going to do it again, I want it to be perfect."

Rabbi Becker sighs. "I'll schedule you for June 2122. It should be beautiful, assuming the Earth has survived."

"I suspect we'll be able to do it sooner than that," Rachel says, still grinning at me. My saying I'd have a religious ceremony seriously meant that much? Why didn't she ever say anything? Or worse, why didn't I know? Right, because she'd never mentioned her religion before our wedding. She sacrificed having the ceremony she wanted because she was scared that I'd hate it. I don't want to ever let her feel like that again. "But we're not here for another wedding. I just wanted you two to finally meet. I know I never shut up about her."

"That's putting it lightly. I think I've heard her name more than Rebecca's."

"Am I really that bad?"

"Between you and your new mother-in-law, she's all either of you talk about."

I can't keep myself from cutting in. That doesn't make any sense. "My mother talks about me? Like, not just to criticize me and how much of a disappointment I am? Or to bitch about how I didn't get sent to one of the nicer prisons with all the white-collar criminals?"

"I know she wasn't always an easy woman," she says. "I wasn't there for a lot of it, but when she met me, let's just say that her biases were obvious, no matter how hard she tried to hide them. I can only imagine what growing up with that was like."

"She threw me out of her house."

She nods, looking far too guilty. I'm not sure I've ever seen a rabbi look guilty. I'm more used to annoyed. "She's come a long way."

"And it's too late."

"She just wants to talk to you."

Something in how she says it raises my hackles. It doesn't sound like she's explaining my mother's behavior or trying to get me to see her. It sounds like she's apologizing for something she's presently doing. That's why she looks guilty. I stand, looking between them. Rachel wouldn't have set this up. I have to believe that. I sniff the air, but while I smell humans, I don't remember what my mother smells like, and I wouldn't have the faintest idea how to tell if she was here. "What do you mean she wants to talk to me?"

"I didn't tell her you were coming. This isn't some setup."

But she is here. I look around for any sign of her and find an old woman in a window. Her eyes look familiar. And so does her face. But it's aged so much in the last thirty years that I can hardly recognize her. Has it really been thirty years? I was fifteen, then, and I'm forty-four now, so it's not far off. She looks so weak and pathetic, like she'd fall over in a stiff breeze.

"You don't have to talk to her," Rabbi Becker says.

I want to snap at her. To tell her that I know what she's trying to pull. But I don't know what I'm feeling. Do I know the way home? I could run it, but I'd have to figure out how to use that phone program without smacking into a wall or being noticed. "I'm not going to."

"Rabbi Becker, you didn't," Rachel finally says.

"I didn't tell her anything. She was already here, and I only realized she was watching us a minute ago."

Rachel crosses her arms, standing beside me, and glares at the old woman in the window. "I told her to leave you alone."

She hasn't come outside. She hasn't said a word. I should give her credit for that, but all I can feel looking into those eyes is the same terror and hatred that I felt when she slammed the front door in my face after she told me never to come back.

Rachel's hand closes over my fist. I didn't even realize I'd clenched it or that it was shaking. She puts her free arm around me. "Thanks for meeting with us, Rabbi."

"We can talk elsewhere," she says.

"Another time. I'm going to take her home."

As we pull away, I swear I hear my mother calling after us, but it's probably my imagination. I've never heard my mother sound that desperate.

Chapter Nineteen

The door closes, waking me from my accidental nap on the couch to find Rachel beaming down at me. "Morning, sleepy head."

I yawn.

"I'm sorry I've been away so much."

"It's okay. You're allowed to work."

"Yeah, but I'm supposed to be your alibi the next time a cop tries to accuse you of murder."

"You're my wife. I don't think they'll believe you."

She grumbles. "It just feels like nothing is going right this month. You've only been out for a few weeks, and I'm already back to work full-time, and your mom keeps calling me, and she was watching us at my synagogue, and people keep dying, and every time I try to do more, I end up trying to completely control your life like I'm your warden."

I shake my head, stifling another yawn so I can look as sympathetic as possible. I don't want her thinking I'm bored of her self-flagellation. "Babe, it's okay. It's been amazing."

"But it should be perfect." She flops onto the spot next to me, tears welling in her eyes.

"Did something happen?"

"Just your mom blowing up my phone all day, and when I finally answered to tell her to leave me alone, a cop was calling to try to talk to me about you."

Did she yell at the cop? "How did that go?"

"I wanted to tell him to fuck off anyway." She groans, leaning into me. "Probably didn't make you look great."

"It's fine. I've been keeping my phone on me, and I haven't left the house."

"You're still a prisoner."

I lean into her, breathing in that beautiful lilac scent as I plant a kiss on top of her head. "I'm not. I'm free, and it's been amazing. I'm just trying to be careful not to be around any murders."

She sighs but doesn't say anything.

"You're being too hard on yourself. You can't control everything."

"Even though I keep trying to."

"Yes, you're trying to look after me, and it's wonderful. I love being here. In *our* house. I never thought I'd be able to say that."

"Yeah?" She pulls back just enough to show me the hint of a smile.

"Yes. And I see you every day and hang out with you at work, and we take all these classes that are really interesting."

She grumbles. "I'm not there for all of them."

"Sure, but you join me for a lot, and you're the one who convinced me to take them. I'm trying to see what's out there and what this new world is like. I still don't know what I'm doing, and it's overwhelming, but I know I have you there."

Her smile grows. "Always."

"Exactly." I squeeze her to me. "There were murders at prison too. I'm used to dealing with suspicious cops. I don't like it, but apparently, that's part of having been a murderer."

"You're not—"

"And none of that is your fault."

She squeezes me. "I could've stopped you from going to prison."

"You're doing more than enough. I'm a month into a life that I already love."

"You do?" She sounds so uncertain, so scared. Does she really think she's making me do all of this against my will?

"I do." I laugh and kiss her again. "So stop beating yourself up over it. Honestly, with the exception of my mother crashing it, the worst day on the outside with you is still better than the best day in prison."

"That's a pretty low bar."

I shrug. I should've come up with something better to say. "Prison wasn't as bad as people make it out to be. You get used to it. You have better days and worse days. Sometimes, things were pretty good, and it's a lot simpler than life on the outside."

"I've certainly been keeping your life simple," she grumbles.

"Babe, stop. You keep acting like you're forcing me to do all this."

"I dragged you to an acting class, I made you drive, I convinced you to meet Rabbi Becker, I picked out your car and our house and your phone. How is it any different than the state doing it?"

Has she really been that worried about that? "If I didn't want to be here, I'd leave."

"You didn't want to be in prison and still stayed there for twenty-five years."

Maybe part of me wanted to stay there. I've picked out so many excuses, but maybe I just wanted to punish myself for what I did. But that's hardly helpful to say now, and I think she's suggested it before, anyway. "Prison didn't care about me. The warden wasn't jumping up and down planning everything because she couldn't wait to show me a taste of the world. You're not forcing me to do anything. You're trying to help me find my way in a world that I never really knew. It's wonderful, and I'm so glad I have you here. Your rabbi is weird, and I still don't get it, but she wasn't the issue there. You didn't tell my mom to spy on us."

"No, I was just her friend for twenty years."

"Because I was gone. Nothing has been that easy, but that's not because I've been out of prison. Nothing has ever been easy. Maybe we're just terrible at being alive—I mean, it would explain why we're dead—maybe we have terrible luck, or maybe this is what it's like for everyone. We've had a rough few decades, but life doesn't go perfectly for anyone. I knew far too many women who went to prison because they had one unlucky day where going a little over the speed limit killed a person they couldn't have seen, or they were in the wrong place at the wrong time with the wrong drugs on them. Things that people do all the time that don't normally send them to prison. Sometimes, you're just unlucky."

She crosses her arms. "So we're unlucky?"

"We did get murdered in our sleep and then arrested a few hours later. Well, only I did the second part. My point is, things don't have to go perfectly."

"I still want them to. I want to give you everything you deserve."

"You already have. I have a beautiful wife, an amazing house I still don't know my way around, a car I intend to never touch, and I can do anything I want."

"And what do you want to do?"

I smirk, and that smile finally spreads across her entire face. "I want to get some food, have some blood, and maybe finally break in this couch."

"I think I can help with that."

"Oh, I have little doubt."

The smile turns playful, and her fang does its adorable thing. "I'll order pizza. Go grab us some blood from the fridge."

"Perfect." A night in with her, without all the hazards and insanity of the outside world, is exactly what I need. The couch sex is a nice bonus.

My life may actually be perfect. I have a giant TV and the most comfortable lap in the world to lay my head in. The couch and the fuzzy blanket are great too, but I'm more invested in the TV and the lap.

"I can't believe you convinced me to watch soap operas," Rachel says for what has to be the fifth time.

"You're the one who kept putting on the next episode."

"I had to know what happened."

I've gotten her hooked. The thought sends a pang of guilt over the last thing I got her hooked on, but soap operas are slightly less destructive. "I'm glad you're enjoying it so much."

"I didn't say that," she insists too quickly and with far too much force to be believable. "They're compelling and manipulative, but that doesn't make them good."

"And yet, you're putting on the next one."

"I need to know if she's really pregnant."

"Oh, if that's all you want, I could tell you. I've seen it already." Her eyes widen. "Don't you dare."

"Admit you like it."

Rachel gnashes her teeth, grumbling.

"Come on."

"Fine. Now stop squirming so much, and let's watch."

I settle in as the titles play, and a car door slams outside. I spent years learning to ignore my senses and focus on whatever I was watching or reading, despite being able to hear everything everyone was watching or saying in the entire prison dorm, but the boots treading the dirt outside worry me. They sound like the guards walking in the grass. It's the heavy leather boots that cops and soldiers tend to buy.

The show starts. I haven't done anything wrong, so I don't need to worry about the cop.

Tires roll to a stop outside, and another set of boots slams on pavement. "*This* is the place?" says a woman with a thick accent like the villain in every movie in the mid-2000s. "I don't see too many vampires in the suburbs."

"This is it, and I had to go through a lot to cover this up for you. That's two precincts and decades of files."

"You'll get your hundred dollars, same as usual." What the hell is going on outside? I glance at the TV to find it paused and look up to see Rachel's head tilted and her concentration clearly on the conversation outside.

"You don't know what this took. This isn't my case, and it had already been reported. I can't make that go away without..." He makes a terrified yelp.

"I'm not Dorenia," she says, her voice oddly calm. "I'm willing to hand over your money and let you walk away because that's your deal with her, and I don't want to step on her toes, but if you want to renegotiate, that opens up several counteroffers. You take money to let monsters go free after they've murdered people. So how about instead of paying you, I take your head, just like I would any other monster."

"Uh," he stammers.

"Last chance, Officer Leopold." A door opens, and more boots crunch outside. How many people are there? I only smell two; that's strange. Oh. The scent of a vampire is always so much milder, so empty, and I'm pressed against another one. Why is there a vampire threatening someone outside and talking about killing monsters?

"It'll just be a minute, Chuck. The machete or the money, Leopold. I have a preference, but I'll let you choose."

Rachel grips my shoulders and pushes me up to sitting. Right. It sounds like they're after me. But why? I don't understand. I look at her, confused, and she seems to think I mean I don't know what we're doing rather than I don't know why the issue is happening in the first place. She points at the back door, just past the living room.

She's right. The reasons don't matter. Someone is after me. Us? We have to get out of here. We move as silently as we can. One of them is a vampire, and that means she'll likely be able to hear as well as we can.

"I'll take the money," the man shouts.

"I was afraid you'd say that." Something thumps, and for a second, I think she cut his head off anyway, but he makes another terrified sound as something trickles onto the pavement before his car speeds away.

Rachel slides the door open, and a blur rushes toward us before we can step outside. Rachel jumps back as a machete shatters the glass.

"Two of you? I was told there was one." The strange woman hesitates, studying us, seeming to not even notice the chunk of glass protruding from the sleeve of her leather jacket. She's smaller than

I'd imagined from how scared that guy had been. Taller than me, but who isn't, though she's a little taller than Rachel too. She's wearing a cowboy hat, and I'd have trouble taking it seriously if the revolver on her hip didn't add a certain threat to it. It's the crazy cowboy from the Community Center. I was right. She is the murderer. She must be.

Rachel backs up slowly, glancing between me and the kitchen like she's trying to tell me something. Grab a knife? Okay, I can do that. "I don't know what you're after, but you can have anything."

I feel guilty running, but it's not to get away. I wonder if this is how she felt all those years ago. I pull open one drawer only to slam it shut and try another. Where the hell do we keep the knives?

The machete carves into the wall a few feet away as Rachel jumps back, shaking. She's probably never been in a fight before. "Please, we don't want any trouble."

"That's what they always say once it comes to this. Maybe the people you killed didn't want any trouble either. Did you think of that?"

What the hell is she talking about? Was I right about her killing criminals too? Rachel gives me another panicked look, and I finally find the right drawer. I pull out a massive carving knife just in time to block a swing from the monster who broke into our home. It stops inches from Rachel's throat. She gasps, her mouth opening, but no words coming out. She's not hurt, but she's clearly terrified.

For that matter, I'm also terrified. I've been in fights before, but those were with humans. I can barely even see what this thing is doing. She moves toward me, her lip curling in some grotesque imitation of a smile. It would look friendly if her eyes weren't so full of hate. The blade shimmers, and all I can do is jerk my hands to the side to try to stop it. The tip of her machete hovers just in front of my eye, barely held in place by my knife, and she laughs. She's not scared or wondering how I'm not dead. She's not trying to talk to me. I manage to put up the barest hint of a fight, and she starts laughing. What is wrong with this monster?

Someone slams at the front door. It must be that other person. He's human, at least. He can't be this terrifying.

"Get away from her," Rachel shouts, and the monster spins, shoving my knife back, slicing my brow, and stops another knife. Rachel must've grabbed one while I was preoccupied. The monster is pushing on it, bringing the knife closer to Rachel with every passing nanosecond. She's too strong. Too fast.

"Let her go," I shout, holding the knife out like I know what I'm doing with it. What can I even do? She's killed so many people, and I've barely even killed one, and that was an accident.

The monster looks between us, confusion in her eyes.

I have to save Rachel. I rush toward the creature, shoving my knife for her throat only for her to kick me off my feet. My head slams into the floor and everything rings.

"Stop," Rachel whimpers.

"You don't sound like I'd expected," the monster says.

"What the hell is that supposed to mean?" she asks.

I try to sit up, but the world keeps spinning. She's going to kill Rachel. I have to stop her.

"You're both trying to protect each other, and you seem to have no idea what you're doing. Have you ever killed anyone before?" She steps back, looking between us.

"We haven't," Rachel says. "Unlike you, we're not murderers." She slashes at her only for the knife to be knocked out of her hand and buried in the wall.

I finally clamber to my feet and try to swing for the creature's head. The vampire picks me up by the throat and slams me into the wall, sending a cloud of plaster and stars raining before my eyes. I think I see her eyes narrow, but it could just as easily be the world doing it. "Where were you last night?" she asks. It sounds hesitant. She's not as murderous and angry as she was a minute ago.

Blood sprays my face, and I think for a second that she stabbed me, but I slump to the floor and find a severed hand still grasping at my throat. I do my best to pry it free, but it's like it's trying to strangle me.

"Drop the knife, or I will make you drop it," the vampire says. "I'm not trying to kill you."

A knife clatters to the floor in front of me just as I pull the hand free and toss it next to Rachel's discarded and bent cleaver.

"You look terrified and confused." She leans down, picking up her hand. "Do you have any blood?"

Rachel whimpers and points at the fridge. Terrified and confused seems to be putting it mildly. Tears are streaming down her face as she helps me to my feet.

The strange vampire sheaths her machete and opens the fridge. It's our chance. We could get the drop on her. She closes it and turns back to us as she takes a sip of one of our blood bags, and her hand fuses back to where it had been. I didn't know we could do that. She gives it a few tentative squeezes. Neither of us attacked her when we had the chance. I really thought one of us would.

"Are you really not going to kill us?" Rachel asks, her voice barely more than a squeak.

"That depends on how you answer a few questions, but it's looking like a no. Did one of you kill anyone last night?"

We both shake our heads.

"Good answer. I believe you. And what about when you were in prison?" she asks, her gaze settling on me. The hate is still there, but it seems tempered with something like suspicion. "Did you kill those girls?"

I shake my head again.

"Interesting. Have you ever killed anyone?"

"One person," I say. "When I first turned. The one I was arrested for."

She nods, turning toward Rachel. "And you?"

"The same person."

"And yet, you didn't go to prison." She sighs and shakes her head. "It's better than most. If I was to go after everyone the law didn't, well, I'd be busier than I already am. If either of you are lying to me—"

"We're not," Rachel shouts.

I nod in confirmation.

The front door bursts open, wooden shards pattering on the wooden floor. "God damn it, Chuck," the woman says. "They didn't kill them."

"They're still vampires, aren't they?" A man groans from our broken door. I can't see him past the wall, but I can hear a chunk of door frame swinging from where it splintered.

The woman looks between the two of us again. "They're innocent. We're barking up the wrong tree."

"Then let's get back out there," he says, still hidden behind a wall.

"You can't just..." Rachel trails off. "You broke into our house and tried to kill us!"

She puts her hand on her hip, far too close to the revolver for my comfort. "Maybe they can tell us something we don't know."

"I'm not talking to monsters."

"Oh, just come in here," she whines, and I finally see the face of the man who broke my door. He's scruffy, with a mustache and close-cropped, graying brown hair and a cleaver in a sheath on his belt. I think I've just met my first vampire hunters.

Chapter Twenty

The strange new guy, Chuck, sits on our dining room table, shiftily glancing between Rachel and me, his hand occasionally darting toward his cleaver, only for him to cross his arms again.

"Could you use a chair?" Rachel says. "You've already destroyed enough of my house."

He glances down, his suspicious expression growing bashful. "Uh, yeah." He stands and pulls out a chair, sitting, adjusting his knife as he does. He doesn't draw it. He smells human, so if he did, we'd be faster, but people wanting to hurt me never gets easier to deal with. "You're sure they didn't do it, Kalila?" he asks the woman for what must be the third time.

"They're far too incompetent for that." She sighs, giving the two of us a look I can't quite place. She keeps insulting me, but given that she probably gave me a concussion, I'm not too keen on fighting her over it, so I sit and calmly drink my blood.

He grumbles. "They're still vampires."

She smiles, her fangs showing.

He grumbles louder. "I've got a friend who can fix your doors." He sounds in pain as he says it. Who would ever be willing to help vampires, am I right?

"And the wall." Rachel points at where I was slammed into the wall and then where the knife had been shoved through it.

"Yeah. It…yeah." He sighs. "How'd we fuck this one up?"

The horrifying monster who tried to kill me, also known as Kalila, mutters, "Bad info. Someone keeps killing these women, and apparently, no one bothered to tell me that she had an alibi for most of them."

"What about the other one?"

"There was a roomful of prison guards and inmates watching both of them during the first murder. Dorenia confirmed it. Our lead just sucked."

"Think they didn't look hard enough, or what?"

She shrugs and shakes her head. "It's tough to say. I tried calling Marsden, but I only got his voice mail. Could be as simple as they were clearly killed by vampires, and she was the nearest vampire. It's not a hard deduction to make."

"And yet, you keep insisting it's a bad one."

"I'm not risking killing another innocent."

"Would that suggest you've killed innocents before?" Rachel asks, sounding increasingly annoyed. There are crazy murderers sitting in our destroyed house, and she has probably never had to deal with that before. Sometimes in prison, it wasn't worth fighting someone who thought they could do whatever they wanted. Even if you won, all it would do was put a target on your back. I'm not sure if Kalila is quite like that, but I don't particularly want to piss her off. She barely even reacted when Rachel chopped her hand off.

I clutch at my throat. There's not so much as a bruise, but I swear I can still feel it, see her severed hand grasping me, blood pouring out. I've been through some crazy stuff in my life, but that's some *Evil Dead* shit. At least, it didn't keep trying to attack me. I'd have had a damn heart attack then. This whole fiend thing is too much. How does Rachel put up with it? I'm used to criminals and murderers and people who want to hurt me but not ones who don't stop no matter what you do to them.

If Kalila decided that I was guilty, I wouldn't have any recourse. She would kill me. I could run, I could fight, I could beg, but no matter how much I hurt her, she'd still get me in the end. That look of annoyance as she lost her hand when she was crushing my throat won't leave my head. She must've already decided that we were innocent, as I don't think for a second that the injury would've made her reconsider. She looked confused, then annoyed, and that entire time, she was strangling me.

If I needed to breathe, I'd be dead.

I feel Rachel's eyes on me, but I focus on the blood. I need to know that I'm okay, and if I drink enough, apparently, I can heal from anything. She reattached her damn hand.

"Babe?" Rachel asks.

I nod.

She rubs my thigh. "You look kinda freaked."

"Are you not?" I ask, finally returning her gaze. She looks annoyed. Just like Kalila had. Not at me but at the interlopers who tried to kill us. I thought I was handling this better than her because I've been through similar, but maybe I was wrong. Maybe I'm just too terrified to do anything, and she's the one who's used to this. What has she gone through at the Community Center? We've spent so long catching up, but I've still missed over two decades of her life.

"Honestly?" She looks between me and them. "I'm shocked anyone actually cares that much. We've had people go missing all the time for years, and nothing has seemed to ever come of it. I'm not used to anybody trying to avenge all the humans who fiends kill."

"I'm trying to get out of the vengeance game," Kalila says. "It makes you sloppy. Now, I'm only trying to keep them from hurting any more people."

"You're the one who tried to break up the slave market, aren't you?" Why does she sound like she admires her? Kalila tried to kill us. Do I need to remind her? I *am* the one who got the concussion, right?

Her eyes narrow. "Why?"

Rachel laughs. Why is she laughing? Did I get brain damage? "I can think of quite a few reasons I might be bothered by a slave market."

"Ah." She doesn't give any more than that.

"I'm sorry it didn't work out. They're still selling people."

"Like I said, it makes you sloppy. If I'd been thinking first, I'd have made sure I could end it rather than get kicked out and blowing my best chance. I just couldn't stand idly by and watch them do that. Especially to a kid."

"My rabbi says we should never seek vengeance as it will only harm us, but we should always seek justice. I think saving a kid sounds a lot more like the latter."

"My imam was killed in an air strike while he was teaching children. I wonder what he would've said."

Rachel gulps, her eyes widening.

"Charlie's doing a lot better thanks to you," Chuck says to Crazy Murder Lady with an oddly grateful laugh. Rachel probably needed that save. Who's Charlie? Isn't that his name? I guess that wouldn't make sense. "Still kinda terrified of you, though."

She nods. "I'd do it again in a heartbeat, but that's kind of the problem. Hard to actually do anything about that damn market if I can't resist chopping off the auctioneer's head my first chance."

"No one else seems to want to do anything about it," Rachel says. "Or much of anything else to minimize harm. A lot of us have to eat people to live, but—"

Her eyebrow twitches. "But it's not much of an excuse. Especially when they seem to do a lot more than that. But I'll happily kill the ones who're eating kids for their health. We're the invasive species. Humans don't even know what they're in for."

"Well, this is horrifying," Chuck says. "I can't take you anywhere."

"You're the one who broke the door after we already knew they were innocent."

"You didn't say anything," he shouts, sitting up.

She snorts. "Call your friend. Get things fixed..." She trails off as her phone starts ringing. "Officer Marsden," she says into it. "Glad to hear from you. Yeah, that lead didn't pan out."

There's a faint sound on the other end. I can normally hear people's phone calls perfectly. I suppose when you have super hearing and kill people all the time, you might keep your phone pretty quiet. The voice sounds familiar, but I can't place anything he's saying.

"Yes, I'm quite certain."

The voice mutters something.

"What do you mean there was another one? Then why are you surprised she's not the killer? Where?"

I can faintly make out the words, "prince" and "Wales." Unless the murder was in another country, that probably means the Prince of Wales Park a few blocks from here.

"I'll be right there. Chuck, we've—"

He stands, raising his own phone and tapping something out. "I've sent the address and instructions. I'll pay for it."

"Dorenia will pay you back."

"She better. It's gonna cost almost everything in my bank account."

"Damn, maybe you should get better at your job." She heads toward the still busted door without a word to us. "Vampires tend to have money."

He chases her. "Some of us don't have superspeed."

"Maybe you're just getting old."

"You're older than me."

Kalila laughs as they walk out into our front yard, and I look to Rachel. She looks as confused as I am. "What the hell?" I ask.

Rachel turns toward the open door. "Did you hear that? There was another death. That should prove you didn't do it."

"I think we already proved that."

"But not to the cops. She was on the phone with one just then. Maybe this will finally convince them."

Wait. She'd called him Marsden, and I knew he'd sounded familiar. She really did rattle my brain. "Fuck."

She stares at me. "Babe?"

This isn't making any sense. Why would he be calling her about a murder in Etobicoke? He's a cop in Kitchener. There's no way it's the same jurisdiction. "Marsden is the cop who kept hassling me about this."

"The one from your prison?"

I nod.

She looks as confused as I am. "But why would he be in Toronto?" She stares at the table. "I don't get it. So he's been going after you for these killings? Why would he be so convinced that you were the culprit? And would he have the authority to investigate one nearby?"

"I'm not sure."

She jumps to her feet, her eyes wide. "We should tell her."

My jaw drops. "The crazy murderer?"

"She's trying to keep people safe."

"By attacking people without checking if they're guilty first."

Rachel stares at me and sighs. "I've wanted to do just what she did so many times, for decades, and I've never had the courage."

"Try to strangle me?"

"I've done that before."

"Rachel, I'm fucking serious!"

She flinches, staring at me, looking utterly shocked. "Babe…"

"She tried to kill us. I thought I'd be the one handling this better, but you don't even seem bothered."

"Of course I'm bothered."

"She. Tried. To. Kill. Us."

"And she stopped when she found out we were innocent."

"You don't think that should've come up first? Maybe you should be sure before you try to kill someone."

She nods, but she doesn't look convinced by what I feel is a pretty strong argument. "I'm not saying she's our new best friend, but she's trying to do something about whoever keeps killing these people. You're the prison superhero. I know you care about it too."

"You kept telling me not to be a superhero."

"Apparently, there's somebody else doing it. And we know something that she doesn't. We have to tell her that the cop she's trusting is up to something."

"We don't even know that."

Rachel puts her hands on her hips. "He's working a case outside of his jurisdiction while telling people that you're the killer when he knew full well that you had an alibi. You'd already gone over all of this with him before, and it was why he tried to arrest your friend."

My stomach drops. My friend, who was the second victim. It hadn't even occurred to me before. What if Marsden is involved? I hope the fucker kills Kalila, but there's too much here that doesn't add up, and it's all coming back to him. "Okay, fine." I groan. This is such a terrible idea.

"So we can go after her?" She grins. "We can investigate a murder?"

"You keep telling me not to get involved in this stuff."

"And that's entirely correct. We shouldn't. Normally. But we need to clear your name if we want to have any chance at a life."

"And you want to fawn over the woman who tried to murder us."

"I'm not..." She reaches for my hand and seems surprised when I don't pull away. She takes it. "I'm sorry."

She always seems to respect women who do horrible things to me. I don't know what to think of that. I shrug.

"I think she's probably a terrible person who's barely holding it together but is trying to do some good with that. I know that feeling."

"You're not a terrible person."

"And yet, I keep seeming to befriend them." She sighs. So she came to that conclusion too. "I know what it's like to do things that you know you shouldn't be doing. To feel completely out of control and unable to stop yourself. It's why I needed Him. Maybe it means I let other people off a little too easily for the things they've done." Is that why? I hadn't even considered that. "I'm not saying that we need to like her, only that she tried to do something good, and now she's trying to stop a killer, and we have information that she needs. Please."

"Do you know how to get to Prince of Wales Park?"

She rushes toward the broken door, grabbing the keys from the bowl still sitting peacefully on its table. "I'll drive."

Chapter Twenty-one

I had assumed that it would be easy to find a murder scene in a park. Aren't they supposed to cordon it off with crime scene tape and everything? There's no way the murder was fake, is there? Or could I have misheard what he said? Maybe there's a different Prince of Wales. We sure have enough locations named after the British monarchy. It could've been Prince of Wales Dry Cleaning for all I know.

I breathe in, closing my eyes, trying to find any trace. There's the lilac and deathlike scent of my wife near me, though it seems stronger than usual. Maybe because she's scared? There's the metal and rust of the gates and basketball court, the wood chips and plastic of the playground, the scents of animals and water; the night is full of smells, and blood is in the air. That murder had to have happened here, but where? The park isn't that big, it should not be this difficult to find them.

"There," Rachel shouts, grabbing my hand and dragging me toward what appears to be a cordoned off crime scene. It's on the other side of the bathrooms. I don't know how I missed that.

No one else is there, save for a body, drained of blood, crime scene tape, and some discarded cigarette butts. Did we miss them? Was it all some trick?

"Where are they?" she asks.

We look around, searching the entire park again, smelling the air, checking every last spot, and all the cars. I never saw Kalila's vehicle, but it sounded big, and all that's here are a few sedans so covered in rust, they may not be able to move any longer. And through all of it, I smell Rachel. There's that same mix of lilac and dead. I know she didn't kill anyone. She'd have smelled like fresh blood. I trust her, and we were together watching soap operas for hours. I don't know bodies that well, but it still smells pretty fresh.

I stop in the parking lot, trying to see if there's anything I missed. Could there be another car somewhere? That Crazy Murder Lady that we're for some reason trying to help probably wouldn't have stayed around without anyone to kill. "We must've just missed them," I say. Rachel would be able to hear me anywhere in the park.

"But what if that asshole is…" She trails off, coming to a stop by me, looking worried, her hair windswept. "I don't know. He has to be up to something."

"Yeah, probably trying to get me killed." I sigh. There's definitely something I'm missing, but I don't know what it is. "I doubt she's in any danger, probably just tracking down another vampire."

What could've happened here? Why couldn't my powers be better for reconstructing crime scenes? Everyone on TV can just look at the scene and know everything. They'd see footprints in the grass and be able to tell who was talking and how the conversation went. But this is a park, and there are footprints everywhere.

Crazy Murder Lady and Marsden were probably both here, likely by the body. I smell again, but there doesn't seem to have been a living person here recently.

He'd originally sent her after me when he should've known better. Could he have told her something that'd make her go back to my place? We left with the door open, so he could've even gone back to plant evidence, but he wouldn't have known that we'd follow.

Would he?

"We can't just give up," Rachel says. "What if he's trying to kill her too? He clearly has something against vampires."

That's true. Or at least, he has something against me. He said that his father had investigated my case. He might've been close to the cop I killed and told him stories about me. Is that all this is about, or is it the vampire thing?

The body still lies there, as dead and empty of blood as before. As Millie had been. Could it really be the same killer? Why would Marsden have tracked it all the way here? Is it because he thinks it's me, and he's decided that we have some personal grudge?

"Why is Marsden in Toronto?" I ask.

"To get revenge?"

"But then, why was he the one investigating this body? And why aren't there any other cops?" That must mean something. Wouldn't they normally stick around to keep away anyone who'd want to mess with the crime scene? They haven't even moved the body. Surely, CSI would've done that, at least.

I step closer, ducking under the tape.

"Dinah, you can't go in there. They're going to think you're the killer."

"You're telling me that they investigated a crime and left the body, taped off, with no one watching over it? And that it's being run by a cop from another city? None of that makes any sense." There's something odd about the body. I move closer, trying to figure it out. It's a woman, just like all the other victims, and her neck is torn open, but there's the slight puncture marks of fangs at the edges of the tear. It was definitely a vampire who killed her.

And there's the faint scent of lilac. Just like when I first got to my cottage. I thought it was my imagination, as Rachel couldn't have been anywhere near me, but he could've been. A cop who kept breaking into that prison for his food. To kill my friends.

The scent had been there when we were at the soup kitchen too. Lilac and death. I thought that she stayed around to keep an eye on me, but it was him. "Babe, why do you always smell like lilac?"

"It's just the lotion I've always used. I know how much you like it. Why? What does that have to..." She trails off, her eyes widening. She smells it too. "What is it?"

Is that really all it is? He uses the same lotion? The body that he claimed to have called in but didn't smells like lilac. Because he's a vampire. I held my breath when I saw him before because I was starving and was scared I'd eat him. It hadn't been a risk. He wasn't food.

How could I have been so stupid? So blind.

I know that I'm in way over my head and that I don't have any training for this, but I'm the one whose life he keeps trying to ruin, and for what? What the hell does he want? "Marsden's the killer," I say.

Her eyes go even wider. "We have to stop him." She doesn't sound excited or even scared; it's simply a statement of fact.

"Worried about Crazy Murder Lady?" How can she act like this? I understand how she feels about the slave auction. It's not like my people didn't go through that too, but Kalila only did it because she's an insane murderer. She's not some superhero, and I don't know how Rachel can act like she respects her. Especially when she always said I wasn't allowed to be a superhero. How has she changed this much? How can she respect the person who was trying to choke the life out of me barely an hour ago? First my mother and then this. Is this really the same person I loved?

She rolls her eyes. "Kalila can take care of herself. I think we learned that quite well."

"Exceedingly."

"I'm worried about *you*. About us. He keeps trying to frame you for...who knows why."

To get revenge? A hatred of his own kind? I guess we'll find out. There's a cop who's trying to ruin my life and keeps killing innocent women. Only one person would both believe me and potentially be able to do anything about it. I pull my phone from my pocket, grateful I remembered it, hit ignore on the call from my mother, and call back the only other person to call me.

"Hello?" A deep voice answers. "I never thought you'd actually be the one to call me. Are you in trouble?"

You could say that. "Uh, Officer MJ..." Where can I begin that won't make me sound insane? "You know how I'm not supposed to be around criminals or anything?"

He stays silent.

"There's a cop who's been harassing me and is a vampire and doesn't even work in this city, and he keeps killing people, and there's a dead woman right here. It looks like a crime scene, but there are no cops, and no humans have been here, and he sent a crazy woman after me, and she broke my doors and I..." Didn't I have a plan? "I need your help to stop him."

There's no answer for long enough that I'm worried he's tracking me and about to call the cops. Does he need thirty seconds, or does he already have whatever he'd need for that from my cell phone alone? "I'll be right there."

"It's Officer Marsden. From Kitchener. Call him. Tell him that you found me or something. I don't know what he's planning, but if we don't stop him, then innocent women will keep dying. I need you to believe me. Please."

"I believe you, Dinah. Like I said, I know you're not a killer."

I breathe out a sigh of relief. I don't know who else I could've turned to. Mia? Maybe she'd have some contact who could help, but the parole officer seems easier. Or maybe this is just me falling on a sword, as usual, and expecting him to take me back to prison to keep everyone else safe.

"Did you leave any evidence on the body? If not, you should call it in, but if there's a chance, we'll have to dispose of it."

Could I have? I stepped near it, and I wasn't careful about my hair. And we walked all over the park, so our shoe prints and hair could be anywhere. "Maybe."

"All right. I'll make some calls and be there soon. You're at Prince of Wales Park, right?"

"I am."

"Go back home, and I'll meet you there. I know someone who'll be more than happy to have a fresh body to eat, but I have no idea what I'm going to say to this cop. Are you sure you need to meet him? If you have enough evidence, we can report him."

"I have his smell."

He grumbles. "Great. Head home and don't move. I'll be there soon." He hangs up, and I'm left still panicked but with at least a glimmer of hope.

Rachel clears her throat. "Are you going to get out of the crime scene now?"

Right. I should do that. I leap over the tape, and we hurry back to her car. Apparently, we're going to confront a murderer. I can't say it'll be my first time, but this one has superstrength, and I'm not liking my chances. Maybe I am still falling on a sword, even if it's not the one I thought it was, but there's no one else who can stop him. It's Rachel, me, and my parole officer against a deranged and corrupt cop and anyone he can convince to do the job for him. What's the worst that could happen?

Chapter Twenty-two

I was expecting a door," MJ's voice calls from the foyer. "I told you they were broken."

His footsteps sound through the house until he finds us in the living room. "Your explanation was a little confusing."

"Well, excuse me," I whine. "I was a little panicked at the time."

"And you're not now?" Rachel asks.

I glower at her. That's just hurtful. I'm somewhat, mostly, moderately calmed down. There's a cop who keeps killing women around me, maybe to frame me, what's there to be concerned about over that? And he's a vampire who's a lot more used to killing people and is clearly way more practiced with his powers and has a gun and the legal authority to kill without any consequences. Nothing to fear at all. "I'm somewhat more collected."

"I know, babe." She wraps an arm around me and kisses my temple. I want to grump or pull away, or at least not look so terrified and weak in front of my parole officer, but I don't think I can bring myself to do it. I've already had one vampire try to kill me today. I'm not up for whatever is about to happen, and yet for some reason, I was dumb enough to decide to confront an evil vampire. Because I always put everyone before me. He'll keep killing innocent women if I don't stop him, and it'll all be my fault, and I need to do something about it, but I'm gonna be terrified the whole time.

MJ towers over the back of the couch, looking down at us. His friendly face looks worn away by anxiety. "I called him and said that I'd talk to you and get you to hand yourself over."

"We're not—"

"I know. It was the best way to get him here."

"Okay." I breathe in, trying not to let the fear overwhelm me. So he invited the monster to our house? Why did I think this was a good idea?

Rachel kisses the top of my head, and it makes it very difficult to focus on my terror. "We can stop him. We outnumber him, and he doesn't know it's a trap."

"He's a murderer, we're not. Don't correct me, Officer MJ."

He laughs dryly and shakes his head. "I wasn't going to say otherwise. I'm not sure you're all that capable of murder."

"I'm going to have to be."

"Is he the one who broke your door?"

"No," Rachel says. "But he sent them. I'm just hoping she's not listening to him now."

He stares at her, not saying anything, clearly waiting for us to elaborate.

"It was some vampire vigilante. She's the one who attacked the slave market."

"Damn. Respect."

"Yeah."

I cross my arms and pull back to glower at her. "She still tried to kill us."

"Yeah, because some cop told her that we were murderers, presumably the same one who's going around murdering people."

"Then she should've figured it out."

"Maybe she should have," Rachel says consolingly. "I'm not saying she's perfect, only that she's trying to do good. Just like we are by stopping him."

I grumble.

MJ looks around with a heavy sigh. "Do you have weapons? Anything we can use?"

Rachel lifts the kitchen knives sitting on the table.

"Great, of course the one parolee to not violate the terms of her parole had to be the one I have to defend from a vampire." He draws his pistol, looking around again. "Do you smell him? Or detect him with any other vampire senses? I told him to give me twenty minutes to talk you into surrendering and then come meet me here, but I didn't expect him to actually wait that long. I'd only made the call right before I came in."

I close my eyes, breathing in, focusing on each of my senses. There's a human nearby, his blood pumping deliciously through his veins, and a too strong musky cologne smell floating from him, there are animals outside, there's the telltale lilac and death of the woman I love, but is there more of that? Why did he have to use the same lotion or at least something else lilac-scented? It makes it so much harder to pick him out.

Wait, no.

Rachel stiffens, gripping my forearm.

There's another scent. It's not quite the same. It's more alcoholic, like a lilac-scented aftershave. No one ever tells you vampires have to keep shaving for eternity.

Is that really him? Where is he? I can't place it.

It's not getting any closer. It's vaguely in the air, and that's it. There're no footsteps or tires grinding on the road outside. There's nothing suggesting he's anywhere nearby except that I can vaguely make out his scent.

"He's around here, I think," Rachel says.

I nod.

MJ raises his gun, pointing it toward the front door. "We should go upstairs. It looked easier to defend. We can funnel him into the hallway."

Right. The couch probably wasn't the best place to wait, but we got home, grabbed knives, and I couldn't even think. I just plopped down where it was comfortable and waited for the fear to pass. "Yeah," I say, forcing myself to my feet. We have to act. He's here. But doesn't that mean he can hear what we're saying?

Is MJ lying to draw him out, or does he really want us to go upstairs? He seems to know more about fiends than I do, so I'd think he'd think of that, but he may not know quite how sensitive our hearing can be. He doesn't seem to know any other vampires.

Or maybe it's because we were already talking like it was a trap, so he thinks that we already blew it?

I may have been overestimating him because he winces and says, "All right, Dinah. Officer Marsden should be here any minute. I appreciate your cooperating."

It's possible Marsden didn't hear us before, I guess.

MJ steps toward the front door and the stairs and jerks his head, indicating we should follow.

Rachel stands, grabs the knives, and hands me one. She forces a smile, but she looks as scared as I feel.

We move after him. The scent still isn't any closer. Maybe he really didn't hear.

MJ reaches the door and starts to go down the hallway to the stairs. Even if we can't make it to the upstairs hallway, this would still help funnel him, right? We just shouldn't have waited someplace with two open doors. And on the first floor, with windows. That was dumb. I've never had to learn tactics, but I should've known better.

He lets out a breath, looking relieved as he turns toward the stairs. We made it. We just need to go up, and we'll have the advantage.

Glass shatters.

It takes me a second to process what it could be. There's no glass around us, and the door is still as poorly closed as it had been before.

But the scent is stronger.

Something rushes from the study and slams into MJ. He cries, but his voice is gargled as fangs sink into his throat.

That cop who's spent the last year tormenting me without my even realizing stands between us and the stairs, drinking the only one of us with a proper weapon. He licks his lips and smirks, letting MJ drop to the floor with a faint groan. Is he still alive? "I've never been one for eating men." He sighs. "But sometimes, it's necessary."

My hands tighten on the knife. I need to attack him. I have to stop him.

Why am I not moving?

Rachel takes a step back and whimpers.

"You're so much more pathetic than I thought," he says calmly. "A fucking cop killer is released from prison, and she doesn't even have the decency to be anything more than a coward."

I open my mouth, but no sound comes out.

He takes a deep breath and steps over MJ, moving closer to me, and I finally manage to move. I back away until my back hits a wall. Some superhero I am.

"You almost take the fun out of it."

"Stay..." Am I talking? I don't know what I'm going to say. "Away." It's not me. I blink and turn my head to find Rachel inching toward him, her knife held all the way out in both hands. She's trying to save me. She's still trying to look after me.

"From her," she finishes with a bit more confidence. Her face is set in a determined glare, but the fear is clear in her eyes.

He sighs. "I tried to keep you where you belonged, Dinah. You're a cop killer. You have no right to freedom." Is that really what this is about? "Once it was clear that you wouldn't be blamed for the deaths, I thought that you'd at least understand that everyone around you would keep dying. When I tried to arrest your friend, I'd assumed that lesson was more than clear."

Wait, but when he had arrested Millie, I was able to compel him. It works. I try to force my will into my voice, needing this to work, just like it did for the parole board. I'm not scared of frying this asshole's mind. "Leave this house and never come back."

"Right." He takes another step toward me, and Rachel pushes toward him with the knife, warning him, still not close enough to fight. "That's not going to work. I didn't want to cause issues when the other officers were shoving me out of the way. They're cops, and I'm not going to hurt a cop."

I stare at the body on the ground behind him. "You just did!"

"He's a traitor to the badge. Helping out a fucking cop killer. There's nothing cop about him."

"Why, because he's black?" Rachel asks, trying to get closer, doubtless hoping that the accusation will make him hesitate for a second.

Marsden's eyes narrow, his fangs showing. "No, this isn't about that, and you know it. Plenty of police are black, but they're all blue first."

Rachel lunges, plunging the knife toward his chest, but he shoves her to the wall and knocks the knife out of her hand with a sickening crunch.

"God, you two are so useless. I thought that you'd understand things, Dinah. We were both vampires, and each time you moved closer to your release, I killed someone. You knew what I was, and you knew what you were. A cop killer. Death was too good for you, but eternity in max, that I could live with. After you killed one of our own, you had to suffer."

I was supposed to know he was a vampire. Wow, I really am dumb. I was so scared that I'd eat him that I couldn't even breathe around him. "Wait, but you're a murderer," I say. "You're the bad guy here."

"I've killed criminals and only criminals." He shoots a disdainful look at my crumpled parole officer. "You killed a good cop. That's how we're different, and it's why I'm going to make you suffer."

"I'm not going back to prison."

His smile grows wider, blood glinting on his fangs. "Oh, that's fine."

Rachel lets out a pained whine and draws my eyes to her hands. They're still attached, but they're twisted at an angle that shouldn't be possible unless she no longer has any bones there. Maybe there isn't. My stomach churns.

"Shut up." He kicks at her, but she jumps back, bumping into a wall and tripping but managing to land clear of him. "We're talking."

I force myself to step toward him, holding the knife at my side. I need to take his head, right? What's the best way to do this? I suppose I just swing for the neck and count on strength and speed to do the rest.

"I think I'll bury you alive. Maybe encase you in concrete. It's the eternity of suffering that I really care about. No blood, no… how the hell did you get blood? I was certain you were feeding on people, but you were locked away in solitary, and nothing changed."

I was starving most of the time. That's why nothing changed. Should I tell him that? I think about how everyone reacts when I tell them how I fed. And he's a guy. He'll react worse than most, I can almost guarantee it, especially as full of himself as he sounds. "It was easy. I bought a bunch of menstrual cups and gave them out and drank the girls' period blood."

"You…" He stammers, his smile finally vanishing. "That's… that can't possibly count as…no, that's disgusting."

I swing. His neck is right there, and the knife is sharp. It shouldn't take much to slice right through him so long as he's too caught up with his theatrics to react in time.

He isn't.

He slams his fist into my shoulder, sending a spidering crack of pain through me, and the knife flies out of my hands. I should've been able to hold on, he only broke my shoulder, but the pain is so much that I can barely even process it through the tears.

The knife keeps flying, and for a second, I think that it may still hit him, but he knocked me off course too much, and it flies past his shoulder, barely scraping him. The trickle of blood on his collar is all we managed to get, and we're both out of the fight.

And so is MJ. I glance toward his body. He doesn't seem to be moving.

"Cement sounds good," he says as if I hadn't interrupted his monologue with attempted murder and periods. "Of course, I'll have to find a good spot where you won't be disturbed." He steps closer while I try to scramble back. I wish I was scared that he was going to kill me, but he apparently has far worse in store.

Rachel shouts something. I'm in too much pain to process her words now. "Babe, no, please," I sob, struggling to get the words out. "Just go. Save yourself."

She rushes toward him and kicks his shin. I expect him to do some fancy move and block it like he did when I attacked him, but he stumbles, dropping to his knee. She pulls her leg back and kicks straight for his head. Could she kick it off? I think we're strong enough.

I hold my breath, watching, needing it to work. I don't want anything to happen to her, and I don't want to suffer for eternity. Please, Rachel, please manage to stop him.

There's another crunch, and I see his fist buried halfway into her calf. She screams.

He pulls it out, wiping the blood on his pants as she keeps screaming. I need to save her. Her knife is still on the ground, but she's in the way, and it's closer to him. I inch toward it, but I have no idea how I'll manage to reach it before he notices.

"Are we finished with this game?" he asks. "Don't get me wrong, beating you two pitiful girls is a pleasure, but I was hoping to have you buried before sunrise."

I grit my teeth. He's looking right at me. I try to force myself to return his hateful gaze and not look at the knife. He can't know what I'm doing.

But apparently, he's not that stupid. He bends and picks the knife up. "Rachel, isn't it?" he asks conversationally.

She whimpers, trying to pull away from him with her remaining leg.

"You're attacking an officer. Now, I get it, your wife is being taken away, but I can't keep looking the other way if you don't stay down. Dinah is leaving with me. There's nothing you can do about that. But if you keep interfering, I'll put a bullet through your head."

"Fuck you," she spits back.

He smirks. "Cute. I'd rather not kill vampires. I was willing to let you two have a quick death when I sent that hunter after you, but she didn't cooperate because she didn't think you were monsters. So I sent her on her way, as she isn't a cop killer, and we're still an endangered species. But that doesn't mean I'm not willing to do what's necessary to stop other vampires from interfering with the law. I will kill you if I have to. Now, are you going to cooperate?"

"Stop it," I say. "Leave her alone." What am I thinking? There's nothing I can do. Am I going to go with him? If it's the only way to save Rachel, then maybe...no, of course I will. I'll do anything to keep her safe. "I'll go with you. Just don't hurt her."

"Dinah, no," she shouts, but it breaks into a sob. I'm in so much pain that I can barely even move, and he only broke my shoulder. I can't imagine what she's going through.

"It's okay." Maybe she'll save me someday. We have eternity, as we keep pointing out. I wonder if there will be enough left of me to be worth saving. I've been in solitary enough times, and it breaks a person. But I could still move. I'll be encased in concrete like Han Solo being given to Jabba, except I'll be awake the entire time, buried alive for years. Maybe she'll manage to find me, but I doubt I'll still be me. I wish he'd just kill me.

His smile looks disturbingly genuine. "That's more like it. Fantastic."

I force myself to move, fighting back the urge to cower. I don't know what he's going to do. If I don't fight, will we simply walk to his car and drive to my grave? My new prison?

The doorbell rings. The repairman must have finally showed up. I don't know if this timing is miraculous or terrible.

We all turn to stare at the door as it swings open to reveal an old crone in overpriced flats, with ugly purple pants and a blouse I recognize. My mother is standing there, looking at a murder scene like she just caught me having sex. Her eyes widen as she looks between me and Marsden. "I saw the door was open and I…" She trails off, her gaze pointed firmly at MJ's body.

"Run," I shout, stepping past Marsden, deeper into the hall. Even after all she's done, I still feel guilty not getting between her and him, but she's a distraction, and I have to take this chance. He has Rachel's knife, but the other one flew past him. Maybe I can find it. I look around, and my eyes settle on MJ's body. There's the faintest movement. He may still be breathing. Or it could be me shaking.

"Dinah?" My mother gasps, and I hear a chain rattling. That doesn't sound like running. "This guy, he's…"

"I suggest you follow the young lady's advice," Marsden says.

I take another step and glance back. Marsden doesn't seem to have noticed what I'm doing, but that doesn't mean he actually hasn't. He's managed to disappoint me every other time I got my hopes up.

She pulls out a Star of David and shoves it toward him. I wince, feeling the burn of it on my skin. But that just means that my recoiling will make more sense. It doesn't hurt that much. It's like a slight sunburn. But I act it up. I cower, crying as I move closer to MJ. I can't find the knife, but he should have his gun.

Marsden's footsteps thud away from me, and my mother gasps. "That little trick doesn't work. See, I'm not a bad guy. I'm a cop."

"But...you're..." What, a monster? A freak? Like my father always called me while she just stood by until she finally threw me out?

I reach MJ and look around him. If he was breathing, I'm not sure he still is. His eyes are half-lidded, and the blood on his neck looks tantalizing. I resist it and risk a glance toward Marsden.

He still hasn't looked my way. He takes the Star from my mother, ripping the chain from her neck as she utters a startled cry, and crushes it in his hand. "This is official police business. I'm taking care of some monsters. I would suggest you stay out of my way, or I'll take you in for obstruction."

I don't think she says anything, but maybe she nods or shakes her head. I find the gun on the floor against the wall. I reach as slowly as I can, not wanting to trigger Marsden's predatory instincts.

"You're a vampire," she says flatly.

"And a police officer."

There's a long pause as I finally wrap my fingers around the gun. "I won't let you hurt her." There's less conviction in her voice than when she told me to never come back.

"Then you're obstructing police business," Marsden says. "And that makes you a criminal."

"She's my daughter."

"You should've raised a better child."

He's going to kill her. It would take her out of my misery. Maybe she'd finally stop calling me or stop spying on me. But I can't stand here and watch her die. "Mom, get down," I say, not able to put much enthusiasm into it.

She drops. Maybe she broke a hip; that'd at least give me some satisfaction. Marsden turns, confusion on his face, his eyes widening as I pull the trigger, and the gun thunders, my eardrums ringing as blood sprays the wall. I shoot him again.

He crumples to the floor, and I stand over him. I've never intentionally killed anyone before. And I don't want to ever do it again. I put a bullet between his eyes, and his motions grow more erratic, his arms twitching wildly. I fire again. And again. Until the gun clicks.

It falls from my hand, and I sink to the floor, tears flooding my vision. I've killed another cop.

"The head," Rachel says, her voice a pained croak. "You have to cut it off."

I bite down the bile rising in my throat as I take the knife from his hand and carve off what's left of his head. I've never felt like a monster before, not really, but in this moment, it's hard to see myself as anything else. The terror in my mother's eyes doesn't exactly help. She can't even muster a word.

But Rachel is hurt, and I don't have time to waste. I run to the fridge and yank the door open, grabbing as many blood bags as I can carry with only one arm before I hurry back. I bite into one, moaning at the taste, but hold it to her mouth. If it can reattach an arm, then a few broken bones should be nothing.

She drinks the whole thing down and still looks like a mess, but she's able to grab another bag herself. "Thank you," she says.

I shake my head. I don't know what she's thanking me for. I killed someone.

"Dinah," she says.

I stare at her, and she shimmers. I'm crying, aren't I?

"He was a monster. You did what you had to do."

"I killed him."

She sighs, and I feel her hand on my forearm. "Babe, it was necessary. He had already killed so many people."

"But—"

"Dinah, it was just. You didn't do anything wrong."

I sniffle.

"Drink your blood."

I don't have the energy to argue. I nod and bite into another bag, feeling my shoulder stitch itself back together. It burns. I've never felt anything quite like it. The pain is almost worse than when he shattered it, but with every second of pain, I feel more whole.

"You saved my life," a strained voice says. It sounds so off that it takes me a moment to realize who said it. It's my mother. She must've cried until her voice went hoarse. I was barely paying any attention.

"It looks like you're the only one." I study my mended arm. I test it out, and it moves exactly as it should. Guilt tugs at me. That monster isn't the only death on my conscience. I got so many women killed. And MJ.

He's still on the ground behind me, not moving. I had so hoped that I was wrong. That he was okay.

"There should still be time," Rachel says. "Give him some blood."

I stare at her, trying to figure out what she means. That's how we were made. We had already died or were close enough to it, and some guy I've never met brought us back. I can do the same for him.

I run to him as fast as I can and sink my fangs into my wrist, then hold it over his mouth, letting it trickle in. "Will it work if I'm not the one who drank him?"

"I'm not sure," she says hesitantly.

There's still blood on his throat. I lean in, tasting it, trying not to give in to my hunger. If I wait too long, there won't be anything left to bring back.

Letting the blood trickle into his mouth again, I lick my lips. Fresh blood is so much better than bagged, or my old source, but it's not a luxury I intend to allow myself. I won't be a monster like Marsden was.

I sit there, waiting, hoping.

Rachel sits with me, resting her head on my shoulder.

Eventually, the blood stops running, and she hands me another bag. I drink it, and we wait.

My mother moves closer, peering into my eyes. She's covered in the dead vampire's blood. "Dinah, you saved me, does that mean you—"

"It means I don't want people to die."

"But I—"

"No." I shake my head, staring intently at my parole officer. If I look back at my mother, I'll start crying. I may even give in and forgive her. Or eat her. "You don't deserve to die. You're a better person now." Rachel rubs my back. "You're okay with your lesbian rabbi, and you supported my wife. You've changed."

"Then you forgive me?"

"No," I say again. "And I never will. I don't want you to die. You're my mom. But that doesn't mean I have to forgive you. I can't even be near you without reliving you throwing me out of your house. I don't want to be around you. I don't want you in my life. And I will never forgive you."

"Dinah—"

Rachel squeezes me. "Josie, please. You've been there for me through a lot, but it was too much for either of us to expect. I know I could never forgive my parents."

"I've changed." She's sobbing now. Her tears fall on the floor by MJ's head.

"I know you have. But you're still the same woman who did this to me. Go be there for other people. Pass on the lessons you've learned so that others don't have to go through the pain that you put me through, but you won't be doing it around me."

"Dinah!" If she has something to follow that, she doesn't say it.

"Josie, please. Leave."

My mother sobs again. "Rachel, you know me. Tell her. Tell her that I've changed."

"I keep telling you, I know." I look up, glaring at her. I thought it would be hard. I thought that I'd give in, but seeing those eyes again, all I can feel is hate. She steps back, more tears falling. "It's not enough. It will never be enough. Now leave."

She doesn't say a word as she walks out of the house, the door swinging behind her.

I press closer to Rachel as she wraps her arm around me, and we both watch MJ, waiting for any sign of life.

And we keep waiting.

Until finally, he opens his eyes.

"Fuck," he says. It's an appropriate first word. I doubt mine was much better. He looks haggard, spent, and covered in blood.

I hand him the rest of my bag, and Rachel grabs a fresh one from the floor. He made it. I got so many people killed, but I was able to save two. It's enough. "How're you feeling?" I ask.

"Like I just died."

"Yeah." I nod. "I've been there."

"Why aren't I killing people?" He sounds worried. "I know that's what happened to you."

"You had blood. It'll be okay. You just have to make sure you feed often enough, then you won't go mad with hunger or pass out when you're trying to compel a fucking vampire you were too stupid to notice."

His expression grows more sympathetic but just as tired. "So that means…I can go home to my wife?"

I thought he was gay. I stare at him, but it's a bad time to interrogate him on his sexuality. "Yeah. She'll be fine."

"Thank God." He winces. "Oh."

I chuckle. I know he hurt himself, and I shouldn't, but he just looks so surprised. "You don't know what your weaknesses are yet, so take it easy. Maybe ask her to invite you in and start with just a finger in the sun."

"Right." He nods, sitting up and blinking at the blood-soaked room. "I can't believe I have to help my parolee dispose of another body."

"It's not like it's the first time."

He sighs. "Do you think she'll…"

"Worried about how your wife will react?"

"I went out to deal with you, and I died. I fucking died."

"You did."

He sighs and seems to grow smaller. "I can't believe it happened. And now I'm…I'm a vampire."

"I'm sorry."

He shakes his head. "You're not the one who killed me. So long as I'm not a threat to Chloe, I'm not that upset to be a vampire. I've always wanted to go to the Community Center. I'm sure James will be excited, but I was still *murdered*. By a cop. Can't say I didn't expect that, but I didn't expect it tonight."

"I know what you mean, but at least we got him back for you," Rachel says.

"I'm sorry," I say again. Is there anything else I could possibly say?

He climbs to his feet, looking even more confused.

"I called Kalila on Marsden's phone," Rachel says. "She was his last call before MJ, so it was easy to find."

"Her name is Crazy Murder Lady," I correct her.

Rachel rolls her eyes, but her lip curls into a small smile. She still loves me. "I told her what happened. She'll make sure the repairman shows up and says she can get a cleaning crew out here to take care of everything. So you can go home." She sounds friendlier toward MJ than she has the other times he's intruded on our house. Maybe dying for us was enough to win her over, or maybe she's just too tired to be mad at him. It's been a very long day.

He pushes to his feet, shaking a little before taking a tentative step. "I feel strong. My knee doesn't even ache anymore."

"Vampirism," I say.

"It's kinda great. Just not looking forward to those downsides. I'll get out of your hair. Oh, could I..." He stares at the bags of blood, realization seeming to dawn on him. "I guess I can go buy some myself now. It feels strange, but I'll get myself some blood tomorrow."

"You can take a bag until then," Rachel says, handing him one as she picks the rest up off the floor. "I don't want you going hungry when you're still getting used to controlling the cravings."

"Thank you." He takes the blood, nods at both of us, and walks back out through the still swinging front door. Rachel and I sink onto the couch, not bothering to worry about bloodstains, and keep watching my, no, *our* soaps until Crazy Murder Lady's friends show up, fix up our house, and finally let us sleep.

It's over. There's no longer a crazy vampire trying to ruin my life and kill people. I stopped him. And my mother may finally leave me alone. I even saved a few lives.

Maybe I am a superhero.

Epilogue

I take the bouquet and set it on my dressing table with the mirror carefully turned away from me, trying not to tear up. I can't ruin my makeup after all the work they put into it.

The roses are beautiful, all a dark red, twined between lilacs. The attached card only reads *Break a leg. I love you. XOXO Rachel.* I can't believe she talked me into this.

I shake my head, grinning at the flowers. As if I took that much convincing. Rehearsal cut into game nights, but I hadn't even thought of that at the time. I knew I didn't want to go onstage in front of a bunch of people, and I knew that I would do terribly in auditions. All she had to say was that if auditions were going to go terribly, I wouldn't have to worry about the audience since I wouldn't be in the play.

And then I got the part.

And now I have to go onstage.

In front of people.

Rehearsals sometimes had a few people there, but it wasn't the same. Rachel came way more times than she could've possibly enjoyed, and that always helped, even if it also made me nervous. She'll be seated already. Will she judge me if I run?

If I chicken out, I'll be making my understudy's day, and Pam is an absolute delight and has more than earned it. She has so much more experience than I do. I still have no idea how I got this part. Granted, I'm playing a prisoner, so maybe my resume looked good.

I sigh and hold my face in my hands, only to immediately pull them away when I realize that I could smear my makeup. Seriously, did she compel me? There's no way I would've agreed to this so easily. I know it's not possible, but still. I have to go out in front of an entire community theater audience, and somehow still remember my lines.

It's like the parole board all over again, and I can't risk compelling everyone. I don't know if that one guy ever recovered from what I did to his brain. So if I bomb, they're going to know I bombed. Even if it means I stand there, stammering, too scared to get out a word.

Rachel will be there. She'll be watching. I can focus on that. Phoebe said she was going to have a friend of hers record it discreetly so she could watch it. It's hard to go to public places with a giant snake tail.

I hope she isn't kicked out for recording. That would be so awkward. At least it would take attention off my terrible performance.

I groan, gritting my teeth. I've honestly loved rehearsals. Exploring my character has been exactly as fun as Rachel pitched it, but that wasn't for a proper performance. I know it's only community theater, and there aren't even enough seats for a real crowd, but it's still bigger than I've ever tried to act in front of.

Who thought this was a good idea again? Oh, right, Rachel, the woman I love and trust implicitly. Great.

"Curtain's up in five," someone says behind me. I turn and earn a smile from Jameela, one of the other actresses. "You'll do great. Just like rehearsals."

Oh no. I didn't think my fear was that obvious. That means the audience will see it too.

"Drinks after? Wait, no, sorry."

"It's fine. I have plans with my wife anyway. Give everybody my love, and I can join you next time. I can still eat nachos."

"All right." Her smile looks more unsure, but she pats my shoulder. "I'll see you out there?" She sounds uncertain. How terrified do I look?

I work my expression into something more neutral and nod. "I wouldn't miss it for the world."

If I don't want to miss my cue, I'm going to have to stop panicking and get out there.

I stand, take a deep breath, and close my eyes. I can hear all the other actors moving into position, the theater full of—or at least containing a few—people. Rachel's there.

I'd better give her a hell of a show.

❖

"She. Was. Amazing," Rachel screams loud enough that MJ winces. He hasn't had long to get used to super hearing.

"No spoilers," Phoebe says, her tail flicking against the counter of Rachel's diner. "Larissa managed to get me the recording. I want to see it after we eat."

MJ smiles, twirling his straw in his bloody milkshake. "Chloe told me to tell you that you were fantastic. It was the best community theater production we've seen in years. And I've had quite a few parolees invite me to these things, so it means something when I tell you that this was the best one. By a lot. A lot a lot."

I chuckle, but I can feel my cheeks heat. I'm not used to all this praise. "I didn't think you were gonna come tonight."

"Here? I told you."

"No, I knew that. You said that after the play." I can't believe I invited my parole officer. We're, like, actually friends now and have even hung out a few times without it being a parole check, though most of that was us teaching him about being a vampire. And I met his demon ex, who is even creepier than him. But MJ is still my parole officer, and it feels wrong. "I didn't think you'd come to the first production."

"I was pretty sure that if I went to a later one, you'd have already quit, and I would've missed my poor sire awkwardly flailing onstage."

I glower at him. I take it back. He's still the worst.

"Hey, it's what you'd been telling me. For weeks. Every single time I met with you."

I roll my eyes and look to Rachel for support.

She shakes her head. "Hey, you shouldn't have been so down on yourself."

Betrayed by the woman I love. I should've been in a Shakespearian tragedy instead. "Are you done?"

MJ smirks. "Oh no, I intend to keep ribbing you forever. You're never getting off this parole, remember."

I look around the Community Center. Where was that fake ID place? "I'll get a new identity. No criminal record, no parole officer."

"Ah, but I have to keep you out of trouble. That's what I promised the courts. And fake IDs are illegal."

"You're the absolute worst."

"You're the one who brought me back to life."

"And I regret it every day."

He grins, and Phoebe laughs awkwardly. "So now that the play has started, does that mean you'll be able to start playing with us again?" she asks.

I suppose we can wait to talk more about the play until she's seen it. I can't believe I'm letting her. I should delete the recording and never go back to that theater. "Yeah. Fridays are still gonna be rough for the next couple weeks until the production has ended, but I can get back to the *Deadlands* game again."

"I can move the other one to Tuesday. I think everyone's free then."

"That would be amazing," I say, finding myself grinning.

"Is it as much like your games as I told you it was?" Rachel asks.

I guess we can't drop the play. "Yeah, kind of. I don't get to ad-lib as much onstage, but honestly, yes. It's still getting into character, the mannerisms and voices I've practiced still help, and it's the same thought process of trying to put myself inside another person."

"Oh, then I do help you practice," Rachel says.

Phoebe snickers.

Everyone is a critic. She's making it very difficult to want to say this. I turn to Rachel, only to get a lascivious look. "Did you want to go practice now?" she asks.

"Kind of," I mutter. "But I was going to say you were right."

She blinks. "Yeah?"

"I didn't think I'd like acting, and I thought my stage fright was proof of that. It didn't make sense for me to like it, but you suggested it, so I tried it. And I guess, even after all this time, you still get me like nobody else does. I...when I was up on that stage, I was terrified, but I still made it through every last scene. I loved it. It was absolutely magical." She still knows me. I don't know how I managed to doubt that. We've changed so much, but she's still my Rachel. And I'm still hers.

"Yeah?" she asks again, her face lighting up, her fangs showing in a goofy, adorable smile.

"Yeah."

She takes my hands. "Babe, I know things have changed. And I thought it was possible I was wrong, that I didn't get why you liked those games, but even if that was the case, all I want is for you to be happy. You didn't have to force yourself to act for me."

"I know I didn't have to, but I trust you, and as ever, you were right."

"Well..." Her smile grows even wider. "I suppose you had to learn that eventually."

"That's what my wife always says too," MJ adds.

"Everyone I've ever dated knows I'm always right," Phoebe says. "It's why I'm the GM."

I turn on her. "Oh, I can out-GM you any day."

"Yeah? That mean you're going to run our *7th Sea* one-shot Tuesday?"

"I haven't even read the books for it."

"Guess you're not that capable of a GM, then." She smirks at me, her tail whipping.

I cross my arms. "All right, fine, you want to test my GM mettle? Let's try a real game. We can keep your little fun one-shots where you get to GM—"

"And the *Deadlands* game?"

"Well, yes, obviously," I grumble. "But if people are up for it, I'll run a *Shadowrun* game. Then you'll see who's the real GM."

"Oh, hell yes," MJ says. "I'll join."

"I…" I stare at him. My parole officer is joining my *Shadowrun* game? That sounds like hell. I bet he's gonna be a Lone Star Officer too. How would that even work for a game? "You know it's not a board game, right?"

"Kid, I was playing when you were…right, you're, like, three years older than me."

He's forty-one? Wow, I would never have guessed that. He doesn't look older than thirty. And he never will. "Fine, you can join the game."

"Can I?" Rachel asks.

I stare at her. "You…want to?"

She shrugs, her fang doing its adorable thing and digging into her lip. "Yeah. I've been curious for a while, but I didn't want to step on your toes. And I had a lot to do anyway. But, well, I know how much you love it, and it'd be nice to try it out."

"Guess you have a full game," Phoebe says. "You'll have to back up those words."

I nod at Rachel. "All right. Fine. But I want your characters all done by Tuesday. I intend to have everything ready for a good session zero."

"Of course, Mistress GM," Phoebe says.

MJ chuckles. "I'll have to find my old books."

"There's probably been a new edition since then."

"I spend so much more on you than I do any other parolee."

"There're a lot more bodies to hide."

He glares at me.

"So what do we do?" Rachel asks.

I don't have any place I have to be until the curtain goes up tomorrow evening, so we all walk her through it and help her build her decker and get MJ updated books from a shop nearby.

It's strange. This isn't that different from prison in the end. I still have a cop keeping a close eye on me. I'm still playing tabletop games. I even could've acted in prison if I'd wanted, but at the same time, I can barely recognize this as the life I had a year ago. I'm married, I have weird nonhuman friends, and there's way more stabbing. That's not a change I expected.

But my wife's going to play my favorite RPG in the whole world with me, so things are kinda perfect. Now if only she'd stop offering to sleep with the GM for extra karma.

About the Author

Genevieve McCluer was born in California and grew up in numerous cities across the country. She studied criminal justice in college but, after a few years of that, moved her focus to writing. Her whole life, she's been obsessed with mythology, and she bases her stories in those myths.

She now lives in Arizona with her partner and cats, working away at far too many novels. In her free time she pesters the cats, plays video games, and attempts to be better at archery.

Books Available from Bold Strokes Books

A Second Chance at Life by Genevieve McCluer. Vampires Dinah and Rachel reconnect, but a string of vampire killings begin and evidence seems to be pointing at Dinah. They must prove her innocence while finding out if the two of them are still compatible after all these years. (978-1-63679-459-4)

Digging for Heaven by Jenna Jarvis. Litz lives for dragons. Kella lives to kill them. The last thing they expect is to find each other attractive. (978-1-63679-453-2)

Forever's Promise by Missouri Vaun. Wesley Holden migrated west disguised as a man for the hope of a better life and with no designs to take a wife, but Charlotte Rose has other ideas. (978-1-63679-221-7)

Here For You by D. Jackson Leigh. A horse trainer must make a difficult business decision that could save her father's ranch from foreclosure but destroy her chance to win the heart of a feisty barrel racer vying for a spot in the National Rodeo Finals. (978-1-63679-299-6)

I Do, I Don't by Joy Argento. Creator of the romance algorithm, Nicole Hart doesn't expect to be starring in her own reality TV dating show, and falling for the show's executive producer Annie Jackson could ruin everything. (978-1-63679-420-4)

It's All in the Details by Dena Blake. Makeup artist Lane Donnelly and wedding planner Helen Trent can't stand each other, but they must set aside their differences to ensure Darcy gets the wedding of her dreams, and make a few of their own dreams come true. (978-1-63679-430-3)

Marigold by Melissa Brayden. Marigold Lavender vows to take down Alexis Wakefield, the harsh food critic who blasts her younger sister's restaurant. If only she wasn't as sexy as she is mean. (978-1-63679-436-5)

The Town that Built Us by Jesse J. Thoma. When her father dies, Grace Cook returns to her hometown and tries to avoid Bonnie Whitlock, the woman who pulverized her heart, only to discover her father's estate has been left to them jointly. (978-1-63679-439-6)

A Degree to Die For by Karis Walsh. A murder at the University of Washington's Classics Department brings Professor Antigone Weston and Sergeant Adriana Kent together—first as opposing forces, and then allies as they fight together to protect their campus from a killer. (978-1-63679-365-8)

A Talent Within by Suzanne Lenoir. Evelyne, born into nobility, and Annika, a peasant girl with a deadly secret, struggle to change their destinies in Valmora, a medieval world controlled by religion, magic, and men. (978-1-63679-423-5)

Finders Keepers by Radclyffe. Roman Ashcroft's past, it seems, is not so easily forgotten when fate brings her and Tally Dewilde together—along with an attraction neither welcomes. (978-1-63679-428-0)

Homeland by Kristin Keppler and Allisa Bahney. Dani and Kate have finally found themselves on the same side of the war, but a new threat from the inside jeopardizes the future of the wasteland. (978-1-63679-405-1)

Just One Dance by Jenny Frame. Will Taylor Spark and her new business to make dating special—the Regency Romance Club—bring sparkle back to Jaq Bailey's lonely world? (978-1-63679-457-0)

On My Way There by Jaycie Morrison. As Max traverses the open road, her journey of impossible love, loss, and courage mirrors her voyage of self-discovery leading to the ultimate question: If she can't have the woman of her dreams, will the woman of real life be enough? (978-1-63679-392-4)

Transitioning Home by Heather K O'Malley. An injured soldier realizes they need to transition to really heal. (978-1-63679-424-2)

Truly Enough by JJ Hale. Chasing the spark of creativity may ignite a burning romance or send a friendship up in flames. (978-1-63679-442-6)

Vintage and Vogue by Kelly and Tana Fireside. When tech whiz Sena Abrigo marches into small-town Owen Station, she turns librarian Hazel Butler's life upside down in the most wonderful of ways, setting off an explosive series of events, threatening their chance at love...and their very lives. (978-1-63679-448-8)

Broken Fences by Jo Hemmingwood. Former army sergeant Seneca Twist has difficulty adjusting to civilian life until she meets psychologist Robyn Mason and has a place to call home. (978-1-63679-414-3)

Never Kiss a Cowgirl by Ali Vali. Asher Evans dreams of winning the National Finals Rodeo in Vegas, and Reagan Wilson wants no part of something that brings back the memory of what killed her father. (978-1-63679-106-7)

Pantheon Girls by Jean Copeland. Cassie Burke never anticipated the detour life was about to take when a meeting with a prospective client reunites her with a past love and reignites the star-crossed passion they shared twenty years earlier. (978-1-63679-337-5)

Roux for Two by Aurora Rey. For TV chef Chelsea Boudreaux and hometown boy Bryce Cormier, love proves as tricky as making a good pot of gumbo. (978-1-63679-376-4)

Starting Over by Nance Sparks. Jennifer has no idea if she can mend Sam's broken soul after the sudden loss of her wife, but it's never too late for starting over. (978-1-63679-409-9)

The Accidental Bride by Jane Walsh. Spinsters Miss Grace Linfield and Miss Thea Martin travel to Gretna Green to prevent a wedding, only to discover a scandalous passion—for each other. (978-1-63679-345-0)

Three Wishes by Anne Shade. A magic lamp, a beautiful Jinni, and a cursed princess make for one unbelievable story. (978-1-63679-349-8)

Undiscovered Treasures by MJ Williamz. For Cyl and her friends Luna and Martinique, life's best treasures often appear when you're not looking. (978-1-63679-449-5)

Curse of the Gorgon by Tanai Walker. Cass will do anything to ensure Elle's safety, but is she willing to embrace the curse of the Gorgon? (978-1-63679-395-5)

Dance with Me by Georgia Beers. Scottie Templeton mixes it up on and off the dance floor with sexy salsa instructor Marisa Reyes. But can Scottie get past Marisa's connection to her ex? (978-1-63679-359-7)

Gin and Bear It by Joy Argento. Opposites really can attract, and as Kelly and Logan work together to create a loving home for rescue cat Bear, they just might find one for themselves as well. (978-1-63679-351-1)

Harvest Dreams by Jacqueline Fein-Zachary. Planting the vineyard of their dreams, Kate Bauer and Sydney Barrett must resist their attraction while battling nature and their families, who oppose both the venture and their relationship. (978-1-63679-380-1)

The No Kiss Contract by Nan Campbell. Workaholic Davy believes she can get the top spot at her firm if the senior partners think she's settling down and about to start a family, but she needs the delightful yet dubious Anna to help by pretending to be her fiancée. (978-1-63679-372-6)

Outside the Lines by Melissa Sky. If you had the chance to live forever, would you take it? Amara Rodriguez did, and it sets her on a journey to find her missing mother and unravel the mystery of her own heart. (978-1-63679-403-7)

The Value of Sylver and Gold by Michelle Larkin. When word gets out that former Boston homicide detective Reid Sylver can talk to the dead, the FBI solicits her help on a serial murder case, prompting Reid to assemble forces once again with Detective London Gold. (978-1-63679-093-0)

When It Feels Right by Tagan Shepard. Freshly out of the closet Marlene hasn't been lucky in love, but when it comes to her quirky new roommate Abby, everything just feels right. (978-1-63679-367-2)

BOLDSTROKESBOOKS.COM

Looking for your next great read?

Visit BOLDSTROKESBOOKS.COM
to browse our entire catalog of paperbacks, ebooks,
and audiobooks.

Want the first word on what's new?
Visit our website for event info,
author interviews, and blogs.

Subscribe to our free newsletter for sneak peeks,
new releases, plus first notice of promos
and daily bargains.

SIGN UP AT
BOLDSTROKESBOOKS.COM/signup

Bold Strokes Books
Quality and Diversity in LGBTQ Literature

*Bold Strokes Books is an award-winning publisher
committed to quality and diversity in LGBTQ fiction.*